In Hot Water

A saleswoman stumbled out of the doorway, her eyes big with panic. She saw the crowd and screamed again and slumped against the wall. Dinah and I rushed into the room she had exited. A crowd of people came in behind us, and then there was a collective gasp. At a large desk in the center of [illegible] wl. Red stuff [illegible]

"O[illegible] g at the crims[illegible]

Ad[illegible] he desk and s[illegible] disgust. "Pink, it's not blood. It's soup."

"A delightful addition to the mystery genre."
—Earlene Fowler,
author of *Tumbling Blocks*

Berkley Prime Crime titles by Betty Hechtman

HOOKED ON MURDER

DEAD MEN DON'T CROCHET

BY HOOK OR BY CROOK

A STITCH IN CRIME

YOU BETTER KNOT DIE

DeaD MeN DoN't CrocHeT

BETTY HECHTMAN

BERKLEY PRIME CRIME, NEW YORK

THE BERKLEY PUBLISHING GROUP
Published by the Penguin Group
Penguin Group (USA) Inc.
375 Hudson Street, New York, New York 10014, USA
Penguin Group (Canada), 90 Eglinton Avenue East, Suite 700, Toronto, Ontario M4P 2Y3, Canada
(a division of Pearson Penguin Canada Inc.)
Penguin Books Ltd., 80 Strand, London WC2R 0RL, England
Penguin Group Ireland, 25 St. Stephen's Green, Dublin 2, Ireland (a division of Penguin Books Ltd.)
Penguin Group (Australia), 250 Camberwell Road, Camberwell, Victoria 3124, Australia
(a division of Pearson Australia Group Pty. Ltd.)
Penguin Books India Pvt. Ltd., 11 Community Centre, Panchsheel Park, New Delhi—110 017, India
Penguin Group (NZ), 67 Apollo Drive, Rosedale, North Shore 0632, New Zealand
(a division of Pearson New Zealand Ltd.)
Penguin Books (South Africa) (Pty.) Ltd., 24 Sturdee Avenue, Rosebank, Johannesburg 2196,
South Africa

Penguin Books Ltd., Registered Offices: 80 Strand, London WC2R 0RL, England

DEAD MEN DON'T CROCHET

A Berkley Prime Crime Book / published by arrangement with the author

PRINTING HISTORY
Berkley Prime Crime mass-market edition / December 2008

Interior text design by Kristen del Rosario.

ISBN: 978-0-425-22500-4

BERKLEY® PRIME CRIME
Berkley Prime Crime Books are published by The Berkley Publishing Group,
a division of Penguin Group (USA) Inc.,
375 Hudson Street, New York, New York 10014.
BERKLEY PRIME CRIME and the BERKLEY PRIME CRIME design are trademarks of Penguin Group (USA) Inc.

PRINTED IN THE UNITED STATES OF AMERICA

10 9 8 7 6 5

For my parents,
Helen and Jacob Jacobson.
You always believed in me.

Acknowledgments

I would like to thank Sandy Harding for all her help and for being so nice to work with.

This book wouldn't have happened without Jessica Faust of BookEnds, LLC.

I would like to thank Leslie Henkel for all of her efforts on my behalf. And a special thank-you to David Brokaw and Sandy Brokaw of the Brokaw Company for their friendship and all their time and great ideas.

Sue Meyer of the Lace Museum in Sunnyvale, California, shared her knowledge and gave me the opportunity to see samples of Irish crochet up close and even touch the intricate stitches.

Paula Tesler remains my go-to person for crochet help and inspiration. The Crochet Partners online list has been a wonderful source of information and insight into the generous hearts of crocheters.

Jean Leinhauser and Rita Weiss are crochet goddesses whose books dazzle me with their possibilities.

Thanks to Homicide Detective Michel Carroll of the Fort Worth, Texas, Police Department for answering my questions. Forensic U put on by Sisters in Crime was fabulous. Where else would I see what a body that had been buried for three years looks like? A particular thank-you to Lee Lofland and Dr. D. P. Lyle for their great workshops.

Thank you, Roberta Martia, for all the support and crochet advice. Appellate Defender Judy Libby offered lots of cheers and explained a lot of legal stuff.

Betty Mehling and Diana Lang have been a constant source of good thoughts.

Thank you, Joe Sugarman, for making it possible for me to crochet in paradise.

And a giant thank-you to Burl and Max for always being ready and willing to join me on some wild adventure.

Chapter 1

"My name is Molly Pink and I'm a yarnoholic," I announced to my crochet group, the Tarzana Hookers, as I put my stash on the table. Okay, maybe there wasn't really any such organization as Yarnoholics Anonymous, and calling myself an addict was a bit of a stretch, but I was feeling a little guilty about the yarn I'd just bought. Even though I was new to crocheting, I couldn't seem to leave a yarn store empty-handed. What was I to do this time? The recycled silk was beautiful, in limited quantity and at a special price. Besides, with the Tarzana Hookers meeting again, I was sure to find something fabulous to make with the three skeins. Well, six skeins if you counted the other three I needed to mix with the first three, because the woman at the yarn store said that recycled silk was too thin to go it alone.

The Tarzana part of our name referred to Tarzana, California. Technically the San Fernando Valley community was part of the city of Los Angeles, but the people on the other side of the Santa Monica Mountains—or over the hill, as it's commonly referred to—looked at us Valleites as at least one step behind them in the sophistication department.

Our weather was a step behind in the comfort department. It was hotter in the summer and colder in the winter, though this May morning it was cool and cloudy on both sides of the hill. I dealt with it by wearing a white shirt with a sweater over it and a hoodie on top of that. As the day progressed and the sun came out, I'd start peeling off layers, then load everything back on as it got dark and the temperature dropped. It was standard operating procedure for May in Southern California.

Three times a week the Tarzana Hookers gathered at 10 a.m. in the event area of the neighborhood bookstore, Shedd & Royal Books and More. A long table was set up in an alcove with a large window facing Ventura Boulevard. We could look out at the street, and passersby could see there was something going on inside. This morning the light was flat and shadowless due to the silvery early-day clouds.

I glanced around the table to see the crochet group's response to my yarnaholic comment, hoping for a smile. Adele Abrams looked up from her work.

"Pink, no matter how much yarn you have, I'm sure I have more."

Some people would have said that to make me feel better, but Adele said it to irritate me; she called me by my last name for the same reason. We had a running rivalry that started when I got my job at Shedd & Royal Books and More after my husband Charlie died. Based on my experience putting on receptions and events for Charlie's public relations firm, Mrs. Shedd, co-owner of the bookstore, had hired me as event coordinator–community relations person. Adele had hoped to get promoted to my job. Instead, she'd gotten story time in the kids' department. She still hadn't gotten over it, and it'd been way over a year.

"And if you thought it was funny, it wasn't—or even original," Adele said with an implied groan in her voice. Adele Abrams had an ample build and an interesting fashion sense. She liked to think she had flair. Today's ensemble was something of a cowgirl look. She wore boots and a long denim skirt decorated with big sewn-on doily-type things. She topped it with a white western-style shirt and a leather vest. Her brown hair had some new highlights and was pulled into a minuscule ponytail, with a battalion of clips keeping up the sides. Even as she talked, she kept crocheting. Adele might be a little weird with her clothes, but she was top-notch with a crochet hook.

I had kind of backed into becoming a Tarzana Hooker. It started with too much caramel corn. It was homemade and totally delicious, if I say so myself, but also totally bad for the fit of my khaki slacks. I'd reasoned that if I could occupy my fingers with something besides ferrying caramel corn to my mouth it might help. The Hookers were already meeting at the bookstore, but I didn't want to be totally green when I joined. Actually, I didn't want Adele to be the one to teach me, so when she wasn't looking I had bought a kids' kit we had in the children's department and taught myself the basics. I'd shared the kit with my best friend Dinah and gotten her to join, too.

I was still a newbie, but totally hooked on crochet. I loved watching a ball of yarn turn into something, even if I had to undo it a lot. It was soothing and relaxing, and somehow always left me feeling restored. And there was something wonderful about wrapping a pretty scarf around your neck and knowing you'd made it.

Adele had accepted that I was part of the group, but never missed a chance to remind me how good she was and how I was still struggling. I noticed she was working with what appeared to be a ball of thin string and a small silver-colored hook. I couldn't see what she was making at first, but as it got bigger, I realized it was a doily similar to the ones on her skirt. Maybe she was planning to start a fashion trend.

"Sorry, dear, but Adele's right about your yarnaholic comment not being original," CeeCee Collins said. "We've all said something similar at one time or another. Let's see what you've got." She reached across the table and emptied my bag. The hanks of multicolored silk tumbled on the table followed by the three companion skeins. The silk ones were shades of reds and warm tones, and the other three were a soft mauve. All were from the Himalayas and promised to help impoverished villagers, which made me feel better about my purchase.

"It's beautiful," CeeCee said, fingering it. "You must give me details about where you got it." Her real name was Connie Collins, but everybody knew her as CeeCee. She was the reason the Tarzana Hookers hadn't been meeting for a while. CeeCee had recently become the host of a reality show called *Making Amends*. The point of the show was to give people a chance to confess to wrongs they'd done, and then the show helped the participants right them. There were a lot of tearful moments and a lot of embarrassing ones, too—a winning combo that had turned it into a hit. It had been too hard for CeeCee to commit to our usual three meetings a week when the show was taping, and though Adele had wanted to keep the meetings going without CeeCee, we had decided to wait until she was free. The production had recently finished making another block of shows and was now on hiatus so the Tarzana Hookers were back together.

CeeCee and Adele were still vying to be head of the group. So far, CeeCee seemed to be winning. As usual

CeeCee's hair was poufed into a stiff bubble. It was that reddish, blondish sort of acrylic-looking color that never occurs without help. She favored velour warm-up suits in jewel tones. Due to the morning chill, she wore a white turtleneck shirt under her jade-colored jacket. She had barely stopped working during the interchange. She was so good at crocheting, I almost believed she could do it in her sleep. But I couldn't figure out what she was making. It was round and brown. I leaned closer and she held it up. It looked like a furry donut with pink icing.

CeeCee was known for her runaway sweet tooth and the battle of the bulge that went with it. "This is the only kind of donut I can deal with right now." She seemed embarrassed as she admitted that she'd gained five pounds. "And I need to lose it starting this second," she said. She gazed longingly at the yarn donut. "This looks so authentic I can almost smell the sugar." She explained that it was going to be a pincushion when she finished it. She had been making them in her spare time on the set and called them zero-calorie donuts. "I'm donating them to the Not Exactly A Bake Sale at Wilbur Avenue Elementary."

CeeCee was always making something for someone else. I'd discovered that crocheters had big hearts and gave away or donated most of what they produced. I wanted to do the same, and the toasty brown scarf I was working on was going to be donated to soldiers when it was finished. I began doing simple rows of double crochet stitches.

As I worked, I waited for some comment from the third person at the table, Sheila Altman, but she never glanced up from her work. I could tell by the hunch of her shoulders she was having a nervous moment, which was not uncommon for her. I had to give her credit. She never gave up trying to lessen her anxiety and had taken up crochet, thinking it might help. Her crocheting was fine as long as her mind was clear, but if something was bothering her it showed up in her stitches. Like now. I watched her trying to jam her hook into stitches so tight they looked like knots. Whatever was upsetting her this time had to be something big. Without missing a beat, Adele handed her a smaller-size hook. It might help her stitches but probably wouldn't do anything for whatever she was thinking about.

"What's up, ladies?" Dinah Lyons said as she came up to the table, tote bag in hand.

"Pink was just venting about her yarn habit," Adele said, shaking her head and rolling her eyes.

Dinah looked at me with surprise. "What's the problem?" Dinah was a ball of energy. I pointed to the hank of yarn on the table. Dinah picked it up and ran her fingers through it while saying, "Sorry, I'm late," before settling in. Dinah taught English at Walter Beasley Community College and claimed that teaching college freshmen had made her ready to deal with anything. She loved silk scarves and today had twined a long kelly green one with a purple one and wrapped them around her neck. As usual, she wore almost-to-the-shoulder dangle earrings and had her short salt-and-pepper hair bristling with gel-encased spikes. She took out a ball of yellow cotton yarn and a pattern book. She thumbed through the pages, then took out an F-size hook.

"What are you making?" Adele asked. Without waiting for an answer, she pulled the pattern book toward her and looked at the open page. "Not another washcloth."

"Dinah, dear, you really should think of moving on to something bigger, say a baby blanket," CeeCee said.

Dinah took back the pattern book and proceeded to make a slip knot and start doing a foundation chain. "Not yet."

"Okay, so how many have you made now?" Adele said, leaning over to get a view inside Dinah's bag, since she carried all of them with her.

"I'll show you." Dinah stopped with the yellow yarn and dumped out her tote bag, revealing a cornucopia of washcloths in varying colors and stitch styles. There must have been fifteen or so.

"These are lovely," CeeCee said, picking up several. "But enough is enough."

Dinah loosened her green and purple scarves. "How many partially finished projects do you have?" she said to Adele.

Adele looked slightly uncomfortable while she calculated in her head. "Just a few, maybe ten or a few more."

"And you?" she said to CeeCee.

"What's your point?" CeeCee said defensively.

I noticed Dinah didn't bother asking me. She knew the answer. I had turned one of my sons' rooms into a crochet room in which there were now at least three partially done scarves, a half-done afghan, an almost-finished hat, and two squares for a baby blanket.

"My point is, I don't want to have a pile of half-done things. If you notice, all the washcloths are complete." Dinah went back to her chain stitches while Adele and CeeCee traded glances. Still Sheila didn't say a word. It was beginning to make me tense.

"Ladies, remember we're supposed to be hooking for charity," CeeCee said, obviously dropping the washcloth issue. "We need to come up with a new project. Anybody have any ideas?"

The mission of the Tarzana Hookers was to make projects to either give directly to those in need or to help raise money at a charity sale. It was because of the mission that Mrs. Shedd had invited the group to meet at the bookstore. And it was why she paid for the yarn for all the projects.

We all looked up from our work, except Sheila. She had managed to dig into the stitches with the smaller hook.

CeeCee had reminded her to keep the next row of her stitches loose, and Sheila seemed to be mouthing the words as she worked. It appeared to be a kind of meditation for her, enabling her to put whatever was bothering her on the shelf.

"Is this some kind of meeting?" a woman's voice asked, distracting us from CeeCee's question. The speaker was dressed in what I'd call country-club casual: taupe slacks and white polo shirt with a navy sweater tied around her shoulders. I recognized the not-a-hair-out-of-place look that always made me pat my hair hoping to eliminate the usual flyaways.

"Hi, Patricia," I said with a welcoming smile. "We're the Tarzana Hookers." I held up my hook and scarf as a visual aid. "Want to join?" I thought since it was a bookstore event and I was in charge of such things it was okay for me to do the inviting. "This is Patricia Orrington," I said before introducing everyone at the table. I explained that she was the author of *Patricia's Perfect Hints*, which was a big hit at the bookstore. I didn't mention that it was self-published and the main reason Mrs. Shedd was so happy to stock it and host book signings was because Patricia had gotten a wine stain out of Mrs. Shedd's designed-in-Paris white blouse.

"It's Bradford now, Molly. You keep forgetting. As in Benjamin Bradford who is running for city council." At that, she put a campaign button down for each of us. Everyone looked at theirs, except Sheila. She hadn't even glanced up in acknowledgment when I told Patricia her name. Was I the only one noticing she wasn't participating?

"So, you're the Tarzana Hookers." She walked around the table, examining our work. When she passed Sheila, she gave us all a raised-eyebrow look before moving on. "I would like to join you. This is just the sort of thing I need. You know, involving myself in some neighborhood thing."

"Do you crochet?" Adele asked.

"No," Patricia answered, turning her attention to CeeCee and asking more about the group.

When CeeCee explained we made things for charity, Patricia seemed even more interested. "Even better. What are you working on?" She checked out our varied projects, giving CeeCee's donut a particularly puzzled look. Adele explained these were our own projects and that we were looking for a group project.

"Well, I have the charity," Patricia said, sitting down. She opened up her large purse and took out some yarn. That seemed a little odd, as if maybe she knew all about us and had planned to join before she even got here. "The Women's Haven. It's a shelter for abused and homeless women and their children. It's Benjamin's pet charity. Bradford Industries donated the building they're housed in."

Adele's eyes bugged out at what Patricia did next. She took out circular knitting needles on which hung the beginning of something sunny yellow. "This will be fun."

"That's not crochet. And this is a crochet group. A crochet-only group," Adele said, looking like she was going to blow. "If we were a knit-and-crochet group we would be called the Tarzana Hookers and Needle Heads."

CeeCee gave Adele one of her cease-and-desist looks. We all agreed we were crochet only and that we liked it better than knitting, but Adele was rabid about it.

"If you want to join us, you'll have to crochet," CeeCee said in a pleasant voice. "Adele or I would be glad to teach you."

Patricia put her needles away and moved closer to CeeCee. "I think I'd rather have you teach me." So far she hadn't made any reference to CeeCee's celebrity status, but I had a feeling the wheels were turning in her head, trying to figure out a way to get CeeCee's endorsement for her husband. Patricia turned to me. "Didn't I hear you were the one who solved Ellen Sheridan's murder?"

"Right now, the only mystery Pink should be concerned with is what happened to the missing stitches," Adele said, holding up my work in progress and pointing out how the brown scarf was getting narrower and narrower. "You're missing the last stitch on each row," she added with just a touch of triumph. "Time to unravel." She turned her attention to Patricia. "That's one of the beauties of crochet compared to knitting: the ease of undoing your mistakes."

Sheila seemed to have lost the meditation aspect of her crocheting and was back to hunched shoulders and tight stitches. Suddenly her head shot up, and she threw her work in the center of the table. Her hook pinged against the hard surface. "That's it. I can't do it. I can't do this anymore."

She pushed back from the table and stood up. CeeCee picked up the royal blue yarn from the middle of the table and began to unravel it while at the same time suggesting Sheila sit down. "Is there something bothering you besides your crochet work?"

Sheila's face said it all. Her brows were scrunched together, her eyes were filling with water, and her mouth quivered with sadness.

"Yes," Sheila said in a tremulous voice.

"Why don't you tell us about it," Dinah said.

"Maybe we can help," CeeCee offered. Then we all started encouraging Sheila to talk.

Patricia rapped on the table. "Girls, if you all talk at once we're not going to be able to hear Sheila." The talking stopped and everyone looked expectantly at Sheila, except for Dinah and me. We traded knowing smiles. Just what the group needed: another person who wanted to be boss.

It took a bit of doing, but CeeCee got Sheila to sit back down at the table. Sheila started drumming her fingers on the table, a sure sign she was really close to the edge. I went over and hugged her, both to make her feel better and to try and stop her fingers. Between the vibe she was giving off and the finger tapping, I was getting nervous. Patricia subtly edged her chair farther away from Sheila. She always seemed to keep herself under complete control, so I supposed seeing someone having a meltdown was upsetting for her. I stood behind Sheila and laid my hands on her shoulders, which for some reason seemed to have a calming effect. I urged her to take some deep breaths, and gradually I could feel her extreme tension release.

"Okay, dear, we're all ready," CeeCee urged.

Sheila had chin-length brown hair that hung straight and usually covered part of her round face. She was in her early thirties and the youngest in the group.

"I didn't want to tell you," she began finally. "I mean, you all have such good jobs. CeeCee with your TV show, Molly does the event thing with the bookstore, Dinah is a college professor."

"Just an instructor," Dinah corrected.

"Whatever, it's still a good job. And Adele runs the kids' department here at the bookstore," Sheila said.

I noticed Adele didn't correct her. But she didn't quite run the kids' department. She only handled story time. Mrs. Shedd did the buying, and any book signings went through me.

"So, I thought you wouldn't understand." She stopped and took a few deep breaths. "My job as receptionist at the gym doesn't pay that much. I tried to get more shifts, but it was a no-go. Something about they don't want me to be full-time because they'd have to pay benefits. So, I thought maybe I could sell some of the scarves I've made." At that she took one out of her bag, and as usual we all oohed and aahed.

It was hard to believe the beautiful scarf was made by the same person who had just thrown her work across the table. Patricia picked it up and examined it.

"You made this?" She didn't have to say more. We all knew what she meant. We had had the same reaction the first time we saw one of Sheila's creations.

"When I'm alone I'm more relaxed when I crochet, and I use one of these." Sheila produced what looked like a plastic crochet hook on steroids.

It wasn't the stitches that stood out on Sheila's scarf—they were just single and double crochet. It was the different yarns and the way she'd mixed them. The scarf on the table had a base of a royal blue ribbon mohair, but then she had made a pattern by mixing it first with a mauve eyelash and a delft blue worsted. Farther up, she'd taken out the blue worsted and changed to a green. The subtle change of color and texture created the effect of an impressionist painting. She had finished it with a blue fringe beaded with tiny crystals that caught the light.

"It's beautiful. I don't see why you had a problem selling them," Patricia said.

"That's not the problem. They have actually been selling very well. It's just . . ." Sheila swallowed a few times and appeared agitated again. "I've been selling them at the Cottage Shoppe, and it was fine as long as Mrs. Brooks was running it. She kept meticulous records and always paid me on time. But she died." Sheila's eyes welled up again, and she did her best to fight back the tears. "Her nephews are running the place now. Really, one of them seems to be the boss. His name is Drew Brooks and, and . . ." Sheila sighed. "He gave me a whole story about the scarves not selling and he had to lower the price and some of them got lost, and the check he gave me was for half of what it should have been." With everything finally out in the open, Sheila seemed spent but calmer. I gave her shoulders a squeeze and sat down.

I knew the store she was talking about. It was located in a house on Ventura Boulevard that had been turned into a business a long time ago. In ancient times in Tarzana, which was like the 70's, there had been a number of houses that were turned into businesses along the main street. Most had since been replaced by bland-looking storefronts. Only the Cottage Shoppe had survived, probably because Mrs. Brooks had been the original owner. It was a Tarzana landmark that sold antiques, some eclectic new items and things on consignment. I hadn't realized the new owners had branched out into selling handicrafts, but then, I hadn't been in there for a long time.

"That's terrible," Patricia said before turning to the rest of us. "It's such a wonderful store. I placed some things there myself. Before I found Benjamin, I was struggling as a single parent. But of course, I only dealt with Mrs. Brooks, and she was always wonderful."

"Well, everything's changed," Sheila said. "And on top of it, I had already given him more of the scarves before I knew about the money issue. I don't know what to do. I really need to sell them, and there aren't any other options."

"That's terrible that this Drew person tried to cheat you," Dinah said.

"I don't think he tried; I think he succeeded," Adele chimed in.

Then suddenly everyone started talking at once again. Patricia rapped on the table and opened her mouth to speak, but CeeCee beat her to the punch. "We can't let him get away with that," she said, laying a hand on Sheila's shoulder.

Patricia seemed miffed at having been ignored and said something about needing to leave. She was volunteering at the senior center. As she got up to go, she went on about her commitment to the community and how even though it was Benjamin's name on the ballot, she and her husband were really a team.

"I have an idea for our next project," Dinah said. "I don't know if you noticed how Molly put her hands on Sheila's shoulders to comfort her, and then CeeCee did something similar. The feeling of having some weight on your shoulders seems to have a comforting effect. What if we crocheted shawls for the Women's Haven? They would be like comforting hugs."

"And we could call them 'hugs of comfort,'" Adele suggested.

We all liked the idea. Sheila said it was true that having something on her shoulders had made her feel calmer and if anyone was a good judge, it was her.

"Well, that's taken care of, but we still have to do something about Sheila's problem," CeeCee said.

CHAPTER 2

SINCE THERE WAS NO EVENT AT THE BOOKSTORE that night, I left in the late afternoon. Mrs. Shedd knew I was likely to work more rather than fewer hours, so she let me make my own schedule. I was still thinking about Sheila as I headed for my car. It was great that she had found a place to sell her scarves, but terrible that the guy was shorting her. I, more than the rest of the crochet group, knew how important selling those scarves was to Sheila. The crochet group knew only part of her story.

Sheila came to a lot of the events at the bookstore. And after the program for the book *Tea and Sympathy: An Anecdote to Stress and Anxiety*, she had hung around talking as I handed out samples of the author's special blend of herbal relaxation tea. Sheila had looked forlorn as she told me how adrift she still felt since the death of the grandmother who'd raised her.

"I know it's silly since I am thirty-one, but I feel like an orphan without Granny Annie," she'd said, tossing her paper cup but making no move to leave. I told her I certainly understood the feeling. I didn't feel like an orphan, but I certainly felt adrift. Even though my husband Charlie had been dead almost two years, I still sometimes woke up in the morning and forgot. And then I'd realize he wasn't there and feel a hollow emptiness that just ached.

"You have the crochet group and your boyfriend," I'd said, hoping to make her feel better. I'd never met him, but she talked about him often. Frankly, he didn't sound like much of a bargain. They seemed to be always off and on again, and he was always pushing her to take drugs for her anxiety.

"And I have school and my plans for the future. But taking one class at a time at night is making it take forever. I just want to finish and get a job as a costume designer at one of the studios." At that she had sighed and smiled at me. "I don't mean to sound so pathetic. Sometimes it all just gets to me." She'd looked down and then met my eyes again. "Please don't tell the rest of the group about my living arrangements. It's so embarrassing."

I had kept her secret, not even telling Dinah, though I didn't think anyone would think the lesser of her. So, she rented a room in a house in Reseda and had to babysit for the owner on the weekend to pay part of the rent. Sheila had a lot on her plate, and it was no wonder she was nervous. And no wonder she was so upset about the scarves. I got angry just thinking about it.

I glanced at the Cottage Shoppe as I drove past on my way home. The wood-frame house was painted a blue gray, and the large windows that faced Ventura Boulevard had window boxes overflowing with red, white and deep purple petunias. How could a place that looked so charming on the outside be run by a total jerk?

We had continued talking about Sheila's problem after

Patricia left. Everyone agreed that Sheila should take back the check and insist on the fair amount. She seemed to go along with the idea, but I wondered if she could handle it.

My house was in an area raised off the Valley floor but still flat enough to have a big yard. A few blocks behind me, the land rose upward and became the Santa Monica Mountains. Houses dotted the slopes, and then it turned wild and green where the Santa Monica Mountains Conservancy began.

I pulled the greenmobile into the driveway. My older son Peter had a fit every time he saw me driving the car. I called it vintage. He called it too old. It was a 1993 190E in a shade I called teal green that was so unusual that whenever I saw another car the same color we waved in solidarity. It was a good car, and I hadn't seen any reason to replace it.

I stepped out of the car and headed toward the backyard, my usual path to my kitchen door. As I opened the gate still deep in thought, I heard rustling coming from inside. Somebody was in the yard. My breath caught, and I started to backtrack toward the driveway while reaching for my cell phone. Suddenly a ball of black fur roared up and dropped a ball at my feet. I felt my lungs release, the air pouring out in a gush. Was I ever going to get used to this?

"We didn't scare you, did we?" The voice belonged to Barry Greenberg, my sort of boyfriend. The *sort of* was only in *my* mind. He saw us as a couple.

"As a matter of fact, you did," I said as my heart rate returned to normal.

"I stopped by to drop off some dog food, and while I was here thought I'd give him a little playtime." Though Barry shrugged defensively, his smile seemed self-satisfied. "Cosmo wants you to throw the ball," Barry said, pointing at the red sphere at my feet.

I bent over to pet the little black mutt, and he did a happy dance in response. I lobbed the ball far into the yard, then walked in, shutting the gate behind me. Cosmo ignored the ball and followed me.

"Didn't you see my Tahoe parked out front?" Barry said. "I'd think you'd be used to my visits by now."

"I guess I didn't notice your SUV." To me all SUVs looked the same; besides, I'd been thinking about Sheila when I drove up, and there was a part of me that didn't want to see his SUV parked there.

"I left more food for him in the kitchen. As long as I'm here I might as well feed him."

Barry was a homicide detective—and very clever and very stubborn. His idea of calling before coming over was using his cell phone at my door—a problem for me. His excuse was that the nature of his job made it hard to make advance plans.

As we walked into the kitchen, Barry pointed out the cabinet door he'd fixed. He was a master with his hands and repaired anything in my house that seemed broken.

"Where's Jeffrey?" I asked. Barry had been divorced for a number of years, but only recently had his soon-to-be fourteen-year-old son come to live with him.

Barry gritted his teeth. "At a rehearsal." Jeffrey wanted to be an actor and wanted to be known as Columbia Greenberg, which he thought was a star name. Barry hated the name and the idea, and kept trying to steer him toward some kind of criminal justice career.

So, why was Barry in my backyard with Cosmo? The only way Barry and Jeffrey could adopt Cosmo was if they had backup. The adoption people knew that homicide detectives often worked odd hours and almost fourteen-year-olds weren't always dependable when it came to remembering to walk a dog or feed it. Since I had a house with a dog door and a big yard, and I was a total soft heart when it came to animals or kids, I'd agreed to be their backup.

At first Cosmo was just an occasional visitor, and I gave Barry a key so he could drop off the dog. Then Cosmo's visits began lasting a few days at a time, and eventually he moved here full-time, but since he was Barry's dog and Barry wanted to be a responsible pet dad, he kept the key and the right to come over whenever so he could look after *his* dog.

Quite frankly, though, this whole dog thing was as transparent as chiffon; I knew Barry was totally pleased with himself for figuring out how to get a key and full access to my house and my life.

Barry asked me about my day as he got the dog's bowl, and I told him about Sheila's problem. "That's what small claims court is for," he said. He didn't seem happy when I didn't jump at the idea. "Molly, don't get involved," he warned. "Just tell her to take it to small claims court."

Blondie came into the kitchen when she heard Barry open the refrigerator. Blondie was my dog. I'd adopted her shortly after Charlie died. She was a strawberry blond terrier mix who had been in a shelter for a year and a half and had never quite adapted to life outside a cage. She mostly kept to herself and had adjusted to Cosmo's presence by ignoring him.

Barry reached for a can of dog food, but his hand stopped on the amber bottles of Hefeweizen. "You should get rid of these; they probably aren't any good anymore." He started to take the bottles out, but I stopped him. He didn't look happy. The wheat beer was Charlie's favorite, and I'd bought it without thinking when I saw it on sale. It had been sitting in the fridge for months and months. Barry was probably right about it being bad, but I couldn't bring myself to toss it.

He shrugged, took out the dog food and put some in

Cosmo's and Blondie's bowls. Then he showed me some supplies he'd left for Cosmo and a bottle of wine he'd brought for us. He grabbed two wineglasses, and we went into the living room. He was dressed in his work clothes: a suit, blue oxford cloth shirt and striped tie.

"You're still thinking about Sheila and the problem with the store, aren't you?" he asked.

I nodded and told him how upset she was. Barry knew she was juggling a make-do job with going to school and that she had anxiety issues. He opened the wine and poured us each a glass, and we sat down on the couch. He pulled his tie loose and me close. "I think I know how to get your mind off of her," he said suggestively while he checked his watch.

"Sure you can squeeze it in?" I teased. These days any time we had alone and naked was pretty much like fast food: standardized and over quickly. He always had to rush off to question some person of interest or take Jeffrey to the dentist or just be home with him.

"If you'd let me make an honest woman of you, there wouldn't be any problem," Barry said, kissing my ear. He put his hand on my thigh, reminding me of how good his hands were at other things beside cabinet repairs. But I also thought, here we go again. It wasn't that I didn't like him. Actually, I thought I loved him. But there were a few things that stood in the way of me going along with his plans. For one there was the issue of me trying my wings: I needed some solo flying time to see that I could do it before I shared the controls with somebody else again. And there was the issue of my freedom. Right now I had no one to answer to if I decided to take up juggling or jet off to Paris. Not that I had done either, but I knew that I could. And the final thing was Charlie. I figured that as long as I had his favorite beer in the refrigerator, I wasn't ready.

But I wouldn't say no to an afternoon passion pit stop. Barry slipped out of his jacket and pulled me toward him while I started to unbutton his shirt. He showed off his exceptional kissing skills, and I sighed. Then the doorbell rang.

"Ignore it," he said in a low growl.

"I can't." I pulled away from him and pointed to the open shutters on the large window. We couldn't see who was at the door, but they surely had seen us. Maybe not clearly enough to know what was going on, but enough to know somebody was home.

Cosmo flew to the door in a barky fury. Blondie walked behind him, letting him do the talking. I walked past the dogs, and Barry stayed on the couch, hoping it was just a FedEx delivery.

When I opened the door, a young woman was standing there, holding a suitcase. Barry wasn't going to be happy. This wasn't just a package to take in and then shut the door. I had met the young woman only a few times, but I recognized her as Morgan, my younger son's girlfriend.

These days my sons usually kept me out of the loop because in the past I had gotten too attached to some of their previous girlfriends and it had made them uncomfortable.

"Didn't Samuel call you?" she said, picking up on my surprise.

I explained I'd just gotten home and suggested maybe he'd left a message. What could I do but invite her in?

"Hey, babe, the couch is getting cold," Barry called from the living room. And time was running out before he had to pick up Jeffrey. He did a double take when I walked in with Morgan and her suitcase.

And sure enough, when I checked, Samuel had left a message on my house phone. I had a feeling he'd avoided calling me on my cell because he didn't really want to talk to me directly. The message was vague on exactly why, but Morgan needed a place to stay for a couple of weeks. Samuel said she couldn't stay with him because he was sharing a place with three other guys and there were already too many people. So he asked if she could stay with me. Like I said, I'm a total soft heart for animals and children, even when they are grown up.

"Morgan's going to be staying with me," I announced in a slightly forced bright tone.

Barry was already picking up his jacket and tie and heading for the door.

"I'll take a rain check," I said, following him to the back door. I kissed him long and deep enough to remind him of what he was missing. He threw a hopeless look toward Morgan and offered me one last bit of advice.

"Remember, small claims court, and you stay out of it with Sheila."

Chapter 3

Barry just didn't understand. No way was I going to stay out of it with Sheila. She had turned to the Tarzana Hookers in her time of need. I wasn't totally discounting the small claims court idea, just putting it off on the back burner in case nothing else worked.

I had shown Morgan to Samuel's room. He thought since he was offering his old room to her, it wasn't really an imposition to me. In his mind, no matter where he lived, his room would always belong to him. Luckily Peter didn't feel the same, or he would have had a fit with what I'd done with his old room. I had taken out most of the furniture and all his sports trophies and stuck them in the garage along with all the sports equipment he insisted on leaving here. Then I'd turned the room into my crochet space.

I'd also shown Morgan the kitchen and told her to help herself to anything. She took a glass of water. From the first time I'd met her I suspected she might have an eating problem. She had that sort of waifish thin body dancers often had, but reminding myself to mind my own business, I headed for the phone.

"We have to do something for Sheila," I said to Dinah. I had already told her about my houseguest, expecting some kind of comment, but Dinah had said nothing. That wasn't like Dinah as she usually had something to say about everything. She mumbled something about not being able to deal with Sheila's problem just then. I heard noise in the background. How stupid of me to assume she was alone.

Dinah was divorced and unlike me, anxious to find a new partner. She'd been trying online stuff and coming up with nothing but duds. Maybe her luck had changed. I apologized for interrupting and said I'd thought maybe we could all go to the Cottage Shoppe with Sheila the next morning to give her moral support. I suggested we arrive when the store first opened, and I ended by telling her with a wink in my voice to "have fun."

All she said was, "It's not what you think," before she hung up.

I tried CeeCee next. She was gung ho about doing something for Sheila as long as she didn't have to be part of it.

"Dear, I have to be concerned about my image. And there's the issue of the paparazzi. All I need is someone to get some photo on their cell phone of me in the middle of some kind of fracas. Sometimes being a celebrity is such a pain."

I gave her the details anyway, even though I wasn't sure she was listening.

I didn't know whether to include Patricia since I wasn't even sure she was really going to join the crochet group, but I didn't want her to feel left out, so I called her. Someone answered the phone and took a message.

I had put off calling Adele until last. Things never went

smoothly with her, and this was no different. When she heard I'd basically been turned down by everyone, she said, "I guess majority rules, Pink. You're on your own."

I was glad I hadn't called Sheila first to propose the idea. It would have been a real punch in the gut to tell her everyone was going to come and then have to call her back and say they'd all begged off. So, I called and just offered my services.

"Oh, Molly, thank you," she said with a gush of relief. "I want to confront Drew Brooks, but I wasn't sure if I'd be able to do it. He's a nasty guy. But if I know you're there, it'll be easier to face him."

THE NEXT MORNING AT THE APPOINTED TIME, I stood outside the Cottage Shoppe. Banners on every window blared enticing messages. One urged people to come in and check out the unique merchandise, another mentioned there were new arrivals daily, and the last one announced the coveted items from the Hearston Estate were coming soon. I didn't remember Mrs. Brooks being so hard sell.

It was another silvery morning, and I was glad to have my jacket protecting me against the damp chill. I glanced around wondering if Sheila had gotten cold feet, and saw a woman approaching the shop.

"I know I said I wasn't going to come," CeeCee said, coming up next to me. "But I couldn't leave you two alone. Sometimes my status comes in handy. Maybe it'll mean something to that jerk." She zipped up her amber velour jacket and glanced around. "Where's Sheila?"

Before I could answer Dinah showed up. I opened my mouth to ask her about the background noise from the night before, but she beat me to the punch. "I'll tell you about it later," she said with a hint of distress in her voice. She looked around for Sheila, too.

Adele marched up with a knowing nod. "I knew it. I thought the rest of you would come, and I wasn't going to be the only one who didn't show. So, what's the plan?"

"First, we need Sheila," Dinah said.

I was about to say that perhaps she'd gotten cold feet, but CeeCee gestured. "Here she comes."

Sheila was walking across the parking lot with Patricia.

"I was just giving her some advice," Patricia said when they reached us. "I told her to just go in there with her mind set on the outcome she wants. And not to give up until he gives in. And if all else fails, maybe if we all came in it would help."

"I want to speak to him on my own," Sheila said. "But it really helps to know you'll all be here."

Adele led the way up the two steps to the tiny front porch. The bell on the door had a jingle fit from so many of us going in at once.

I told Sheila to go ahead and that we'd be hanging around waiting for her. I squeezed her hand for good luck, and with her hair swinging, she walked toward the sales desk. Rather than just standing around, we all started looking around the store. "If there's something rotten going on here, it sure doesn't show," I said to Dinah. The inside of the store was as charming as the exterior.

Dinah and I stuck together as we walked into the first room. Since the shop was a house, the items for sale had been arranged in the rooms for which they were suited. We had entered the living room, where a pair of antique maple rockers sat in front of the small fireplace. Both had knitted throws draped over the arms. One was a heathery blue that was soft to the touch. I looked at it quickly, afraid Adele would make a scene if she saw me admiring it. There was also a wood bench with purple velvet cushions and shelves with all kinds of interesting doodads. I already owned enough doodads and kept my distance. In an alcove off the living room a gorgeous leaded glass lamp in shades of green sat on a craftsman-style table next to a love seat covered with needlepoint pillows. Everything had a price tag.

I pointed out Sheila's scarves displayed on a mannequin and on top of a dresser in the "bedroom." A case held some vintage jewelry pieces and an array of perfume bottles. Dinah admired a sequined evening wear top that was draped over one of the drawers. There were a few other articles of vintage clothing, all of which were unusual and in mint condition.

I had to admit it was a lovely store. Everything was displayed in an artful manner. Even the floors were nice—hardwood throughout with a dark stain and an occasional oriental rug.

"Whoever arranged everything did a wonderful job," Dinah said, looking at a basket filled with picnic items complete with a compass and a book on local parks.

"I have a feeling it wasn't Drew Brooks," I said as we made a full circle of the display rooms and came back to the entrance hall. The dining room was across from us and had been turned into a small refreshment area. A number of wrought iron bistro tables and chairs were placed strategically about. A bar had been built into the room and was set up with a selection of bakery items covered with glass domes. It also featured an espresso machine and a chalkboard listing the coffee and tea options along with an announcement they now had "Soup by Kevin." Today's offering was lentil.

The door to the kitchen was behind the bar. Apparently it was actually functional rather than another display area for merchandise.

Dinah and I went in and found a table. Dinah still hadn't discussed the night before and seemed tense, but every time I asked her what was wrong, she said it wasn't a good place to talk. She laid her leather tote on the table and pulled out some papers and started to grade them.

Gradually the rest of the group drifted in and pulled up chairs. CeeCee took out her crocheting. She must have finished the donut pincushion because she was now working on an iridescent white baby blanket. Patricia was checking her watch and going over her calendar. Being a candidate's wife appeared to be a busy business. Adele was crocheting red flowers out of the stuff that looked like string. Judging by the way she kept holding them up to her ear, I gathered they were going to be earrings.

Sheila reappeared a few minutes later. All of her good spirits were deflated.

"I asked to talk to him." She was talking fast, the words tumbling out. "He and his brother have offices upstairs. One of the saleswomen went up there to tell him I was here, but he said he was busy and I would have to wait. I finally figured out it was just a stall."

We all started talking at once, offering advice, but we were interrupted when a tall bald man wearing a well-fitting dark suit and carrying a Harrods shopping bag roared through the store. We could hear him bellowing as he found a salesclerk and demanded to talk to the owner.

"I guess that's the kind of voice you have to use," CeeCee said.

I saw one of the clerks come out from the small sales office and rush toward the stairway. Before she'd gone up three steps, the bald guy pushed past her and went up on his own. "I'm guessing you're not the only one Drew Brooks tried to cheat," I said.

A few moments later, the same man came down the

stairs, this time with another man who I assumed must be Drew Brooks.

"You're not going to get away with this," the bald man said.

Drew was short with a solid build and a flop of brown hair. What he lacked in size he made up for in a sense of power. He ushered the bald man to the door and in a phony voice thanked him for his business. As he walked back past the tearoom, he saw all of us sitting there, crocheting, checking calendars and reading student papers—everything except eating or drinking.

"This is for customers only," he said in an unpleasant voice. Sheila took a deep breath, stood up and separated herself from the rest of us.

"I need to talk to you," she said in a surprisingly forceful voice. "That check is unacceptable." I guess the moral-support thing really worked.

Drew dismissed her with a shake of his head. "Sorry, no time. I'm on my way out."

Before any of us could say a word, he had gone out the front door. It shut with a bang and an angry jangle of the bell.

"If he thinks he can just avoid dealing with me, he has another thought coming," Sheila said and banged on the table for emphasis. We all jumped.

Another man, maybe a little younger than Drew, came down the stairs. He had similar features and the same brown hair, but it looked different on him. Drew had more of a sneer, while this man, who I assumed must be the other Brooks brother, seemed to have a more genuine smile.

"Ladies, I hope you noticed we're now featuring some homemade soup," he said, apparently oblivious to any problem we were having. He checked the refreshment bar, noting the tea was low and the creamer empty.

"Kevin Brooks," he said as an introduction, holding out his hand to CeeCee. It was really meant for all of us, but she was closest.

"Your brother owes our friend an apology and the rest of her money," CeeCee said. I guess she had made sure there were no cell phone or paparazzi cameras aimed at her and decided to go for it.

His innkeeper smile faded, then he looked at CeeCee again as who she was began to sink in. "Ms. Collins, I wish I could help, but my brother handles the money." His gaze moved over the rest of us, and he sucked in his breath when he saw our fierce expressions. "How about a bowl of soup for each of you? On the house, of course." When he didn't get any response from us, he rethought his offer. "Maybe it's a little early for lentil soup. How about some coffee or an espresso drink and a pastry?"

"A cappuccino would be nice, with low-fat milk, of course," CeeCee said. Once she'd opened the door, the rest of us spoke up. Kevin made the coffee drinks, set them up on the bar and invited us to help ourselves to the pastries. CeeCee muttered something about not wanting to be rude as she took a raspberry croissant. We carried our goodies back to the table. I was pleased when my red eye was nice and strong and a perfect complement to the sour cream danish.

"Then everything is fine now?" Kevin Brooks said, coming by to check a few minutes later.

Sheila surprised us all by hitting the table with her fist and saying it wasn't. "If you think giving us a caffeine-and-sugar rush is going to make me go away, you have another thought coming. My friends and I'll be back, and your brother better make good on what he owes me or else."

Kevin took a step back and appeared uncomfortable with her outburst. I was also surprised by it. Sheila always seemed soft spoken, with her head down and her hair covering her face. I didn't know she had the ability for such a confrontation. The other customers had heard her, too, and we suddenly had become the center of attention.

"I think it's time to go," CeeCee said, scanning the crowd for anybody with a camera. These days, with everything on the Internet in a few minutes and the public hungry for anything embarrassing about celebrities, she was always on guard.

As we filed into the entrance hall, Sheila said she really meant what she'd said: She was coming back, and next time Drew Brooks was going to have to deal with her or else.

"We're with you," Adele said. "That was a fabulous cappuccino, just the right blend of foam and espresso, but it'll take more than that to buy me off."

CeeCee was hesitant about agreeing to another go-round, but she finally patted Sheila's hand and said she was in. Dinah's eyes were flashing, and she told Sheila she'd done good by standing up for herself. Of course, she'd be back. There were some problems with us meeting at the shop the next day, so we decided to do it the day after at the same time. We'd started out just wanting to help Sheila, but now Drew Brooks had gotten all of us mad.

Patricia excused herself, saying she had to get to some volunteering thing at the hospital and left ahead of the rest of us.

As we were leaving, I noticed a familiar face admiring the heather blue knitted blanket I'd noticed earlier. She looked up and our eyes met.

Detective Hea—I mean, Gilmore," I said. Her face showed recognition but not the open smile of someone really glad to see you. No wonder—we weren't exactly friends. We did have something in common. Barry Greenberg. She wanted him and I had him. And it really bugged her.

"Were you with the brown-haired woman making the scene?" she asked.

I tried to shrug it off, but she stuck with it. "Didn't I recognize the crochet group? What is it you call yourselves?"

"We're the Tarzana Hookers," I said in a low voice, realizing that seeing her shopping like a regular person was weird. Detective Heather was dressed in a dark suit with a pencil skirt and heels, and had pulled her white blond curls back into a more serious style. I only called her Detective Heather in my mind and to my friends. Saying it directly to her sounded too much like calling her Detective Barbie Doll. She already didn't like me, and I didn't want to make it worse. The truth was, she had a lot going for her. She was not only hot looking, but also very smart and a good detective, according to Barry.

Detective Heather asked what the problem was. I knew it was foolish, but since it wasn't for me, I explained, thinking she might do something, like wave her gun at the nice Brooks brother and get Sheila her money. No such luck.

"Tell your friend to take him to small claims court," she said, brushing some lint off her purse. I didn't have to ask to know she'd knitted it. It was the replica of some bag featured at Neiman Marcus that you'd have to take out a mortgage to buy. Detective Heather was knit only and no fan of crochet or the people that did it.

CHAPTER 4

TWO DAYS LATER, I WAS AGAIN WAITING OUTSIDE the Cottage Shoppe, but things were different. According to the banners on the windows, the Hearston Estate items had arrived. I didn't know what they were, but they seemed to have attracted a crowd. People kept passing me and going inside. I thought the crochet group had agreed to meet outside, but after standing alone for a while, I began to wonder if I'd misunderstood, so I went inside, too.

Once I got past a clump of people in the entrance hall, I saw CeeCee standing in the dining room, admiring a three-tiered tray of scones.

"I thought we were going to meet outside," I said, walking up to her.

"It's so much more interesting in here, I came inside," CeeCee said. I asked about the others, and she mentioned she'd seen Patricia looking around. "And here's Dinah." My friend stepped around a woman carrying a butter churn.

I was determined to get some information from Dinah

this time about the other night. I'd since tried calling her a number of times, and either she hadn't answered or she'd told me she couldn't talk. Today she was wrapped in a rust-colored shawl and had on brass earrings that jangled when she moved her head.

"Okay, so what *is* going on?" I asked. Dinah hesitated. There was a buzz from all the chatter, and it was obviously not a good place to have an intimate conversation.

"I'm really not trying to stall you. I'll tell you about it, but let's take care of Sheila's problem first." A woman jostled Dinah as she showed off a crystal decanter to her shopping companion. "Here comes Sheila." We waited while Sheila moved between some people and came over to us. She had a determined look on her face, but I noticed she was twisting her fingers, a sure sign she was nervous.

Adele waved and then came over. CeeCee came from the dining room and joined the group. We huddled and all agreed that Sheila's best bet was to simply go upstairs to Drew's office rather than talking to either of the saleswomen first.

"And be firm," Dinah said. Sheila took some deep breaths and marched toward the stairs.

Adele held up her find to show us. It was some sort of deep purple turbanlike hat with a tall black feather. She modeled it, but it made her look like a kooky fortune-teller.

"It was Gloria Hearston's. You know who she was, don't you?" Adele directed her question at CeeCee, but the name didn't seem to register. "She was this really famous silent movie star. I can't believe you don't know who she was. Her family just released a select number of her belongings." Adele showed off a sheet of paper that had the Hearston story on it.

As I looked at Adele's hat again, I noticed the tall bald man from the other day. He was wearing another well-tailored suit and had the same Harrods shopping bag. But his manner was different. He walked toward the door with an expression I could only call satisfied.

A few minutes later, Sheila burst into the middle of the group. She was close to tears and even deep breathing didn't help. "He laughed at me," she said, her voice cracking.

We moved into the empty dining room, where Sheila repeated the whole encounter with Drew as we tried to calm her. Kevin walked into the room and didn't even seem to notice us. I didn't care what he had said about it being all his brother's domain. I reached out to grab his arm and get his attention when suddenly a hair-raising scream cut through the drone of conversation. It seemed to have come from upstairs. Everybody froze and glanced up just as another scream erupted.

I expected Kevin to do something, but he seemed glued to the floor, so I nudged Dinah and we took off toward the stairs, joined by half the people in the store. We stopped at the top of the stairs, confronted by a small hallway and several doors. A saleswoman stumbled out of one of the doorways, her eyes big with panic. She saw the crowd and screamed again and slumped against the wall. Dinah and I rushed into the room she had exited. A crowd of people came in behind us, and then there was a collective gasp. At a large desk in the center of the room, Drew Brooks was facedown in a bowl. Red stuff was splattered everywhere.

"Omigod, there's so much blood," I said, looking at the crimson marks on the rug, wall and desk.

Adele, still wearing her Gloria Hearston hat, pushed through the crowd. She looked at the desk and surroundings and shook her head at me with disgust. "Pink, it's not blood. It's soup." She mumbled something about precious time being lost while we were standing there like idiots, and pulled Drew's head up. It was covered with something red, which I now realized was too thick and lumpy to be blood. Adele was right. There was still soup in the bowl.

To her credit, she dragged Drew onto the floor and started CPR. By then the assembled gawkers all had their cell phones out and were calling 911, which apparently froze the system temporarily. Finally one person was designated as the caller.

A few moments later sirens filled the air.

"WHAT THE—" A UNIFORMED LOS ANGELES police officer said after squeezing into the room and seeing Adele crouching on the floor, pumping Drew's chest. When everyone tried to answer at once, he yelled for quiet so he could get on his radio.

His female partner pushed in behind him and then looked around, shaking her head. "We have to clear the room."

As much as Adele and I have had our differences, I think Officer Lucy Hernandez could have been a little nicer to Adele when she pulled her off the floor. After all, Adele was trying to resuscitate Drew, but I guess seeing a big woman wearing a turban-style hat with a quivering feather, hovering over a body, with all of us as an audience, must have looked strange.

After Officer Hernandez moved Adele away, she checked Drew's pulse and her expression dimmed.

The crowd was exiting the room, but I kept moving back so I could have a longer time to look around. I knew that right now all the clues to what had happened were right in front of me and once I left I wouldn't have another opportunity like this. My first thought was that it wasn't my problem, but a voice in the back of my head said to check it out anyway. And recently I'd been reading and rereading *The Average Joe's Guide to Criminal Investigation*, so I was becoming more observant.

Like not all of the red stuff was soup. I'd seen the back of Drew's head for only a moment before Adele pulled his face out of the bowl, and there was a lot of red stuff clumped in his hair. Then I looked at the desk. Along with the regular desk stuff, I saw a bunch of paperweights scattered on it. One seemed to be a globe and another a brass bust of Teddy Roosevelt. The rest appeared to be made of glass with colorful stuff suspended inside. One of Sheila's scarves was lying next to the soup bowl. Instinctively, I almost made a grab for it, but just then Officer Hernandez came up next to me to make sure I left. As I took one last look at the desk, I noticed something white and lacy hanging off one of the drawer pulls. It looked as if something had caught on it and ripped. Even as I headed out the door, I kept my eyes on it, imprinting its details on my mind.

There were more uniforms downstairs, and they held us back while the paramedics rushed past. Barry had told me once that as long as the head was still attached to the body, the cops called for a rescue ambulance. I couldn't blame them. It was better to err on the side of optimism.

Then we were escorted outside to the parking lot as yellow tape was strung around the perimeter, apparently to corral us in.

"Just stay put and no talking to each other," another uniform said. "We need to get statements from all of you and fingerprints and hair samples."

A police helicopter hovered overhead. The noise level grew as several helicopters from news stations arrived and hung in the air off to the side.

CeeCee was surrounded by a cluster of people who

were apparently ignoring the no-talking order. I passed by close enough to overhear them and figured out they were wondering if this was all part of her reality show. Patricia was also ignoring the no-talking order and was handing out campaign buttons to two women. I heard her say something about Benjamin being serious about reducing crime. Dinah was helping Adele clean up. She had gotten soup on her face and arms and the hat. I guessed the shock of what had happened had set in and she was acting frantic and stunned. When I looked back toward the store, Kevin Brooks was talking to a uniformed officer. Even from a distance I could read his body language: He was in shock.

Beyond the yellow-tape perimeter, I saw the Channel 3 News van pull up. The door flew open, and Kimberely Wang Diaz got out, dressed in slacks and a blazer and wearing stage makeup. I was distracted from her by a black Crown Victoria pulling up behind two police cruisers. When I saw Barry get out, I waved.

He didn't appear to see me. He was dressed in a suit, wore sunglasses and had a closed expression. Barry was totally serious about his job, and I was sure his mind was already ticking with whatever details he'd been given.

I'd asked him once how he could handle what he had to handle. I didn't really even want to think about what he saw on a daily basis. At first, he'd been macho and said it was all in day's work. Then he got real and said he'd had to learn to keep an emotional distance.

Even though he wore sunglasses, I knew he was looking over the crowd. When his head stopped moving, I knew he'd seen me. I waved again. He hit his forehead with the heel of his hand and shook his head. I saw him take out his cell phone as he stepped over the yellow tape and moved toward me.

"Tell me you were just on your way to the post office and you stopped when you saw the crowd and wanted to find out what was going on," he said when he got close.

His mouth settled into a straight line when I shrugged in a hopeless gesture.

"I didn't think so." Directing his attention to the rest of the crowd, he spotted Dinah, CeeCee, Adele and Sheila. He knew who Dinah was, recognized CeeCee and figured who the others were. He got the picture.

"This is the store you were talking about the other day, isn't it?" he asked. I couldn't see his eyes because of the sunglasses, but I was sure he was looking heavenward with exasperation. "Molly, you didn't tell your friend about small claims court, either, did you?"

"It was my suggestion of last resort. We thought if we all came here together Drew Brooks would just pay Sheila what he owed her and she wouldn't have to go through the whole court hassle. Sheila's kind of shy and gets nervous over anything. If she had to stand up and talk in front of a judge, even that TV guy who seems so friendly, she'd be a basket case. Drew Brooks is really dead, isn't he?"

"I'm not sure," he said. Then he sighed. "Yes."

When I'd been upstairs with everyone else, my adrenalin had kicked in and I'd thought only of what *The Average Joe's Guide* had said about being observant. That had helped me to keep a distance and pay attention to details instead of getting emotionally involved. But now, as the reality of Drew's death began to sink in, I thought I was going to be sick. Barry must have noticed I'd gone green. He held my arm for support and told me to take some deep breaths, and he gave me a piece of peppermint gum. I chewed for a moment and with each deep breath felt a little more stable.

"It was murder, wasn't it?" I said.

'Not your problem," Barry answered. I told him about the blood on the back of Drew's head. "Also not your problem."

Barry's cell phone rang, and he turned and walked away a few steps. He was flipping it shut when he came back.

"I have to step down—again. I can't be the lead detective if my girlfriend was in the room with the victim."

"It wasn't just me. There were lots of people up there. I didn't touch him." I pointed vaguely in Adele's direction. She was still wearing the hat. "Adele's the one who put him on the floor and tried to do CPR."

He was shaking his head and probably rolling his eyes behind the sunglasses over the last part. "Yeah, but I'm not dating them, so you're the only one who counts—or counts me out."

"But I'm not a suspect or a person of interest. I was just an innocent bystander," I said as he turned to go.

"We'll talk about it tonight."

"Tonight?" I repeated.

Barry had a smug set to his mouth. "I bought some dog toys for Cosmo, and I was going to bring them by." Before I could make any comment about possibly having plans that interfered, he went back into full-out work mode, gestured to his partner Darren Keltner and pointed toward the car.

I should have figured who'd replace Barry as lead detective. He and Darren were leaning against their car when she pulled up. The first thing I saw was the white blond hair as Detective Heather Gilmore got out of the Crown Vic with her partner Rick Allen. He was no trouble; she was nothing but.

The four detectives had a conversation. Well, Darren and Rick listened while Detective Heather and Barry talked. Barry gestured toward the crowd, probably explaining something. Then Detective Heather looked my way. There was a certain déjà vu to all this, but this time there was no way she could try to pin the death on me.

Like I said, Detective Heather and I had issues. Well, one issue. She wanted Barry. Who could miss the way she flicked her hair and touched his arm as they talked? He had always claimed not to be interested. I was curious about why he wasn't and had asked him about it shortly after we'd started seeing each other again following a brief breakup. She was blond, younger than I was, had a better body and was in the same line of work as he.

"She's not my type. We had coffee once, twice, ah, a few times," he'd stammered. "And it didn't work out."

I'd gone into shock mode when I realized he'd actually gone out with her. He'd always claimed not to notice she was interested. "What? You went out with her? When? How?"

"Remember when we broke up? I was a free guy then. You kept saying how you thought she had the hots for me, so I thought I'd see what was up."

"What about Jeffrey?" I'd demanded, trying not to look pouty-faced. He was so protective of Jeffrey, at first not even letting me meet him because we weren't in some permanent sort of relationship.

"He never met her," Barry had said as his lips curved into a grin. He knew he'd gotten to me and was enjoying my upset. "It never got that far. She isn't like you." He tousled my hair and touched my cheek. "You are my comic relief, the person who shows me a life away from work," he had said, wrapping me in his arms. "And you're nice to cuddle with, and," he added, licking his lips, "there's always your cooking."

He was right, there. I never used anything-helper or packaged cake mixes. I was one hundred percent from scratch. And I knew I was a good cook. The extra padding on my hips was a testament to it.

He'd said something about Detective Heather needing a cookbook to boil an egg. I'd wanted to ask how he knew. It sounded way past a cup of coffee to have gotten that kind of information. But I had decided it was better to just leave it be.

"Well, well, look who's here," Detective Heather said when she finally walked up to me. Barry and Darren had left, and Rick Allen was talking to some uniforms.

"I was just in the room with Drew Brooks. There were all those people, too." I waved my hand over the crowd. "I'm not a suspect or a person of interest."

"That's for me to decide and you to find out," she said, taking out her notebook and pen. "I might just as well start questioning you now. Let's start with the personal stuff, like your age and your weight. I know your name." She made sure her pen was working. "Aren't you like fifty-something?"

"Forty-eight," I corrected.

"And your weight?"

"What do you need that for?"

"For identification purposes," Detective Heather answered.

"What? So you can tell me apart from all the other Molly Pinks running around Tarzana?"

Begrudgingly, she said maybe she didn't need that information after all. But she did need to know what I was doing there and what I'd seen. I tried to say I was there like everybody else to see the Hearston Estate items mentioned on the window banner, but she stopped me.

"I saw you and your group here the other day. As I remember there was some kind of problem. Didn't somebody say something about not getting away with something?" She turned away from me and checked through the crowd until she found Sheila. "She was the one making the threat, wasn't she?"

"I'm sure she had nothing to do with what happened to Drew Brooks. You should really be much more concerned about that tall bald man with the Harrods shopping bag." I told her how he'd been in there the other day, and again just now. "And he was sure steamed about something," I said.

She scribbled in her notebook. "And his name is?"

"Oh, I don't exactly know," I said with a shrug.

Then she asked me to point him out.

'He's not exactly here," I said, a little uncomfortable.

"And maybe he doesn't exactly exist," she said.

"Of course he does. I'm surprised you didn't see him the other day. Go ahead and ask my friends. They saw him. They'll vouch for me."

Detective Heather didn't appear convinced. "Your friends would probably say they saw a bald green Martian in the store to back you up."

"Wow, you think they're that loyal?" I said, surprised. There was something in Detective Heather's voice. Was she jealous of my friends, too? "To put your mind at ease, just ask them when I'm not around."

"How about I just see what they say on their own." She held her pen poised. "Do you want to tell me what happened?"

I told her everything starting with the scream. She listened with an impassive expression as I told her how we'd found Drew and how Adele had tried doing CPR. She asked if I'd give my fingerprints and a hair sample. As soon as I was done, I was escorted to the edge of the parking lot, and the officer waited as I climbed under the tape and walked away. I'd have to catch up with Dinah later.

Kimberely Wang Diaz zoomed up to me since apparently I was the first one let go.

"I remember you," she said, sounding too enthused. "Aren't you the one they call the crime scene groupie?"

"MOTHER, TELL ME THAT'S NOT YOU." IT WAS MY son Peter calling my cell phone. Peter was a William Morris television agent who took his image very seriously and got upset when anyone in the family, which basically meant me and his younger brother Samuel, did anything he thought reflected poorly on him. He claimed he'd had the TV in his office on mute and by the time he turned it up, the story was over.

If you're watching Channel 3, it is," I said, relieved he had the sound off and had missed the "crime scene groupie" comment. It was ridiculous to have that label just because I happened to show up at a few crime scenes in the past. By now I'd walked down the street to the bookstore parking lot and gotten in my car.

"Mother," he said, stretching it out to two syllables of disapproval. I explained what had happened and assured him I was fine, even if I was still feeling a little fuzzy headed over it all.

He gave me a minilecture about "that's what happens when you start dating cops." Peter wasn't happy about Barry and used any opportunity to try to knock him out of the picture. At first, I thought it was the idea of my dating that bothered him, but when he tried to fix me up with Mason Fields, a lawyer he was working with on a reality show, I began to think it was more about who.

"Mother, you're not a suspect, are you?"

Finally something I could answer in a way that would make him happy. "Of course not," I said, trying to sound peppier than I felt. The whole experience was finally getting to me.

"Maybe you should talk it over with Mason. Just in case," Peter said. Mason and I had a little flirting thing going, and I did like him. He had a sense of humor about being a lawyer, he was fun and he seemed to like me. But I wasn't quite up to juggling men, and so far I hadn't taken him up on his offers of dinner. I told Peter I'd keep it in mind and clicked off.

Then I called Dinah's cell to see what had happened to her. I got her voice mail and left a message to call me ASAP. It was about then that it struck me: I'd gotten in my car as if I were going to go somewhere, but I was on my way to work and the bookstore was in front of me. Chalk it up to being unnerved by the morning's occurrence.

Adele called in to say she had to go home and change since her clothes had gotten messed up when she was working on Drew. When she finally came in, she spent most of the day in the bookstore's café telling everyone how she'd tried to save Drew Brooks. I was glad she wasn't wearing Gloria Hearston's hat.

Luckily it was a slow day because I was definitely not my usual self. I'd be okay for a few minutes, but then I'd get a bad feeling in the pit of my stomach as I relived walking into Drew's office and seeing him. Along with the eerie flashbacks, one thought kept surfacing: What had really happened?

I left Shedd & Royal in the late afternoon and drove home, still not having heard from Dinah. By some quirk of timing Barry and I arrived at my driveway at the same time. He pulled his Tahoe in behind the greenmobile. The sun was fading, turning the sky a soft apricot as we walked into my yard together. For once I didn't care that Barry had just dropped over.

"Are you okay?" he asked, putting his arm around my shoulders.

"I've had better days." It felt nice to have some support, and if anybody could understand how I felt it was Barry. He dealt with crime scenes all the time.

"You couldn't get your mind off seeing Brooks, right?" When I nodded, Barry squeezed my shoulders. "The best thing you can do is concentrate on something else." He glanced around the yard. "Think about how beautiful those flowers are," he said, pointing at the orange and yellow pansies filling the planters that ran along the patio. "Think about your friends, your crochet stuff—me," he said, as his lips curved into a grin.

"Actually there was something I kept thinking about," I said. His expression warmed—he obviously assumed it had to do with him. It did, just not the way he thought. "I bet you know all kinds of inside information about what happened to Drew Brooks," I said.

"You call that thinking about something else?" He shook his head with dismay. "If I didn't know better, I'd think you just liked me for my information," he teased, putting the bag of dog toys down on the patio table. I suspected he had just picked them up on his way here as opposed to having purchased them this morning, when he'd mentioned needing to drop them off.

"I just wondered what happened after I left. Well, you left, too, but you must have found out how Drew Brooks died and who Detective Heather thinks did it." I opened the kitchen door, and Cosmo ran out the door and tried to decide who to greet first. Clearly the dog knew which side his toast was buttered on because he rushed up to me, putting his floppy paws on my knees.

Barry appeared hurt. "Have you forgotten who your daddy is?" he said, holding up a rawhide chew. Cosmo was a regular dog diplomat. After a quick hello lick to me, he ran over to Barry and grabbed the chew. Blondie came out to see what was going on. Barry offered her a chew and she snatched it and ran back into the house.

Before we went inside Morgan drifted into the kitchen, Barry did a double take, then his expression dropped.

"How long is Princess Sad Face staying?" he said in a low voice.

He was right about the sad face part. Morgan always seemed to have a certain melancholy air about her. Today she was dressed in pink tights and leotard with a sweatshirt tied around her waist. When I did that it was to keep a sweatshirt handy. Morgan told me she did it to camouflage her hips—if you could call those tiny things hips. She went to dance class every day and worked at a kid's gym and at an after-school program. Also, she went to auditions for music videos and stage productions. She had one coming up in the next couple of days.

"Just for a couple of weeks," I said, watching her open the refrigerator and take out three slices of apple on a plate and a bottle of sparkling spring water.

Barry didn't seem happy with the information. Her

presence was a definite obstacle to his plans to show up spontaneously on my doorstep and then morph it into a whole other kind of encounter.

"What happened to that whole thing about your freedom and wanting to live alone and have ice cream for dinner if you wanted?" he asked.

"I still can, as long as I don't make her eat any," I said. "So, are you going to tell me about Drew Brooks, or not?"

"Not. I don't know anything. It's not my case, remember?"

"But you do know how he died—he drowned in the soup, didn't he?" I mentioned seeing the blood on the back of his head. "I bet somebody hit him on the head and he fell in the soup."

"I'm not talking, and besides, until there's an autopsy nobody knows for sure."

"Okay, then, if it was your case, who would you investigate first?"

Barry groaned and shook his head. "Hey, Sherlock, I see where you're going and keep out of it. Have you ever heard the term *obstruction of justice*? If Heather thinks you're getting into things—" He grabbed my hand and pretended to handcuff it.

"I was just curious, that's all."

He rolled his eyes in response and carried the dog things inside.

THE NEXT MORNING WHEN I WENT INTO THE bookstore office I was surprised to find Mrs. Shedd sitting at her desk. Our paths crossed only occasionally since she mostly came in before the bookstore opened or after it closed. She was in her late sixties, but her blond hair, cut to frame her face and strategically cover certain spots, made her look at least twenty years younger. The actual color was chemically enhanced, but the thick, shiny texture was all good genes.

Everyone called her Mrs. Shedd. I only recently found out her first name was Pamela. I had never met Mr. Royal. Whenever she mentioned him, Mrs. Shedd gave the impression that he was on an extended trip. It was obvious he was her silent partner—very silent, like dead or nonexistent.

A mug of coffee sat next to her along with a little pile of cherry-almond cookies. The newspaper was open on the desk. Even upside down, I could tell what article she was reading. It was the same one I'd already read about the Drew episode. Since it was a local murder, it was a big story on the third page. The article mostly described what I'd seen firsthand. The cause of death was still unknown pending the autopsy results, but the police were still investigating. There wasn't a lot of personal information about Drew other than that he was divorced with no children. What a surprise.

There was an accompanying picture that showed the crowd corralled in the parking lot, waiting to be questioned. Thankfully, the photographer had been more interested in catching how many people were there rather than who they were, and nobody's face, including mine, was recognizable.

"Talk about freaky," I said, pointing at the article. "It was quite a scene."

"You were there?" Mrs. Shedd asked, perking up with interest. When I nodded, she wanted details, and I told her the whole story of Sheila and her scarves.

"This didn't have anything to do with the projects you're doing at the bookstore?" Mrs. Shedd said, seeming concerned.

"No. She made them all at home. She just brought them in so we could drool over them."

I mentioned that Patricia had joined the crochet group. Saying her name to Mrs. Shedd was like pushing the play button on a recording. Whenever I mentioned Patricia, Mrs. Shedd told the same story in the exact same words.

"She's a genius. She got the pinot noir stain out of that blouse I had made in Paris. I don't know what I would have done without her. You know I had that dinner with the mayor that night. She saved the day. Saved the day." Mrs. Shedd always said "saved the day" twice. Then she went into the part about how she was happy to host events for Patricia because she knew from experience that the things in her book worked. I smiled and nodded, acting as if I were hearing this story for the first time.

"You must have known Ramona Brooks," I said, trying to change the topic. "I hadn't thought about it before, but it only made sense since Shedd & Royal was just down the street from the Cottage Shoppe."

"She was a lovely woman," Mrs. Shedd said. "And she adored that store. It started out as just an antique and vintage store. She had a knack for finding unusual items at garage sales and flea markets. Then she would add a little polish, display them to their best advantage and get a nice price. She started taking in things on consignment because it was easier. But she was particular about what she'd take. It had to be unusual and something that would pull in a big price. It was only recently she also started taking handicraft items on consignment. But they had to be special, like those scarves you mentioned."

"Did you go in there much?" I asked, hoping Mrs. Shedd would keep talking. Who knew what information she might have that could come in handy?

She laughed. "Too much for a while, and I have the stuff to prove it. Ramona was a good saleswoman. She always pointed out that everything was one of a kind and that if you didn't buy it when you saw it, the next time it probably wouldn't be there."

"I suppose she knew all about antiques and the values of things," I said.

"She definitely knew a lot about the things she sold, but when it came to the consignment things, she really went by what the seller claimed." Mrs. Shedd ran her thumb along her coffee mug and appeared thoughtful. "I was really sorry when she died. She was a lovely woman, unlike her nephews."

Mrs. Shedd described how she'd stopped in the Cottage Shoppe shortly after Drew and Kevin had taken over. "I wanted to introduce myself and wish them good luck. I ended up walking in and out in almost the same move. The two men were having a yelling match in the living room. It seemed so out of place with such a genteel backdrop. I couldn't hear who was saying what. One sounded viciously nasty and the other just seemed upset. I didn't hear the details, and frankly I just wanted to get out of there."

"I'd bet money the really nasty one was Drew," I said. "He told Sheila if she didn't like what he was offering, she could take her scarves somewhere else. He knew there wasn't another place like it around here doing consignment. Kevin seems more pleasant." I shifted my weight. "Maybe you should tell that story to the police."

"I don't want to get involved, and neither should you," she cautioned. "You're not a suspect, I assume, so the best thing you can do is keep a low profile."

I tried to look as though I agreed. Mrs. Shedd was my boss, after all. It was just about ten and time for the crochet group to begin. Needing her approval, I told her about our plan to make comforting shawls for the Women's Haven. She liked the idea immediately and said to go ahead and get the yarn. As I walked toward the door, she casually said, "By the way, a local children's author offered to come to story time. I told Adele to handle it. I hope you don't feel I've stepped on your toes."

I just smiled and said I was sure it would be fine. As I passed the children's department, I noticed the sign for story time had an extra sheet attached announcing in bright multicolor letters what Mrs. Shedd had just told me. Obviously, Adele had made the poster and whatever arrangements needed to be made.

Why was I upset?

THE CROCHET GROUP WAS ALREADY GATHERED around the event table when I got there. But when I saw Dinah wasn't there, I began to worry. She hadn't answered the message I'd left yesterday. Something was up that she really didn't want to talk about. Everyone else was busy trading notes about the events of the day before and being questioned. While it appeared that life was going on, I think we all felt a little uneasy.

I brought up the man I'd noticed both times we'd been at the Cottage Shoppe. "Did you tell Detective Heather about the bald guy with the Harrods shopping bag? I don't recall seeing him in the parking lot," I said to CeeCee.

"Bald guy? I don't recall seeing a bald guy anywhere," CeeCee said. "Thank heavens I didn't go upstairs with the rest of you. It must have been awful." She turned toward me and made a strange segue. "Molly, I saw you on the news. Dear, when are you going to take my advice and get some of that makeup that doesn't make you look so pasty? I always wear it when I think I might end up on camera."

I shrugged off her comment. Not only had I not been expecting to end up on the news, but in my book, if you'd just seen a dead person with his face in a bowl of tomato bisque soup, it would be weird if you didn't look pasty.

CeeCee didn't seem to notice that I didn't respond, and continued on. "Luckily, that Detective Gilmore helped me slip out through the alley so I didn't have to deal with the press." CeeCee took out some printed papers and handed them out. "Let's move on to why we're here. This is a pattern for a basic shawl. It's easy enough even for a newbie like you," she said to Patricia.

"Well, you certainly must remember the bald guy," I said to Sheila. She shook her head and looked over the instructions, listening as Adele suggested it would be best to use a worsted-weight yarn.

I expected Adele to have something to add about Drew's death, but she was uncharacteristically quiet. Was it my imagination or was Adele keeping a low profile? She'd said nothing about seeing or not seeing the bald guy or about anything else for that matter except her yarn suggestion. I had a feeling it had to do with the upcoming children's author appearance and her concern that I might try to step on her authority.

"Mrs. Shedd gave us the go-ahead on the Women's Haven project," I said as Dinah finally arrived and slid into a chair.

"You remember the tall bald guy, don't you?" I was relieved when she nodded. "We have to talk," I said. Then I noticed there were a couple of children standing a little behind her chair.

"Are they with you?" I asked, joking, but my smile faded when she nodded in agreement. I thought back to the background noise from a couple of nights ago and rethought my impression that Dinah had had a hot date. "Okay, then, who are they?"

Dinah looked over at them and introduced Ashley-

Angela and E. Conner to everyone, but she didn't explain who they were. The both appeared to be about four years old, though the girl seemed more mature. Dinah looked at the table longingly but said she couldn't stay. Then she took the shawl instructions and left. I mouthed "call me" as she walked away with the kids in tow.

Once they had left we started discussing Drew Brooks again.

"Oh, lets focus on something more positive," Patricia said, making a slip knot with some yarn CeeCee had given her. She was still crocheting practice swatches. The rest of us took out our own projects.

CeeCee was working on something round and white. I laughed when she said she was making a birthday cake. CeeCee didn't bake them, but apparently she did crochet them. "Best of all, it has zero calories," she said, sliding the directions across the table. Actually it was crocheted, then glued to cardboard. When finished it would have pink roses on top and *Happy Birthday* embroidered on it. It was another donation for the Not Exactly A Bake Sale.

Sheila was quiet. She had been more involved with Drew Brooks than the rest of us and probably was still processing all that had happened. I wondered if she had noticed the scarf on the desk in his office. She seemed to be staring into space while her fingers worked the same royal blue yarn she used at our last meeting. Her stitches weren't tight this time. If anything they were inconsistent, one loose, the next one tight, and the edges were completely uneven.

"Sheila," I said gently, pointing out how the side seemed to be getting bigger. Her gaze went down to her work and she almost jumped.

"What am I doing?" she mumbled and began unraveling.

"You probably have a lot on your mind," I said, getting

dirty looks from CeeCee and Adele, since they were usually the ones who gave her smaller hooks or comforted her.

"You have no idea," she said, putting the hook and yarn down.

"Then why don't you tell us, dear," CeeCee said.

"I think I might be in trouble," she said softly. "My fingerprints are on the murder weapon."

Everyone's head shot up. "Murder weapon?" we said in unison.

Sheila explained that one of the gym members' close relatives worked at the West Valley Division of the Los Angeles Police Department. "When she came in this morning, she told me she'd heard they thought Drew had been knocked out with a paperweight before he fell in the soup."

"So that's what happened." I told the group about seeing blood on the back of Drew's head. "I saw a bunch of paperweights on the desk. How do you know your fingerprints were on the one that hit him?"

Sheila let her breath out and sat back in her chair. "When I went up to see Drew about my money, I was really nervous. You know how I sometimes tap my fingers? Well, I was trying not to do that, so I picked up one of the paperweights. But before I could stop myself, I started tapping it. So, I put the first one down. It was very heavy and large. I picked up the next one, and then I was tapping again. You get the idea. I went through all of them.

"I shouldn't say this, but I was mad enough to do it. He just laughed at me when I asked for the correct amount. He said where else was I going to sell my scarves. The worst part is he was right. I could try to sell them online, but unless you see them and touch them, they don't seem that unique."

"Nonsense, dear," CeeCee said. "Your scarves are lovely

and special. I'm sure you could sell them somewhere else." CeeCee did a few stitches on the birthday cake. "So they think Drew died from a blow to his head?"

"She said they won't know for sure until the autopsy, but they think he drowned in the soup. Still it was getting hit with the paperweight that made him fall in the bowl."

There was a collective gasp in the group.

"Oh my," Patricia said. "It's true a person can drown in just an inch or so of liquid."

Sheila stared at the table. "I don't know if the rest of you noticed, but one of my scarves was on his desk."

"Does Detective Heather know about your fingerprints?" I asked, laying my hands over Sheila's.

"Maybe not, but she's going to. After an officer questioned me, he asked if I'd let them take my fingerprints and a hair sample. I said sure when he explained it was so they could exclude my fingerprints when they were looking for the suspect. It's just a matter of time before they match them up." She looked up at me. "I'm scared."

And Sheila didn't even know that Detective Heather had overheard her threaten Drew.

Chapter 6

THROUGHOUT THE REST OF THE MEETING THE crochet group did their best to reassure Sheila that nobody could possibly think she killed Drew Brooks. After everyone left, I took down the long table and set up rows of chairs and a demonstration table for the evening's event. Then I left the bookstore and headed to Dinah's house. I had decided not to wait any longer to find out what was going on with her. When I saw her car was in her driveway, I pulled up behind it.

Dinah's house was in an area called Walnut Acres, largely because at one time it had been a walnut farm. Just as there were orange trees in my backyard left from when the whole area had been an orange grove, there was a walnut tree in her front yard.

I knocked on the door, and a moment later she opened it.

"You can't hang up or run off this time," I said, trying to seen inside.

She opened the door wider and motioned me in. "I'm sorry. I should have explained at the crochet meeting." She looked worn out. Even her spikey salt-and-pepper hair seemed deflated.

Like Dinah's clothes, her house had an arty look with interesting color combinations. She had a deep purple couch with a chartreuse throw over the arm and colorful pillows. There was a wing chair with a floor lamp next to it and a side table that held a stack of books and her crocheting. However, the coffee table had been cleared of the usual items. I wondered at first, but when I heard the giggly voices from the other room, I realized she had kid-proofed the place.

I glanced through to the added-on den. The walls were lined with bookcases, and there was a TV and a soft leather couch in a warm chestnut. A sliding glass door at the back of the room led to Dinah's compact backyard, which she kept low maintenance by having a garden of native plants. I sat down on the couch, and she walked over to one of the bedrooms, looked in and then came back.

"Okay, who are they and why are they staying with you?"

"This is so embarrassing," Dinah said, sitting on the arm of the couch. Being embarrassed was so unlike her. She was the gutsy one, the one not afraid to tell her students that when it came to her class she was queen and they followed her rules or they flunked. What could possibly make her embarrassed?

The answer was simple, but one I never would have expected. "Jeremy showed up," she said, referring to her ex-husband. "And he wasn't alone. E. Conner and Ashley-Angela are fraternal twins and his children with the new Mrs.—or should I say the new ex–Mrs. Lyons." The irresponsible with the more irresponsible. What a couple.

"He's been living up north. He lost his job just about the same time his wife took off, leaving him with the kids. He's down here about a job." Dinah shook her head obviously upset with herself. "I can't believe I'm letting him stay here. . . . Well, he's actually gone now. He went to San Diego about a job. I must need my head examined to have let him leave his kids here."

"Well, who am I to talk? Samuel's girlfriend is staying with me, and I think she's anorexic."

Dinah knew about Morgan but not her eating problem. She looked at me with understanding and hugged me. "I was afraid to tell you. I thought you'd think I was an idiot."

"Or softhearted." I smiled at her. "Or softheaded. Maybe that's what we both are. Whatever. I'm just glad to have my friend back."

Now that her secret was out in the open, Dinah relaxed. After checking on the kids again, she made us some tea, and I told her about what had happened at the crochet group.

"Are you sure Sheila didn't do it? I mean, she is full of surprises. Who would have guessed she'd make those beautiful scarves?"

"She couldn't have. Besides, if she was going to do it, why would she want all of us to be there?"

"Unless it was one of those disorganized crimes," Dinah said. I had told her a lot of the stuff I'd learned from *The Average Joe's Guide*. There were crimes that were carefully planned, and there were some that were totally spontaneous, and then there were some that were planned but something went wrong. The ones that were unplanned or went askew were called disorganized crimes.

"If you're so sure she didn't do it, who did?" Dinah said.

"We know who had opportunity. Everybody who was there."

Dinah looked at her watch. "I have a class and I have to get the kids ready to go. Thank heavens Beasley Community

College has child care." She got up and walked me to the door. "I wonder how many people have a motive?"

"If he cheated Sheila, he probably did the same to other people. So anyone who sold things on consignment could have had it in for him. The bald man was sure mad at him. Kevin Brooks seems like a nice guy, but Mrs. Shedd overheard him and Drew in the middle of a bitter argument." I thought back to the office. "And there's something else. There was something white and lacy hanging off a drawer pull, as though something had caught on it and torn."

"I didn't see that. Lacy like how?" Dinah said.

I closed my eyes and conjured up the image. When I had been catching that last look at it, I had tried relating it to something familiar. What had I thought of? And then an image floated forward and grew clear. It reminded me of the doilies Adele had sewn on her skirt.

DINAH WASN'T THE ONLY ONE WITH THINGS TO do. I had arranged to meet CeeCee later to buy the yarn for the shawls, but I stopped home for lunch first. Cosmo rushed toward the door as I came in, with Blondie in close pursuit. What a change. When I only had her, she sat in her chair all day unless it was walk time or I offered her some cheese.

As I put my keys down on the counter, Morgan came out of her room and startled me. I'd gotten used to dog noises but not the sounds of another human. She came up and suddenly hugged me, wanting to make sure I was all right. I had told her about the murder the night before when my younger son Samuel stopped over during the break between his day job as a barista and his evening gig playing piano at a restaurant. He'd already gotten the basics about the incident from his brother.

"As long as you're okay," Samuel said when I'd finished giving him the details. He had taken his father's death harder than his brother, and I knew he worried about something happening to me. With that settled, he and Morgan had exchanged awkward glances, and then he had left to go to his night job.

"I was going to have some lunch. Want to join me?" I asked, hoping my smile and cheerful voice would brighten her expression. She looked more melancholy than usual.

"That would be nice. What are you having?"

"When in doubt grilled cheese sandwiches always work," I said, washing my hands and starting to take things out of the refrigerator. She agreed to eat with me, but only if she could make her own. I stepped aside as she extracted a package of no-fat American cheese product, which was as close to cheese as plastic was to cashmere. She had some bread, too. Sliced so thin, light shown through it. It was extremely low in calories and high in fiber thanks to the secret ingredient. The label called it by some fancy name like cellulose specialo, but I looked it up. It was basically wood fibers.

I used bakery egg bread and Muenster cheese. She made hers in the microwave, while I sizzled some butter in a frying pan, which filled the air with a delicious aroma. When I added the sandwich, it smelled even better.

When our sandwiches were ready, we sat at the little booth in the kitchen and I asked her how things were going.

"Not so good," she said, taking a tiny bite of her sandwich. "I went on an audition for a music video this morning, and they said I didn't look ethereal enough. That means five pounds too heavy." She put down her sandwich as if it were its fault and drank some sparkling water.

"I'm sure you don't need me to tell you that you're already almost too ethereal," I said. "The next audition will go better."

She slumped and looked glum. I decided the best tactic was to let her know there were people who had worse problems. I told her about Sheila and how Drew Brooks had cheated her and she'd confronted him just before he got killed.

"And now she's worried because her fingerprints are on the paperweight that hit him on the head, and she doesn't even know that this police detective overheard her threatening him. I'm just hoping the detective doesn't start treating Sheila like a suspect."

"Wow," Morgan said, sitting up. "I guess some people do have bigger problems. I bet I've seen her scarves at the Cottage Shoppe." I asked her if she shopped there often and if she knew anything about the Brooks brothers.

" 'Brooks brothers,' that's funny," she said. It was amazing how much better she looked when she smiled. She said she had liked the store better when their aunt owned it. "She had all kinds of unusual and wonderful things. Somebody had made a shadow box out of an old dance program from *Swan Lake*. It was autographed by Margot Fonteyn and Rudolf Nureyev. Next to it was a dried pink rose with the stem still on and a pair of her white satin toe shoes. They were even autographed." Morgan almost swooned. "But it was way too expensive for me. And I saw this fabulous hanky that had belonged to Lady Somebody. It was really beautiful but completely out of my price range. I love all the handcrafted items. Did you see the knit blankets in the soft heather tones?"

"They are beautiful," I said. Since she liked the handcrafted things so well I thought maybe she'd like to learn how to make some and asked, "Would you like to join the crochet group?"

"That would be nice except I don't know how to crochet," she said. When I assured her someone would teach her, she said she'd come with me to the next meeting.

Morgan had become all animated, and I enjoyed having a daughter-age person to talk with. The only down moment came when I got a cookie for dessert and offered one to her. You would have thought I'd offered her a cockroach.

An hour later, with the dishwasher taking care of the cleanup, I left to meet CeeCee at the Super Craft Mart to buy the yarn for the hugs of comfort project. She was waiting by a display of craft books when I got there. She kept looking around as we walked back toward the yarn department, and I finally asked her what the problem was.

She glanced down an empty aisle. "You have no idea how it is now. Everybody is looking to catch you doing something embarrassing and stick it on the Internet. Now that I have a hit show, it's even worse." She leaned close and lowered her voice. "I practically have to sleep in stage makeup. The other day somebody got a picture of me in my robe, getting the Sunday newspaper. My hair looked like I stuck my finger in an electric socket."

I hadn't seen the photo she was talking about, but I could just imagine it. I'd always kind of laughed at CeeCee's obsession with stage makeup and posing herself just right if there were any paparazzi around, but I suddenly saw it in a different light. Her situation made me glad I was a nobody.

As soon as we got to the yarn department, she pointed out the worsted acrylic and said each shawl would take about six skeins. We both started counting skeins and eventually filled two carts with yarn.

"We'll start them in the group, but then everybody is going to have to do a lot of the work on their own. I promised the shelter twenty shawls," CeeCee said, wincing. "That's how many women are at the shelter now. Then I said we would keep providing them, so when someone new came, they'd have one to give her." CeeCee seemed upset. "I hope nobody lets me down."

Was it my imagination or was she looking at me?

I mentioned that Morgan was joining the group, but had to add that she didn't know how to crochet. At the end of the aisle I noticed shelves of what looked like balls of string.

"What's this stuff?" I asked, pulling down one of the orbs of material.

"That's what you use to make thread crochet, dear. Lacy bookmarks, doilies, that sort of thing."

She took down one of the balls and showed it to me. "Number 10 is the most common kind. It's also called bedspread weight. The higher the number, the finer the thread." CeeCee took off a package of slender steel hooks. "These are the kind of hooks you use."

Near where she'd found the hooks there was a display of pattern pamphlets. The pamphlet cover showed a linen tea towel with a delicate crocheted edging. Something about the design caught my attention. I kept starring, trying to place it. Then the answer came to me. "That looks kind of like what was hanging on Drew Brooks's desk drawer," I said, picking up the book and moving it around to see it from another angle.

"Something was hanging on a desk drawer?" CeeCee said, perplexed.

"Didn't you see it? When we found him in the—"

"Remember, I didn't go up there. Thank heavens. Hearing about it was enough. And then being kept in a parking lot to be questioned. That blond detective was giving me a bad vibe. She asked me if you knew the victim. She really doesn't seem to like you." CeeCee's voice changed tone. "But she's certainly a beautiful knitter. Did you see her bag?"

I did a double take. CeeCee complimenting a knitted project?

"I know. You think all I care about is crocheting. Personally, dear, working with a pair of needles leaves me cold, but I can appreciate other's work, like that heathery knitted blanket at the Cottage Shoppe."

"You mean the one hanging on the rocker?"

"Wasn't it lovely? Of course, there were lots of lovely things. I was going to buy one of the needlepoint pillows. The one with irises. But I never got a chance."

"Do you think I could do thread crochet?"

"Maybe, with some help."

I asked CeeCee the obvious question—would she give me the help? A sly smile appeared on her face.

"I've been on this diet forever, and I've had enough with yarn pastries. I'd just about kill for something delicious." I got her drift. I put a ball of the bedspread weight thread and a set of the steel hooks in a separate part of the cart.

"Sure, when I come I could bring over some bake goods." I was about to suggest setting a time when I noticed some movement down the aisle, in front of the yarn by the pound section. Two women were looking at us and talking to each other. *Looking* wasn't really the right word. It was more like they were studying us. I tried to ignore them, but it was as if I could physically feel their eyes on me. I looked down to make sure I didn't have my pants on backward or toilet paper stuck to my shoe.

CeeCee picked up on my discomfort. "Don't worry, dear. They're not staring at you." She glanced at them and kept talking to me. "In the old days when I was doing *The CeeCee Collins Show*, you never would have found me in a store like this." She laughed at the absurdity of it. "I had assistants to buy my yarn. In those days, there was more privacy if you were a celebrity. Fans might approach and ask for an autograph, but they were polite and kept a certain distance. Now everybody wants to get a picture of you with spinach in your teeth or in the middle of some clothing malfunction."

CeeCee was wearing garnet-colored velour pants and a high-necked white knit shirt. She seemed pretty safe from clothing malfunctions.

"Of course, since the new show, dear," CeeCee continued, "I've been getting a lot more attention. I have a whole new generation of fans." She acknowledged the women with a regal smile and a gesture that was something like a wave. Their eyes widened as they giggled and moved closer. When they reached us, one of them held out a skein of kelly green merino wool and asked for CeeCee to autograph the label. I thought it was kind of strange, but CeeCee didn't seem to have a problem with it and just happened to have a permanent marker handy.

"You knit, then," one of the women said to CeeCee after noting her cart full of yarn.

"No, dear. I crochet," CeeCee answered in her sweet, high-pitched voice. There were no hysterics like Adele would have pulled. In her sugary voice, CeeCee just pointed out the virtues of crochet. The women listened with interest, and apparently she gave a convincing sales pitch because they rushed off to the display of hooks. Both came back with a package of assorted sizes and wanted CeeCee to sign those, too. When they left, CeeCee picked up our conversation as if nothing had happened. But then she was used to being stopped by strangers.

"You were saying you thought the piece of something hanging on the drawer meant something," CeeCee said.

"Yes, but I don't know what. And I'm worried about

Sheila." I told her how Detective Heather had overheard Sheila when she was saying that Drew Brooks was going to pay her what he owed her or else.

"Oh dear. And then her fingerprints being on the murder weapon . . . Do you think that detective is going to try to pin it on her?" CeeCee's expression grew serious. "I feel terrible bringing this up, but did it ever occur to you that she might really have done it?"

"Maybe for a moment, but we're talking about Sheila. Shy, nervous Sheila," I said as we moved closer to the check-out counter.

"Of course, you must be right. She couldn't have done it. I'm glad I didn't go up there with the rest of you. Imagining that man with his face in the soup is bad enough. I've been in my share of detective dramas, but 'the body' always got up when the shot was done."

Chapter 7

By late afternoon I was back at the bookstore. I inhaled the welcoming scent of paper, bookbinding and coffee as I walked in. It took two trips to bring in the bags of yarn. When I saw how many balls of yarn it took to make a shawl, I knew we had a lot of work ahead. After stowing the bags in the office, I turned my mind to the evening event and the preparations still to be made.

As I walked past the children's area, I couldn't miss the life-size cardboard cutout of Koo Koo the Clown. It had a display shelf holding a supply of the book *Koo Koo Goes to the Dentist*. The author's real name was William Bearly, and this was the seventh in the Koo Koo series. Adele was clearing off cups from the small table. She'd gotten her wish and handled an author—in this case, an author dressed as a clown—all on her own, though most of her "handling" had probably entailed helping him walk through the crowd of toddlers so he wouldn't trip on them with his huge red shoes, and then having to serve the juice and cookies. Adele didn't particularly like children or their books, but this event was a step up from just reading them stories or running activities. The kids had all left, and Koo Koo was scarfing down the last of the cookies with several juice chasers.

I moved on to the event area without stopping and glanced out the big window. There wasn't much action on Ventura, just two boys with backpacks playing with a hacky-sack ball as they walked toward the bus stop.

The sweet smell of something chocolate perfumed the air. Bob, our main barista, must have just taken out a batch of cookies in the café attached to the bookstore. What bookstore, or any kind of store, these days didn't have some kind of food and drink service? Even the Cottage Shoppe had Kevin's soup. Our angle was the smell of Bob's cookies. They acted like a magnet pulling people into the café. Whenever we had an evening event, he always made sure he baked something extra aromatic.

I put a sign in the window facing out. There hadn't been room for the full title. All I could fit was *Potty Training*. The full title was *Potty Training: A Beginner's Guide to Container Gardening*. The author, Poppy Roeback, hosted an indoor gardening show on PBS and promised to demonstrate planting a patio salad garden. I expected a mess.

Adele came my way as Koo Koo flapped his way to the door. I was on the floor unrolling plastic around the bottom of the demonstration table. In anticipation of Poppy's rather excited approach to handling dirt, I'd set up a separate table to hold copies of her book.

"How did it go?" I asked, holding on to the table and pulling myself off the floor.

"I don't know, Pink; you be the judge. Let's see, I sold all the copies of the book except for the ones on the display, which I'm pretty sure will move by tomorrow. Oh, and Koo

Koo asked me out on a date. Have any of your authors ever asked you out?"

I started arranging books while I processed the information. Her success was a bit of a surprise, and I hated to admit that I felt a twinge of upset. What if Adele's event did better than mine?

Adele stood a little taller with self-importance. "Oh, and Detective Gilmore called. Since I was the one who did CPR on the victim, she wanted to know what position he was in before I tried to save him." Adele by nature had a loud voice, but as she recounted her first-aid efforts, she seemed to ramp it up even more, causing a couple at a nearby display to look up. "She thinks I'm an important witness. She asked a lot of questions about you and if you knew the victim, and of course, she wanted to know about Sheila."

"Like what about Sheila?" I asked as I finished with the signing table.

"Like if she was prone to outbursts of anger and if I'd seen her the whole time we were in the store. I just told the truth. Pink, you'll be happy to know I didn't say anything to implicate you in the crime. All I said was that you were trying to help Sheila get the money owed her. She wanted to know if I'd seen Drew Brooks after Sheila went up to his office. I had to tell the truth. I didn't see him. Did you?"

"Don't tell me that now you think Sheila did it, too." It was worrisome that our own group had doubts about Sheila's innocence.

"I don't think so, but she could have. Didn't she say she was mad enough to have done it? Add that to the fact that she was upstairs alone with him and her fingerprints are on the murder weapon." Adele had settled on the edge of the table and was fiddling with her skirt. Her outfit would be perfect to wear if she went out with Koo Koo. She reminded me of a snow cone. Her gauzy skirt had strips of yellow that morphed into orange, red and finally a grapey purple. She had teamed it with a lime green peasant blouse.

"That's why I have to find out who really did it." I said it under my breath, but Adele heard it anyway and rolled her eyes.

"Well, I guess Sheila can relax then, since Nancy Marple Holmes is on the case."

Let Adele make her comments, I thought. I had, after all, already solved one murder.

"CeeCee and I got the yarn for the shawls," I said. I guess I knew what I was doing. I'm not proud of it, but between her gloating about the book signing, and making fun of my investigative abilities, I wanted a little revenge annoyance. She went off like a firecracker. How could we have gone without her since she was at least cohead of the group?

Adele insisted on seeing what we'd gotten immediately. There wasn't a choice but to follow her as she took off toward the office. Once there she started rummaging through the large white plastic bags. She just kind of grunted until she looked inside the small one that had the things I'd bought for myself. She pulled out the tiny hooks and ball of ecru thread.

"Even you would know this wouldn't work for shawls," she said, waiting for an explanation.

It seemed like a perfect time to bring up what I'd seen on Drew's desk handle. I asked her if she'd noticed anything.

"I was too busy trying to save Drew's life. And if he hadn't been dead, I would have." She started to walk away but turned back to add, "My book event was so successful I bet Mrs. Shedd lets me do another one. I bet she lets me handle Milton Mindell. After all he is a kid's author."

I forced my mouth not to fall open. Mrs. Shedd wouldn't. She couldn't give Milton Mindell to Adele. I'd been the one who had convinced him to do his first signing at Shedd & Royal. I'd been the one who had run his appearances so well, he kept coming back. And I'd be the one to look bad if Adele messed things up. All the bookstores in the area wanted to get him away from us. And why not? He wrote a new book every three months, and kids ate up the combination of horror and humor. And when the kids came to one of his events they bought his new book, his old ones and other people's books, too. A book event with Milton was like money in the bank.

All his good points came with a few drawbacks. Milton was a handful to deal with. His events were more like productions, and he insisted everything had to be his way. But I had managed just fine. And if I ran his upcoming appearance, it would be fine, too. After all the work I'd done it wouldn't be fair to hand it over to Adele. But I kept the emotion out of my face and told Adele not to get her hopes up.

"We'll see," Adele said, walking away in a huff.

When I'd finished with the setup for the gardening event, I headed to the café for a red eye to recharge me for the night. The coffee with a shot of espresso always did the trick.

Patricia Bradford blocked my path. "Molly," she gushed. "I want you to meet Benjamin." He was nice-looking in a bland-brown-hair-and-even-features kind of way, and there was a definite warmth in his smile as he reached out to shake my hand. Patricia pulled him away before his hand made contact. "I want to show Benjamin where my book signing is going to be." She led him toward the event area, explaining that, of course, there would be more chairs for her appearance.

My confusion must have shown in my face.

"Mrs. Shedd didn't tell you, did she? She took one look at the new edition of *Patricia's Perfect Hints* and set up a date for my signing. It's next Friday. Please go to the office immediately and mark it on your calendar."

Benjamin patted her hand. "Honey, I think you're a little frazzled. I'm sure you didn't mean that to sound as demanding as it came across. You've said nothing but nice things about Molly, and I'm sure she'll put it on the calendar." He turned toward me and nodded. "By the way, Patricia told me about your group making shawls for the Women's Haven. I guess she told you it's my pet charity. I want to thank you." Despite the bland looks, his dark eyes were sincere and he had some charisma.

Patricia hugged him. "You're so right, hon. I am frazzled." She hugged me next. "Of course, Benjamin is right. I know you'll take care of everything."

Benjamin walked toward some people looking at magazines and began introducing himself, while Patricia stayed close to me. "The whole thing at the Cottage Shoppe has left me feeling permanently upset. I can't seem to get that picture of Drew Brooks out of my mind. And then all the questions by the police." Patricia looked at me and sighed. "You realize you must have seen whoever did it."

"We could have walked right by them," I said. We both shuddered at the thought. I again brought up the bald man with the Harrods bag.

Patricia thought a moment. "Maybe I do remember him." She looked up and saw Benjamin pointing toward the door. "We'll talk about it again. We have to get to a fund-raiser at the country club," she said and then followed her husband to the exit.

I finally got my red eye and added two of the just-baked chocolate cookies, which would have to suffice for dinner. I settled into one of the easy chairs by the window in the café and sipped my coffee. Bob took out a batch of carrot spice bars, and their sweet cinnamon scent mixed nicely with the pungent smell of fresh coffee. He brought one over and said my "dinner" needed some vegetables. It was a relief not to have to worry about anybody else's meal. Morgan had her own stash of food, however low calorie, and took care of her own eating—or not eating. I'd already fed Blondie and Cosmo during a pit stop on the way back from the yarn store.

When I returned to the event area, a crowd had already started to fill in the chairs. Who knew so many people were into container gardening? My gaze stopped on two figures toward the back. They were a particular surprise.

"I didn't expect to see you here," I said, stopping next to Barry and his son Jeffrey. More than not expect, I didn't want him here. What happened to the idea of some space in our relationship? It wasn't enough he kept stopping by whenever he felt like it to take care of his dog—now he was frequenting bookstore events, too?

"I thought some plants might be, ah, nice on the patio. You know, they say dealing with nature is good for your soul."

Jeffrey was looking at his father as if he were nuts. While Barry tried to come up with more reasons why they were there, Jeffrey pulled out a page from his school paper and handed it to me proudly. It was a review of the drama club's production of *Carousel*, and it mentioned that Columbia Greenberg was outstanding as Curly. Barry groaned with frustration as I congratulated Jeffrey and handed back the article. I knew he kept hoping Jeffrey/Columbia would forget about wanting to be an actor and join the Junior Forensics Club.

"Well, enjoy the program," I said with a just a little roll of my eyes. "I expect to see your patio full of plants."

I walked away, but Barry caught up with me and pulled me into the space between the bookcases in the travel section.

He held both my hands and tried to look me in the eye, but I avoided his gaze.

"Barry, I'm working," I said, trying to pull away, but he had a tight grasp, probably from hanging on to all those suspects that tried to run off.

"Okay, maybe I'm not as interested in starting a container garden as I implied. But I needed to see you. How about we all get some dinner later?" When I didn't respond right away, he clenched and unclenched his jaw a few times, a sure sign he was upset.

"Look, babe, I spent my afternoon telling a woman with two small kids that her husband had been killed. I need something positive to balance it off." He was usually able to maintain a benign expression, but this time he looked drained.

I was a little stunned. Barry generally didn't give away that many details about his job. Sometimes he looked more haggard and I knew he'd dealt with something particularly awful. And on the occasion when some case had worked out well, he seemed to have a sense of satisfaction. But it was usually reading between the lines on my part. Barry's comments tonight were enough to get my full attention. I touched his shoulder.

"Can we talk about this later?" I said gently. I was on the lookout for Poppy. She wasn't there yet, and it always made me nervous when authors cut it close.

He moved so his face was in front of me. "Please just give me a minute. This is important. You're important. I can't begin to tell you what it does for me to see you. It's like I rejoin a world where people are happy and dogs play ball, and people plant lettuce in their kitchen. I like what I do, but sometimes I just hit empty. When I see you, it's like hitting the refill button." He grinned. "You even help me not to be so upset about Jeffrey calling himself Columbia."

It was hard not to be touched by what he said, particularly since I did care for him. But it was all about timing. Poppy Roeback was just coming in the door, pulling a wagon full of supplies. And there was someone else. Someone tall, bald and wearing a designer suit.

I couldn't take my eyes off of him. Was he the man from the Cottage Shoppe? The one who'd been so angry? True, bald seemed to be in these days, and frankly I can't say I blamed men for going that way. If I had to choose between a bald spot surrounded by a fringe of hair that made you look insipid, or all-bald-by-choice that gave off a certain macho vibe, I'd go for the naked head. I strained to see better, which didn't please Barry, particularly when he turned and realized I was looking at another man just as he had poured out his heart.

"He's the one. I'm sure he's the one," I said, pulling away and moving toward the front.

"The one, who?" Barry said in close pursuit.

Poppy Roeback saw me and pulled her wagon in front of me. "Molly, I'm all set," she said, pointing at the bags of dirt and stack of pots along with some flats of plants.

When I looked up again, the bald man was gone.

CHAPTER 8

I WAS STILL PICKING UP BALLS OF DIRT THE NEXT morning. No matter how much plastic I'd put down, the dirt had rolled farther. I was under the table trying to clean up as the crochet group began to arrive.

"Hey, there," Dinah called, peeking under the table. "What are you doing?"

I explained that Poppy had gotten more enthusiastic during her book signing than she was on her PBS show. She had rolled the containers out into the crowd and demonstrated planting tomatoes with a trellis that could grow even in a sunny spot in a kitchen. She'd been using plants that already had fruit since she wanted the crowd to get the real idea, and some tomatoes had broken loose, and of course, somebody had stepped on them. She'd also used some special ball-shaped clumps of dirt that expanded when you added water, and some had fallen out of the pots.

"Sorry I missed it. Sounds like fun," Dinah said, picking up a gigantic dirt ball. Now that she had unloaded about her ex, she wasn't avoiding me anymore. What a relief!

"Jeremy called before I left. He's going to be delayed coming back from San Diego. I want to see him get a good job, but his kids are wearing me out." She did look tired around the eyes, and the spikes in her gelled hair seemed to be drooping again. "Those kids are out of control. Believe me, if they were staying longer, I'd have a thing or two to say."

I could just imagine. Dinah was not sentimental and gushy about little kids. She'd been known to make caviar and cream cheese sandwiches for her own kids when she ran out of jelly. Even when they were small, Dinah's children had manners and were nice to be around. They had interesting things to say and knew the world didn't revolve around them. I was guessing E. Conner and Ashley-Angela thought it did.

"All I can say is thank heavens for Beasley's child care. It's really part of the preschool teacher program. They take in faculty kids to let the students practice on them."

I filled her in on everything that was going on. She sparked on Barry and Jeffrey's appearance.

"How can you fault the guy for showing up and saying all that sweet stuff?" she said, mystified. "All he wants is a serious relationship. Do you know how hard that is to find? I never had that with my ex even when we were married." Dinah helped me up as I finished with the cleanup. "I know, you need your space," she said, understanding even if she didn't agree. That was the cool thing about best friends: You might not always agree but you backed each other anyway.

Morgan walked in the bookstore and I waved her over. As usual, she was wearing dance wear, this time with a skirt over it. She laid a bag from the craft store on the table.

"If only I could have talked to the bald guy," I said to

Dinah as Morgan situated herself. "I would have liked to ask him why he was so angry at Drew and what he had in the shopping bag."

"Did you find out who he was at least?" Dinah had taken out some cotton worsted yarn and was starting another of her washcloths. This one had a cluster pattern, and she was doing it in a sea foam green that would go with her bathroom.

"I asked Rayaad," I said, refering to our main cashier. "She didn't even know who I was talking about. It's kind of hard to find him without knowing his name."

"Oh well, maybe you'll see him again somewhere."

Morgan had laid out a selection of crochet hooks and some cream-colored bargain yarn.

"Maybe you could show me how to crochet before the others come." She was as bummed out as ever. Another audition hadn't gone as she had hoped, and she was even more convinced if she were five pounds lighter she would have gotten the part. I suspected she was impatient to learn how to crochet because she thought it would burn calories.

Dinah and I looked at each other and I shrugged. "I'm afraid it's kind of like the blind leading the blind, but I can show you how to do the basics." I did a slip knot in slow motion and made a bunch of loose chains as an example. Once Morgan had done the same, I showed her how to dip her hook under the two strands of yarn, then yarn over and pull it through. "Then you just put your hook through both loops, and voilà, you've done a single crochet."

Morgan seemed to have a knack for it. Even more surprising, considering how hard it had been for me, she could do it while talking. "Does the bald guy have something to do with the murder at the Cottage Shoppe?"

When I nodded, she continued. "I was thinking about it. Whoever went up to Drew Brooks's office last has to be the killer." By now she had made a whole row of single stitches, and I showed her how to turn her work and begin another row.

"Good thinking, Morgan," I said, noting that she had gotten right to the heart of the matter. She might look waifish and like her head was off in the clouds, but she was obviously smart, too. Not a surprise. My son Samuel had always gravitated toward girls with brains.

"So, who went up there?" Morgan said as she moved onto a third row. Her stitches were even and in the perfect place between too loose and knots.

I had to think for a minute. "Well, there's the bald guy. I know he went up to Drew's office the first time we were there, and I have a feeling he went upstairs the day Drew was murdered, but I don't know when. The saleswoman went up there for sure. She's the one who screamed. And Kevin Brooks probably did to bring up the soup. There were a lot of people shopping. Any one of them could have gone up there, too."

"But certainly all those people didn't want to kill him. Do you know anybody who had a reason?" Morgan asked.

"Shei—" Dinah said, but I put my hand over her mouth before she could get out the *la*. None of us had noticed that Sheila had come up to the table as we were talking. She was looking through her craft bag and thankfully didn't seem to have heard us. As always she was wearing her business suit since she came during a break from work. It struck me as funny that the gym required its employees to wear dressy black suits while all the members came in wearing tee shirts and stretchy pants.

While I was getting the yarn for the shawls from the office, CeeCee and Adele had arrived. When I got back to the table, I introduced them to Morgan. Then CeeCee took the yarn I'd brought out and began to separate it by color.

"I talked to the director of the Women's Haven, and she's very excited about the shawls," CeeCee said. "She'd like to make some kind of an event when we give them out. I hesitated to give her an exact date since we really haven't even started. I'm sure we're all agreed we want to get them ready soon."

I mentioned that now that we had a new member the work would go faster.

Adele looked at the practice swatch Morgan was making. "Who taught you how to crochet?"

When Morgan indicated me, Adele burst out with a sputtery laugh. "Pink taught you to crochet? She just learned herself and already she's giving lessons." Adele got in another laugh at the absurdity and then offered to give Morgan a real lesson since she was a pro. To prove her point, she held out her arms to show off the black-and-white-striped warmers she'd made for them. Actually, they seemed like a good idea for May weather, though they were at odds with the rest of her outfit. I'd begun naming her outfits, and this one I called Queen of the Pampas. She wore black leather boots with rust-colored gaucho pants and a black camisole. The arm warmers went from the base of her hand to slightly below her shoulders. She'd let her hair go back to light brown and had it in tiny pigtails. Adele didn't know the meaning of the word *subtle*.

Adele took Morgan to the end of the table, promising to teach her the right way to crochet. The rest of us started choosing yarn for our first shawl. At that moment Patricia rushed up out of breath, apologizing for being late. She took out a completed aqua shawl. It appeared to be made of mohair yarn, but she insisted it was synthetic and machine washable.

Sheila looked at it. "What a beautiful shade of blue-green. But it looks almost—" CeeCee made a shush move with her fingers and angled her head toward Adele. Sheila didn't finish the sentence, but I knew what she was going to say. Knitted. The shawl looked knitted.

Patricia kept her voice low. "I know how you feel about you-know-what, but I'm so much more comfortable with a pair of needles and it is going to be hard for me to commit to being here all the time. And it is such an important project."

"Of course, dear. All that really matters is that we get enough shawls done," CeeCee said, doing a double take as Patricia pushed away from the table. "You aren't leaving already. You just got here."

"Sorry, but I have to do a demonstration of some of my hints at my daughter's school." Patricia was already halfway to the door by the time she got to the end of the sentence.

"Well, ladies, lets get going on the shawls," CeeCee said with a sigh of resignation.

We all started making our foundation chains. I glanced CeeCee's way and she seemed to be working a much bigger clump. At first I thought she'd gotten ahead of us since she was such a skilled crocheter, but even working faster didn't explain it.

Adele finished playing teacher, and she and Morgan rejoined the group. Adele told Morgan to make a practice swatch and then she'd help Morgan start a shawl. Adele saw the clump of worked yarn coming off CeeCee's hook and wanted to know what it was.

"Just the next big advance in crochet," CeeCee said. "They are called extended stitches; you do the foundation and the first row at the same time. No more pesky trying to force your hook into a twisty chain stitch."

"That's just the rabble-rousers spreading rumors. It's nonsense to think of giving up the foundation chain. It's . . . its historic," Adele sputtered. "And I'm a purist. I say the old way is the best way."

I added not opened minded onto my description of Adele. Luckily CeeCee had already put away Patricia's contribution or Adele would have gone ballistic, probably yelling something about us not being needle heads and keeping our group pure. Adele always went nuts when confronted with anything about knitting. I suppose there was some dark secret in her past. Maybe a bad experience with a sweater knit by her grandmother or something. As if calling yourself a hooker all the time was some kind of step up.

With all the commotion, nobody was paying any attention to Sheila. She had positioned herself at the end of the table, and her head was bent over her work. I was the first one to check out what she was doing. She had the directions for a shawl and six skeins of dark navy yarn. But she seemed to be stuck on making the foundation chain. From my vantage point her stitches looked like knots. I didn't have to ask to know she was upset.

CeeCee noticed next. She put a hand on Sheila's arm to stop her struggle, then suggested she unravel, do her foundation with a bigger hook and then go back to the K-size hook on the next row.

Sheila stopped her work and took the larger hook, then she began to tap it on the table, another sure sign she was upset. CeeCee reached over and put her hand on the hook, making it impossible for Sheila to continue tapping it. Undaunted, Sheila began drumming her fingers.

"Just tell us what's wrong," Adele said impatiently.

"You're all very nice to me and I hate to be a crybaby, but I'm worried about losing the place where I live." She looked at me and I shook my head, indicating I'd done as she asked and not told anyone about her living arrangements. "You might as well all know. I rent a room in a house in Reseda, and I babysit on the weekends to pay part of the rent. The woman who owns it said she's uncomfortable with me being there since Detective Gilmore asked her a bunch of questions about me. I talked her into letting me stay for now, but she said if I get arrested, I'm out." Sheila tried to take a deep breath. "The detective has decided I'm a person of interest. She said she overheard me threaten Drew Brooks." By the end, Sheila's voice was cracking.

"Don't worry, dear," CeeCee began. "Molly will take care of it. She'll find out who killed that nasty man and get you off the hook."

"What?" I said as Sheila rushed over to hug me in gratitude.

CHAPTER 9

"I CAN'T BELIEVE CEECEE SAID THAT. SHE MADE it sound like a done deal. What if I can't find out who killed Drew Brooks?" Dinah and I both had the morning off, and I was pacing around her living room. Several days had gone by since CeeCee had made her pronouncement that I'd get Sheila off the hook, and I just didn't know if I'd be able to do it. The kids were playing in the other room, and Dinah seemed angry.

"He said he'd be back last night for sure," she said seeming totally unaware of what I had been talking about. "I've called and called his cell phone, and I'm just getting his voice mail." She ran her fingers through her short hair. She might not be listening to me, but I knew she was talking about Jeremy and his so far failed promise to return from his big job hunt. Dinah didn't look like her usual self. Not only had she kid-proofed her house, she'd kid-proofed her appearance. No long scarves, because the kids tended to step on them and almost choke her whenever she bent down to their level. Gone were the long earrings, too, since E. Conner started playing with them when she took the kids out for lunch. All she had left was her gelled salt-and-pepper hair and her attitude. Poor Dinah. She was used to her house and life being orderly.

"C'mon kids, you're going to see Miss Trudy," Dinah said in an upbeat tone.

"We don't want to," E. Conner said, dragging his feet as he walked through the living room. It made an awful noise and probably left scuff marks. Ashley-Angela followed him, hanging on to a beat-up stuffed elephant.

"We want to stay here. They won't let me talk to Wonkie," she said, hugging her elephant.

Dinah had been pretty easygoing with them, but between their father not showing up and their poor behavior, she'd reached the end of her patience. Dinah was an expert at shaping up immature freshmen. She did it by being direct and leaving no wiggle room. It was her way or the highway. I had a feeling the kids were about to get a taste of this technique.

"No discussion. We're leaving in five minutes," Dinah announced. "Wonkie's not going." She started to snatch it from Ashley-Angela's arm, but the little girl's face crumbled. Dinah was tough but not mean. "Okay, he can go, but you both have to do what Miss Trudy says." E. Conner tried dragging his feet again. Dinah told him to stop it or else. Her tone was strong enough that even I didn't want to ask what the *or else* was.

She got them in the car, making sure they were belted in, and we headed off for Beasley. Dinah didn't have a class until late in the day, and she kept muttering something about how she hoped no one checked her schedule since child care was supposed to be used only during office hours and class. I hoped they didn't, too, because it wasn't a day to mess with Dinah.

As we walked them in, Ashley-Angela ran back to hug Dinah and give her Wonkie.

"He said he wants to go with you," she said in a serious voice.

"Freedom," Dinah said, sticking the elephant under her arm before doing a little dance as we walked away. "I need coffee."

"Me, too. Then maybe we can come up with a plan," I said, relieved to have my friend all to myself.

"Plan? Plan about what?" Dinah asked, and I realized she hadn't been paying any attention to what I'd been saying. After I reminded Dinah of why I needed a plan, we discussed where to go for coffee. Dinah didn't think I'd want to go to the bookstore café since I didn't have to be at the bookstore this morning. However, the coffee was the best and I got a discount.

It was hard to find a table. Two men were using tables as offices. They had their laptops, phones and BlackBerries spread out, and looked as though they might be there all day. Another table was taken up by two women from the building next door, who were talking about someone named Lannie who apparently had messed up something. Several student types occupied a big table. Their textbooks were propped open and they were discussing an upcoming exam.

We took the only vacant table, next to some guy with blond hair that looked like yellow cottage cheese, who was writing a screenplay on his computer. I was going to have to tell Mrs. Shedd she ought to put up signs with time limits for the tables.

Dinah took a long drag on her coffee and sighed with pleasure. "At last I can think again."

"Good. Because I have to figure out how to proceed."

Dinah drank more of her coffee and pointed at the window. The Cottage Shoppe was down the street, and Kevin had just stepped outside to put up the "Open" sign. "Why not start there? That's where it all happened."

It was a good point, and since this was the first time the store had been open since the murder, it seemed like a good time to have a look around.

"Maybe we can also find out who the bald guy is and what he was so mad about," I said. Dinah nodded in agreement as she drained her coffee.

As we walked down the street toward the store, I noticed that it appeared to be the same quaint place it had always been. The only hint that anything had gone on was the scrap of yellow police tape stuck on the door handle. The banners about the Hearston Estate offerings were still on the windows, and the bell tinkled when we came in the door.

It was pretty dead inside. Then Kevin Brooks came down the stairs. His face brightened when he saw us, and he immediately came over.

"May I help you find something?" His voice sounded a little too anxious. He seemed to study our faces, and then he smiled with recognition. "You were here the other day, weren't you? The day that Drew—" He swallowed hard. I could understand how that would be a hard sentence to finish.

I told him I was sorry about his brother; Dinah did the same.

"Thank you, ladies. I wasn't sure about opening again as soon as the police finished, but I think Drew would want me to. It is important to keep going, don't you think?"

Personally, I thought it was a little fast. I couldn't imagine having gone back to work a few days after Charlie died, but then who knew how close Kevin and Drew were. Hadn't Mrs. Shedd mentioned something about overhearing the brothers arguing?

Kevin invited us to look around at our leisure and

mentioned there was complimentary coffee, tea and soup in the dining room. I just hoped he'd had the good sense not to be serving the tomato bisque again.

"Dorothy will be glad to help you with anything," he said, gesturing toward the clerk half hidden in the living room. I knew her slightly. She was one of the regulars from Romance Night at the bookstore, and as I recalled she preferred paranormals, particularly anything with a vampire. She was past typical retirement age and appeared overdressed by current standards—a mark of her generation.

Dinah and I walked into the room. Dorothy didn't seem quite to know what to do with herself and was sitting in one of the rockers, rocking at a frantic pace. It made me tense to watch her. But at the mention of her name, she stopped short and jumped up. The chair continued on its own with a loud thwack-thwack. I grabbed it, bringing it to an abrupt stop. The tension level was high enough already.

"I'm sorry to have startled you. It's no wonder you're feeling jumpy—after what happened." I touched her shoulder in a sympathetic gesture as Dinah gave me a go-for-it nod and wandered off. "I was here. I saw him." I pointed at the ceiling to indicate upstairs.

She shook her head with dismay. "Thank heavens I missed that sight. Trina—she's our other salesperson—is the one who found him. She's been having nightmares about giant bowls of soup and says she doesn't know if she'll ever be able to come back to work. Frankly, I can't believe Mr. Kevin reopened already. They've barely had the funeral. He said something about life has to go on."

"I'm sure Mr. Drew will be missed," I said in a somber tone, curious how she would react. I added the *Mr.* after hearing her refer to Kevin that way. Personally, I thought it sounded kind of pretentious.

She looked around, then stepped right next to me. "I

know they say you shouldn't speak ill of the dead, but he was not a nice person." She again checked to make sure no one would overhear her before continuing. "As soon as they took over the place, he crowned himself boss. All he cared about was money, money and more money—for himself. Not like his aunt. Don't get me wrong, she did okay, but she did it in a fair way."

I wanted to ask for details and maybe segue into the bald man, but Dorothy didn't stop long enough to breathe, let alone for me to interject something. All the talking was obviously some kind of vent for her tension.

"Cut everybody's salary, he did," she said with a grunt of disgust. "It wasn't so much a problem for me. My Henry left me very comfortable. I do this more to keep busy, but Trina counts on the money, and she was devastated." Dorothy shook her head in dismay. "You know what he said to her when she complained? He said if she didn't like it, there were plenty of fast-food places looking for another burger flipper."

Dorothy had begun to walk as she talked. She stopped at a basket full of sachets and started nervously running her hands through them. "I was going to quit on principle. I have my pride. But Mr. Kevin apologized and reinstated my salary."

I wondered if he was doing the same for the other cuts his brother had made. I'd have to be sure to tell Sheila. Dinah had gone off to the Kids' Korner and as she came toward me, I noticed she was carrying a cloth doll and a wooden truck. No matter what she'd said about Ashley-Angela and E. Conner, apparently they had gotten to her. When she rejoined us, Dinah just hung back and listened, while Dorothy went back to complaining about Mr. Drew. She seemed very upset that he had installed an alarm on the back door to prevent shoplifters from escaping.

"Shoplifters?" she said, putting her hands on the hip portion of her mint green pants outfit. "This is not a shoplifter kind of business." She pointed to a card that proclaimed no refunds or exchanges and all sales were final. "Shoplifters want to bring the stuff back and get cash. Not going to happen here." She let out a big sigh. "Well, at least we won't have to listen to them fighting anymore."

"Fighting?" I said, finally getting to say something.

She said the two brothers argued loudly and continually.

"For someone so worried about business, Mr. Drew certainly should have known to keep his voice down. More than once I saw a customer walk out. Maybe they thought nobody could hear them, but this is a small place and sound travels."

Now that she had brought up customers it seemed like my chance to steer the conversation toward the bald man. "I suppose you're familiar with most of the customers and sellers," I said when she finally took a breath. She opened her mouth to say something, but the bell on the entrance jangled and some customers came in.

Dorothy seemed to have lost her train of thought and walked toward them. "Look around," she said to Dinah and me with a dismissive wave.

For a moment we stood there. "Do you think she'll come back?" I asked Dinah. We watched as more people came in the door, and then we both shook our heads.

"You can pay over here," Kevin said as he stepped behind the counter in the converted closet under the stairway that served as a cashier station. Even more people had arrived.

Kevin rang Dinah up and put the toys in a bag. We stepped away to make room for the new customers, but I wasn't ready to leave.

We moved back into the living room and pretended to be

looking around. Maybe not totally pretending. There were a lot of interesting things to look at. I stopped by a dark wood library table. It was for sale along with the items on top of it, which included some of Sheila's scarves. On the floor next to it was a large basket with an appealing arrangement of art supplies somebody was selling. There was a sketch pad and two books on drawing, some colored pencils and pens, along with a wooden hand and a wooden figure of a person to use as models.

Dinah nudged me and asked if I'd gotten any good information. I told her about the salary cuts and how the saleswoman whose screaming had gotten us all upstairs had been devastated by the pay cut and Drew's treatment of her. "I think that puts Trina on the suspect list. Maybe she hit Drew with the paperweight, and when his face hit the soup she just waited until the soup had done it's deadly work and then began to scream. And there's Dorothy, too. She claimed not to be upset, but maybe she just said that. She could have gone up there earlier and smashed him on the head."

I watched Dorothy picking up a brass lamp to check the price. No question, even though she was well into her sixties, she had the strength to swing a paperweight with some force. More people came in the shop, and the buzz of conversation got louder. I recognized some of the regular customers from the bookstore. Dorothy was being pulled in all directions by the crowd.

"Can you believe all these people," Dinah said. "You'd think they were giving something away."

"Are those *the* paperweights?" a woman asked, pointing to a group of objects on the mantelpiece. She was wearing casual pants and high heels, a look I never understood. Someone else was apparently interested in them, too, and pushed next to her, asking the same question. It took a moment for it to make sense. Then I realized they were talking about the paperweights that had been on Drew's desk. Ugh. There was some discussion about which of the ones on display had been *the one.*

"None of these," Kevin said. "The police have the one that hit my brother. It's evidence, you know."

The woman in the heels said she really wanted to buy one since they were a part of history. I rolled my eyes to myself. I had this thing about people and their desire for a part of history. Or what they thought was a piece of history, anyway. A paperweight from the desk of a dead guy didn't qualify in my book, even if he was murdered.

She picked up a brass bust of Teddy Roosevelt and a tall glass piece with a green jellyfish suspended inside. I remembered seeing them on the desk. Someone asked Kevin what *the one* looked like.

"It was a globe inlaid with semiprecious stones on a silverplate base. It was quite heavy for its size," he said. Then he looked uncomfortable with what he'd said. The mention of it stirred my memory, and I shuddered as I recalled seeing the globe lying on its side. I realized the red I'd seen on it wasn't pieces of ruby.

Meanwhile, I heard rumors starting to circulate among the growing group of shoppers. Someone mentioned that one of Sheila's scarves had been on Drew's desk, too. Suddenly there was a run on those. I wasn't sure if that was good news or not for Sheila. She might make some money, but it only brought more attention to the fact that one of her scarves had been in the room when Drew died.

Dinah and I slipped into the dining room to get away from the crowd. Apparently they hadn't put it together yet that the free samples of soup were prepared by the same person who had made the soup Drew drowned in. Dinah and I took some soup samples and sat down at one of the small bistro tables. Kevin had made a nice cream of asparagus with a touch of curry. From our table, we could see that Kevin had joined Dorothy in dealing with the crowd.

Everyone seemed occupied, which gave me an idea. I pointed upstairs. "What do you think? There may never be another chance like this. I'd like to see Drew's office. Maybe the white lacy stuff is still hanging on the drawer."

"We have to be stealth," Dinah said with a twinkle in her eye. She crumpled her soup cup and got up.

"Wait a second," I said, sitting back down again. I'd worn no-show white socks with my slip-ons, but somehow the socks had slipped down and were in a bunch right at my arch. I pulled off both socks, stuck them in the pocket of my khaki slacks and put the shoes back on. I could practically feel a blister forming as we threaded through the crowd toward the stairs.

My heartbeat picked up as I checked to make sure no one was looking in our direction. A rush of adrenalin surged through me as I started up the stairs with Dinah right behind me. We moved quickly, and when we were out of sight, I let my breath out. We'd made it.

It seemed eerily quiet after all the racket downstairs.

The first time I'd been up here, I hadn't paid much attention to the hall. Now I noitced that the second floor went over only the front half of the building. There were two open doorways and one closed one, which I guessed led to a bathroom from the ancient days when this was a house.

I was curious to see what Drew's office looked like now that the crime scene investigators and detectives had finished with it. The desk was cleaned of tomato bisque residue, and the paperweights had been moved downstairs. The CSIs must have taken the bowl and the rest of the soup. I wondered how they handled keeping a bowl of soup as evidence.

I didn't see Sheila's scarf. Did that mean they'd taken

that as evidence also, or was it just so soup soaked it had gotten trashed? This time I noticed there was a desk lamp, a three-tiered paper holder and a telephone. I supposed last time I'd been in the office they had all been on the floor. Someone had tried to clean the carpet, but residue of the red still showed in the beige pile. There were some shelves in the back with books about antique and collectible prices. I noticed a printer on the bottom shelf with a USB cord to nowhere. I guessed Drew must have brought in a laptop.

What I didn't see was anything hanging off a desk drawer.

"Maybe whatever it was is in the drawer now," Dinah whispered.

I hesitated. So far all we'd done was look at what was readily seeable; opening drawers seemed to be crossing a line. What was that saying—in for a penny, in for a pound? It seemed silly to sneak up here and not check out everything. Besides, if I was careful, no one would know. I took out one of the no-show socks and used it as a hand cover so I wouldn't leave fingerprints.

"Clever move," Dinah whispered.

The drawers were mostly empty. One had a bunch of blank labels and some postcards. I looked at one. It was lime green and announced that a new shipment of goodies had arrived and encouraged the recipient to make sure and come in. Another had some pencils and pens, stamps and a copy of *The Greed Machine*. We'd had a signing for it. The author had bragged that he knew how to grow money, which basically amounted to diverting it from other people's pockets into his. I had a feeling it must have been Drew's personal bible.

I stood back and looked around again.

"I think we've covered it here," I said softly. I walked out and headed for the other bedroom/office. "I wonder what

Mr. Kevin has," I said, slipping inside. His office was slightly smaller and the furnishings were plainer. The desk was antique, but plain wood rather than the inlaid squares of Drew's desktop. There was a bookcase with a few books. All appeared to be cookbooks, and the one that seemed the most handled was on restaurant design. There were some restaurant equipment catalogs and also a binder. I flipped open the binder and saw it held a collection of recipes, including one for the tomato bisque soup.

Dinah sat down on the love seat while I continued to looked around. I took out one of my no-show socks again and used it to open the desk drawers. There was a phone book, some pens and pencils and two packages of fruity mint gum, which I thought sounded like an upset stomach waiting to happen.

I was sliding the drawer shut when I heard noise on the stairs. Voices that were growing louder. I turned toward Dinah. She'd heard them, too. I think we must have had matching panic faces. Operating on instinct, she slid behind the love seat and I crawled under the desk, grateful that it had a modesty shield across the opening, so no one could see me from the other side.

This was the problem with snooping around. You could get caught. I squeezed under the desk as far as possible, but I still had a view of the feet and pants' bottoms of the two people who came in the office. Two legs had faded jeans and not the kind thrown in vats of bleach or washed with rocks to look that way. These appeared authentically paled by countless washings. The feet were in work boots that looked as though they'd seen their share of action. The other legs wore dark olive green dress trousers, and the shoes were loafers with tassels, or as I called them, men's party shoes. I also noticed something white and balled up under the desk. In my panic I must have dropped my no-show sock. I silently snatched it and put it in my pocket.

"So, here are the plans and costs," the jeans-and-boot person said. He was shifting his weight and had a deep voice. "We'd be enlarging the kitchen and dining room by adding onto the side and back. We'd take out the storage room and use the space for another downstairs bathroom."

I listened with interest. I'd already figured out the other feet belonged to Kevin. It was kind of a no-brainer since it was his office and I recognized the olive green trousers from before. So, Drew was barely out of the picture and Kevin already was getting estimates from a contractor. One more sign Kevin wasn't exactly inconsolable over the loss of his brother. Kevin asked some questions about how long it would take to put on the addition and said he needed to be able to stay open during the remodel.

I was so busy listening I almost forgot where I was and started to shifted around to a more comfortable—no strike that, less uncomfortable position. My legs were beginning to hurt from being jammed under my chin. I started to stretch them out, but quickly realized they'd stick out past the end of the desk and probably be in plain sight. Forcing myself not to groan, I wrenched them back. Didn't they want to take their discussion downstairs where they could actually see the areas Kevin wanted changed? I thought longingly. Then I could get up and stretch and we could make our escape.

No such luck. Instead Kevin sat down at his desk, though thankfully he didn't pull his chair in or stick his legs underneath. I had squeezed sideways now so as to take up less space. I peeked under the bottom of the modesty shield and noticed something was moving. I was so contorted by now I could have auditioned for the Cirque du Soleil, but I saw that Dinah had come out from behind the love seat and was crawling against the wall toward the door. Mr. Work Boots was standing in front of the desk and must have been blocking Kevin's view of her because they just kept talking like nothing was going on. Work Boots was saying he needed a check to get started, and judging by the drawer opening, Kevin was going to give it to him. I watched Dinah's feet disappear out the door.

Kevin kept talking—and not getting up from his desk. I was beginning to feel a little panicky, like maybe I'd never get out of here, or worse, be discovered. Then I heard the scrape of his chair as he pulled it closer to the desk. I turned and saw that his knees were moving under the desk and any second they were going to hit me.

And for the life of me, I couldn't come up with a valid reason I could give for being there.

My heart was pounding and the adrenalin rushing, but it wasn't a good feeling this time—more like it was making me nauseous. I took a few deep breaths and prepared to face the consequences. His knees were so close I could smell the cleaning fluid from his pants. I battened down my personal hatches and prepared to hear him scream when his knees made contact.

There was a sound all right and it was loud, but it wasn't human.

CHAPTER 10

KEVIN'S SHOES TOOK OFF LIKE A SHOT IN RE-sponse to the loud whine. Mr. Work Boots followed close behind. I gave them a moment, then race crawled out from under the desk. When I got downstairs there was pandemonium as everyone was rushing out the back door.

I followed the crowd and found Dinah standing with the others in the parking lot.

"Thank you, thank you, thank you," I said hugging her.

"You didn't think I'd just leave you there. It's lucky I was listening when Dorothy mentioned the alarm on the back door. All I had to do was push the door and it went off," Dinah said, glancing around at the frantic faces of the group in the parking lot. "Though, I just wanted to create a distraction, not cause a panic."

Kevin moved through the former shoppers, checking everyone to see if they were holding any merchandise. Dorothy was leaning against the building, looking very pale.

"I suppose everyone overreacted because of the murder," I said as Kevin stopped in front of a woman in designer jeans and heels, holding a lamp. Judging by his body language, I suspected that he thought she'd tried to leave with the lamp and set off the alarm in the process. Too bad he didn't take the time to think it through. I mean, if she was trying to steal a lamp, would she just hang around waiting to get caught?

In the distance I heard the whine of sirens. "Uh-oh. We better get out of here," I said, grabbing Dinah's hand. We took off and as we ran, we both got the giggles. By the time we reached the bookstore café, we were breathless and laughing so hard, tears were running down our cheeks.

"What's up? You two look like you just did something naughty," Bob said as we both flopped into chairs at a table by the window.

"Us?" I said with my best innocent, middle-age widow look, which made us both start laughing all over again. Bob shook his head with disbelief as a hook and ladder roared past the window.

Bob was very serious about his barista duties, and his round body shape suggested that he did a lot of taste testing of the cookies. He had a small clump of hair on the bottom of his chin that looked like a shaving mistake. Is that even called a beard? And he always reminded us that he was working on a screenplay—some kind of alien adventure story. Maybe the idea for his face hair came from that.

When we finally regained our composure, I tried twisting my body to get the kinks out. "It wasn't fun being squished under that desk," I said.

Bob brought us drinks and some cookie bars he'd just made using a recipe of mine. Since I'm only a marginal chocolate fan, they were more or less chocolate chip cookie bars without the chocolate chips. Instead I added more nuts and bits of dried apricot. After seeing our condition, Bob must have figured we'd had enough caffeine, so he brought us both camomile tea.

We looked out the window and saw the hook and ladder had pulled around the corner from the Cottage Shoppe. Two firemen had jumped off and were headed toward the front door carrying axes. Most of the shoppers had left, but a few were hanging around to watch what was going on.

"I guess someone must have freaked when the alarm went off and called for the works," Dinah said, wincing with guilt. A rescue ambulance stopped in front of the store and another fire truck followed. Two police cruisers came from the other direction and barely stopped before the doors flung open and four uniforms popped out. A black Crown Victoria pulled up and Detective Heather got out of the driver's side as her partner got out on the other side. Instinctively, I shrank back from the window as if her detective eyes could pick me out from across the street and a half a block down.

Maybe she couldn't boil an egg, but she could sure wear a suit—though I couldn't imagine how she functioned in the pencil skirt and the heels. Barry occasionally made reference to some of the ucky places he had to go. Places with bugs and rodents, and he wasn't talking butterflies and field mice. Personally, I'd want to wear armor.

Kevin Brooks came out and met up with the emergency people. It appeared there was lots of pointing and apologizing. All the uniforms headed back to their various vehicles. Detective Heather made no move to leave and continued talking to Kevin. Her appearance wasn't lost on him. Even from across the street, I could tell he'd be glad to do any egg boiling necessary. I was relieved to see he had apparently let the lady with the lamp go and was now holding it himself.

"I suppose it must be a shock to her that she can't get Barry. She does have a lot going for her besides looks," I said, watching her conversation. "She's smart, focused, ambitious and—"

"Cold as an iceberg," Dinah said, finishing my sentence.

We ate the cookie bars but shunned the tea as we watched the hook and ladder roll past the window, shaking the floor as it went. Neither of us wanted to do anything to mess with the nice afterglow of the adrenalin rush.

"What's going on?" Even though the voice was coming from behind us, I recognized the speaker as Adele. When I turned, she was standing next to the table, following my gaze. Lately, she'd been getting a little more serious about her clothes. They were still outrageous, but ever since the Koo Koo the Clown signing, she'd been going for blander colors. I called this outfit the Butterscotch Kiss. She had on pants and a top in a dark golden yellow with a crocheted scarf the same color tied around her head. She'd barely mentioned their date except to say he really liked her, but she wasn't into dating a clown, even if he was a published one.

"Somebody went out the back door of the Cottage Shoppe and set off an alarm and the cavalry was called in," I said. My lips started to quiver as I looked at Dinah, and I had to fight to keep the giggles from coming back.

"How come you know so much about it?" Adele sounded jealous that we knew what was going on rather than interested in the answer. She sat down at the table before we had a chance to invite her to join us. Leaving out our little side trip upstairs, I told her we'd gone over there to check out the specials. I gestured toward the banners on the windows.

"And probably snoop, too," Adele said. "Pink, I know how you operate." Shocked, I turned my head toward her, thinking she knew what we'd done, but then I realized she meant *snoop* in a general sense, as in talk to people and look around, not in the more specific sense of sneaking into private offices. "So, what did you find out?" Adele demanded.

Why not tell Adele? I told her what Dorothy had said about Drew cutting salaries as well as the money the consignees got. "The other saleswoman, Trina, was the most upset. And Drew and Kevin were fighting all the time about something." I turned to Dinah. "Maybe it had something to do with the plans Kevin has for the place." Dinah nodded with interest.

"Pink, you're sure taking your time solving this. Sheila could be tried and convicted if you don't get the lead out. I'm a better sleuth than you are," Adele said with a snort. "Just from what you said I can see there are two prime suspects. The saleswoman who found him—Trina. How much more prime can you get? Who says his head was in the soup when she got there? Or the other one. Maybe she was telling you how upset Trina was to get the heat off of her. Whose to say she didn't bop him and leave and let her coworker find him?" Adele seemed pleased with herself, but then her eyes widened as if she'd thought of something else even more self-satisfying.

"By the way, I had a little conversation with Mrs. Shedd about the Milton Mindell event. I told her I should handle it all by myself since it's a kids' event."

My adrenalin high faded. Was Adele out of her mind? So many kids showed up, we had to give out numbers in advance. And mixing Milton's temperamental personality with Adele's divaness spelled disaster in red letters.

I'd have to talk to Mrs. Shedd, I thought. Then I stopped myself. Was the potential for disaster the only reason I was so uncomfortable with the idea of Adele handling the event? Or was I afraid that little by little Adele might take away pieces of my job? Bingo. Okay, I never claimed to be a saint.

"I don't know why Mrs. Shedd didn't agree," Adele said. I tried not to be obvious about my relief. Thankfully, Mrs. Shedd had some sense. But only *some*.

"But she said I could work with you on it." Adele gave my arm a friendly punch. "So I guess we're partners, then." It didn't matter that I looked dismayed, Adele wasn't paying any attention. She just went on, saying that Patricia Bradford had dropped off a box of books along with signage for her event. I noticed Adele made sure to mention that the Patricia's Hints program was all mine to handle.

We didn't generally carry self-published books like Patricia's because they were a hard sell, but Mrs. Shedd made an exception for Patricia, who never left anything to chance. Normally, I made signs for author events, but Patricia preferred to make her own, more elaborate ones with more flattering copy. Adele said this time she had described herself as "the first lady of hints."

"So, what did you buy?" Adele said, abruptly changing the subject. "You said you went over to the Cottage Shoppe to check out the specials." Her comment jogged my memory, and I thought of the doll and truck Dinah had bought. Then I realized we'd left the bag on the chair in the refreshment area of the store. Since Dinah had a class to teach, I offered to get it. Adele insisted on coming with me.

The store was considerably quieter than it had been earlier. In fact there were almost no customers for us to blend in with. Kevin was talking to Dorothy. She looked as though she couldn't wait for her workday to end. Who could blame her?

When I glanced in the dining room, I saw the package still on the chair. I picked it up and was heading toward the door, anxious to make a hasty exit, but Adele had gone off to look around. I stopped in the entrance hall to wait for her. Kevin and Dorothy were still talking. I like to think of it as curiosity, though some might call it nosiness, but I leaned a little closer to try to hear. I swallowed hard when I got the jest of it.

Kevin was saying he'd seen someone on the stairs earlier. Because of the overhang all he had seen were a pair of legs in black slacks. It couldn't have been Dinah, because she was wearing rust-colored denims, and it couldn't have been me, because, as usual, I was wearing khaki pants.

Could somebody else have been looking around upstairs, too?

Chapter 11

The May gloom had finally worn off as Adele and I headed back to the bookstore. With the sun burning through the clouds, the air had warmed considerably, and I peeled off my black knit hoodie. Once we got inside, she went off to the children's department and I headed back to the office.

I worked on the newsletter and made sure the calendar in it was up-to-date before printing out copies to leave by the door. I had included a little article about the Tarzana Hookers' hugs of comfort project and mentioned how the director of the Women's Haven was very excited to be giving shawls to the residents. I also put a little note in saying new members of the crochet group were always welcome. More than welcome. We needed them if we were going to get all those shawls made.

After I had put out the newsletters, I cashiered a bit to give Rayaad a break and then helped some shoppers find books. By the time I was heading for home, I was thinking of a nice long bubble bath and an evening of soothing crochet. I really wanted to get a good part of my first shawl done, and while I was working I could think over everything I'd seen and heard at the Cottage Shoppe.

Someone must be having a party, I thought as I turned onto my block and noted the number of cars parked on the street. I was glad I wasn't invited. The bubble bath beckoned, and I was contemplating maybe an ice-cream dinner. I pulled into the carport and walked into the yard. It was empty for a change. No Barry and his dog. Ah, peace at last, peace at last. For a moment, anyway.

Who knew the party was at my house?

I pushed open the kitchen door and there was greeted by the instant noise of multiple conversations and people. Morgan and Samuel were in one corner of the kitchen having some kind of heated discussion over a bowl of lettuce and a bottle of vinegar. Barry and Jeffrey were by the pantry, unloading dog food and assorted treats from a grocery bag. Cosmo was watching at their feet. Barry had been bringing over so much dog stuff, it was taking up all the shelf space. My terrier mix was sitting in the other room, observing everything at a safe distance. Then Peter walked in from the other room along with Mason Fields. When my older son saw me, he marched over scowling. He wanted to know why Samuel's girlfriend was staying with me and why Barry had a key and was acting like he lived here.

"It's only been a few weeks since I've been over," Peter said, gesturing toward the dog food unloading zone. "Who's the kid and where'd that dog come from?" As if on cue, Cosmo dropped his saliva-covered ball on Peter's zillion-dollar Enrico Fabrizio shoe. "Mother, this house is like a circus." Since Charlie's death, Peter thought it was his job to be the man of the family. Sometimes he took the job too seriously.

"Let's see," I said, watching as he glowered at everyone, particularly Barry. "Your brother's girlfriend needed a place to stay for a while, and I have lots of room. And Cosmo, Barry and Jeffrey are all part of the same thing." I explained that Jeffrey was Barry's son and they had wanted to get a dog, but couldn't unless they had sort of a cosigner.

"Mother, you didn't?" Peter was already throwing up his hands in a hopeless gesture as I explained that Cosmo had started as a frequent visitor but had now become more of a permanent guest. The little black mutt dropped the ball at Peter's feet again. He leaned down and ruffled the dog's fur before tossing the ball out the back door into the yard. Cosmo charged after it. To my surprise, Blondie followed him out.

"He's kind of cute. Couldn't you just have said he was yours once he started living here?"

"No. He's really Barry and Jeffrey's dog, and sometime soon they'll be taking him back with them," I said.

"Sure," Peter said with disbelief. "I think the more likely move is the cop and kid are going to try and come here to stay with their dog, Mother," he said, stretching the word into two syllables of disapproval.

Whatever happened to the concept of growing up and being able to do what you wanted? It wasn't bad enough that I had had to deal with my mother's withering opinions of anyone I dated when I was a teen. Now I had Peter, and he certainly didn't give me any slack.

Mason had discreetly stayed out of earshot during Peter's fuss about Barry, Jeffrey and the dog. As soon as he saw we were done, he came toward me with an amused smile.

"So, I finally get to see the famous Pink Manor. Certainly a lively place."

He explained he and Peter had come from a meeting

about a reality show deal they were putting together at some production company in Sherman Oaks. Peter had brought him over because he was worried I was mixed up in another murder and needed someone to tell me how to deal with the police. Personally, I thought the visit had more to do with Peter's efforts as matchmaker than his concern about me being a suspect. Particularly since I wasn't a suspect. However, I was glad Peter had brought him over since I did have something I wanted to talk to him about.

From across the room, as though he had lawyer radar, Barry glanced up, locked eyes with Mason and clenched his jaw. Barry knew how to keep his face impassive, but the jaw thing was his one tell when he was really upset.

I don't think Barry would have liked Mason even if he didn't see him as competition. Mason had a reputation for keeping his celebrity clients out of jail. He knew how to find the reasonable doubt in cases detectives like Barry built. He was high profile and showed up on the news all the time, coming out of the courthouse. He was also on the board of directors of almost every charity. He claimed, in his usual joking manner, he had to do something to make up for being a lawyer. He was divorced and clearly could have his pick of women of any age group even though he was in his fifties. Why not, he had the big three going for him: successful, good-looking and available. Actually, there was also a fourth. He was a total nonjerk. I suspected his interest in me had more to do with the fact that I kept putting him off than anything else. You know, people always want what they can't have.

I did like him. He had a sense of humor about himself and an ability to take care of things without making a big deal out of it, like the way he had helped my younger son line up some gigs playing keyboards at some local bars. So I wasn't saying never about Mason, just not right now.

"I'm glad you're here. I wanted to talk to you about something." I stepped toward the open door and the relative quiet of the backyard. Mason straightened at my comment and got an expectant expression on his face. I was afraid when he heard what I wanted to talk to him about he was going to be disappointed.

I didn't have to see Barry's eyes to know that he probably had a stare so piercing it could burn a hole in a rock.

"So talk," Mason said when we got outside. He had on a dark suit—blue that was almost black—and a creamy white shirt made out of a soft, silky cotton. He wore no tie and his shirt was open, showing a frizzle of chest hair that, like the hair on his head, was mostly dark brown with a little gray. A few strands of hair always seemed to fall across his forehead, giving him an earnest, hardworking sort of look. He stretched one arm and leaned his hand against the house, which placed him at an intimate distance from me.

"No matter what Peter might have said, I'm not about to be arrested. I'm not a suspect, person of interest or anything like that. Well, maybe a witness." I started to explain the whole scene with Drew's face in a bowl, but he'd already heard it. It was serious and all since Drew was dead, but saying the whole thing out loud sounded ridiculous and funny.

"I'm glad to hear you're not a suspect, but you know if you ever are arrested or need a cup of sugar or just a friendly ear, I'm just a phone call away."

I thanked him but told him I wanted to talk to him about somebody else and I began to tell the whole story about Sheila.

"Detective Hea—I mean Gilmore heard Sheila say some threatening things about Drew, and then Sheila was at the shop when the whole soup incident happened."

Mason nodded but didn't seem particularly concerned

until I mentioned the row of paperweights on the desk and how Sheila had said her fingerprints were on the paperweight that had hit Drew on the head.

"How did she know which one hit him, if she didn't do it?"

"You have to know Sheila," I began, then told him about her finger tapping and how she'd tried to appear calmer and started tapping the paperweights and worked her way through all of them.

Mason pulled out a card. "If they start accusing her or anything, tell her not to say anything and to call me."

I gave him a thank-you hug. "And there's another small problem."

He waved for me to bring it on.

"She doesn't have any money."

Mason shrugged. "No problem. I'd do it as a favor for you. But then you would owe me, wouldn't you," he said with a teasing twinkle. "How about dinner as payment?"

"No problem," I said and offered to pay up right away. Of course, I invited everyone else to stay, too. I don't think that was what he had in mind.

CHAPTER 12

"HOW DID YOU FEED THEM ALL?" DINAH ASKED. We were the first ones at the crochet group and had taken out our shawls to work on. Dinah wanted all the details of my impromptu dinner party.

I'd been working on my shawl at home, and even though it was just simple rows of single crochet and double crochet with a space, I kept losing stitches. I hadn't noticed at first and had just kept going, but then began to see there was a certain incline to the edges. I counted the stitches and realized I'd lost ten somewhere along the line. If I continued this way, instead of being a long rectangle the shawl would be shaped like an arrow. I was just glad Adele wasn't there to see it or I'd never hear the end of it. I unraveled row after row until I'd reached one that had the right number of stitches.

Dinah had found a babysitter for the kids. Although she seemed more relaxed, I noticed she kept taking out her cell phone as if she was going to make a call, then reconsidering and putting it down on the table.

"In answer to how I fed everyone, I sent Samuel and Morgan and their argument to the store. I have a gas grill in the backyard, and I told Barry and Mason they were cooking. I had to get them some tee shirts left over from some promotion Charlie did since they both had on nice clothes. They looked pretty funny in suit pants and green tees that said 'Wally the Wonder Worm.' "

"I thought you said Barry couldn't cook," Dinah said, spreading out her work and the ball of forest green yarn. She had tried to convince us to let her make a shawl by joining all the washcloths, but we talked her into following the same pattern as the rest of us. Despite everything she was dealing with, she was still farther along than I was. After hearing about my lost-stitch problem, she kept counting hers every few rows and was relieved to see she still had the correct amount.

"What man can't barbecue? Or would admit it, anyway?" I said. "Besides it was just hot dogs and hamburgers."

"Barry and Mason barbecued together?" Dinah said. "How did that go?"

"Not so well." I laughed at the remembrance. "They argued about when something was done, what rare looked like and whether or not the hot dogs should just be heated or should look all scorched and covered with black. Luckily I had a lot of condiments. You stick it on a bun and pour on enough catsup and mustard and it tastes fine, no matter what."

"What about Morgan? Did she eat?"

"I think so. I heard her mumbling about losing some weight and then all the dance roles would roll in." I looked at Dinah and winced. "Did I really just say that?" Dinah nodded with a laugh and I shrugged. "Whatever. Thank heavens it isn't my problem." I had done another row and counted stitches. I was back at the right amount.

"Do you think Samuel wanted her to stay with you because of her eating problem? Maybe he thought you could fix it," Dinah said.

"I hope not, because that kind of problem is out of my league. I'm better at things like going shopping together at the mall or teaching her how to crochet, not fixing her life."

"Tell me the rest about Barry and Mason," Dinah said.

"How do you know there is a rest?"

"I need there to be a *rest*. It's almost the end of the semester at Beasley and the last chance for my freshmen to shape up." She shook her head with hopelessness. The community college gave everybody a chance and then left it to instructors like Dinah to weed out the kids who couldn't cut it. Some years were harder than others, and I gathered this one was a prize winner in the not-ready-for-college department. "I need some diversion from thinking about my students and the fact that I am still taking care of my ex's kids and he still isn't back. If there isn't something good, make it up."

It wasn't that hard to come up with more, and I didn't have to invent any of it. I told her Barry had made a point of fixing a lamp in front of Mason and turning it off and on numerous times to demonstrate that it now worked. "Barry also kept acting very territorial, showing he knew where everything was and implying he belonged there. Then Mason made a point of loading the dishwasher." I chuckled at the memory of Barry's shocked expression. I hesitated, and Dinah knew I was holding something back.

"C'mon," she urged, putting down her crocheting to listen.

I explained I had told Mason to help himself to something to drink. I was busy gathering stuff for the table and didn't notice at first that Barry was standing behind Mason as he surveyed the drink offerings in the refrigerator.

"Why don't you have a beer," Barry had suggested, gesturing toward the four amber bottles of Hefeweizen on the second self. I knew what Barry was doing and I should have just closed my eyes and left it alone when Mason took one of the bottles.

It was ridiculous to think of it as Charlie's beer, but I couldn't seem to help it.

"You don't want to drink that," I had said, taking the bottle out of Mason's hand. "It's really old and probably flat and has beer cooties. I should throw it out." Despite my words, I had put the bottle back in the refrigerator.

Mason had been clever enough to figure out whatever was going on had nothing to do with beer and took a Perrier instead.

When I finished the story, Dinah rolled her eyes. "Do you still have that beer?" she asked, shaking her head.

To avoid the lecture I knew was coming, I changed the subject and told her I'd gotten Mason to agree to help Sheila and it turned out he was on the board of directors of the Women's Haven.

"That man is on the board of directors of everything," Dinah said. When I started to say something she said it for me. "I know—he has to make up for being a lawyer. What did you have for dessert?"

I told her I'd thrown together something last minute. "I sliced up some apples and mixed them with a little cinnamon sugar, then I'd covered them with a mixture of flour, brown sugar and butter and baked it for a while."

"Sounds good," she said.

"It was even better when I added the vanilla bean ice cream. It was the only time there was any peace. Barry and Mason had their mouths full and couldn't spar."

Adele arrived as I was finishing the story. She gave us a

hurt look as she put down her things. "Why didn't you come get me?" she demanded.

"You seemed busy," I said by way of an excuse. It was true. When I'd gone past the children's department, she seemed to be poring over something.

"I was working on the plans for the Milton Mindell author program."

My jaw dropped. I wasn't even used to the idea that she'd be working with me, and she was already trying to take over. She pulled out a file and started going over her plans. They began with the idea that the program should take place in her section of the store and we should do it differently this time. I put up my hand to stop her. "It's all about what Milton wants. Not what you want or I want. He has his own plans and we just implement them." I wondered if Mrs. Shedd knew what she was unleashing when she said Adele could work on the event.

Just then Patricia walked in with CeeCee. I had to give Patricia credit; she was persistent. She was still working on CeeCee, trying to convince her to appear in one of Benjamin's campaign ads.

As everyone settled in, I could see that none of us had done as much on our own as we'd hope to, and CeeCee clucked her tongue in slight disapproval. CeeCee laid a finished one on the table. It was beautifully made, so perfect it looked almost machine made. I picked it up and examined the sides. They were straight, unlike mine, which kept getting wiggly.

Patricia had an impressive bag for her supplies. She showed us how she had taken a plain tote bag and attached pockets on the inside and outside. She had one for hooks and needles, and another for supplies like scissors and a tape measure, and she had made a special section to hold a skein of yarn. "I'm considering putting this in the next version of *Patricia's Perfect Hints*, though once Benjamin gets elected, I'll probably be so busy with my duties that I won't have time to think about new editions."

I rolled my eyes. He was running for city council, not president. Did she think she was going to be first lady of Tarzana? Patricia started to take out knitting needles, but Adele gave her the evil eye, so instead she placed an unopened packet of crochet hooks on the table. "Which one do I use?" she asked.

Adele put down her own work and pulled out a K hook from the package. Then she helped Patricia with the slip knot and showed her how to keep track of her chain stitches by making a mark on paper every time she made ten. Adele was a little condescending in her tone until Patricia reminded her that casting on for knitting was similar and she knew how to keep track of her stitches.

I glanced toward the entrance. "Where's Sheila?"

All I got were head shakes and shrugs as answers. It wasn't like Sheila not to show or call, and I started to worry. It distracted me from my crocheting, and when I counted my stitches, I found I had lost a bunch and the shawl was again taking on an arrow shape.

"Good work, Pink," Adele said sarcastically as she fingered it. She turned to CeeCee. "Didn't you show her how to keep from losing stitches?"

"Dear, why don't you handle it?" CeeCee said in a cheery voice. Not the answer I wanted to hear. But at the same time I wanted to learn how. "Show her how to handle her stitches of despair," CeeCee added.

"Stitches of despair?" I said, looking at my work.

"That's what I call them. They are the stitches causing you despair," CeeCee said, glancing up from the cream-colored shawl she was working on.

Adele grumbled to herself and told me to begin the pattern row. I was supposed to chain four, which would count as the first double crochet and a chain. Adele stopped me when I'd only chained three and told me to mark the top chain with something that looked like a plastic safety pin. Then she let me make the forth chain.

"Pink, that's your problem. Now when you do the next row, you'll be able to see where the last stitch goes and hopefully you won't mess up anymore."

Adele waited while I finished the pattern row and then told me to do the next row. She stood so close over me that the beaded fringe on the scarf she had around her head kept smacking my face. Who wouldn't get nervous when watched like that? I ended up getting the yarn twisted in my hook and dropping it with a loud ping. Adele threw up her hands as though I were beyond help and went back to her seat.

Without her hovering, I did fine and best of all realized what I'd been doing wrong so I wouldn't keep doing it.

And still I kept checking for Sheila.

"Here she comes," CeeCee said. Sheila came up to the table, looking pale as skim milk.

"This is so terrible," she said, sinking into a chair. She explained Detective Heather had been hanging around the gym asking questions about her. Her boss was upset with her, and she was worried about losing her job.

"Did Detective Heather talk to you?" I asked.

"Of course. She talked to me first. She made it seem casual, but it was like she had a script. She said one of the salespeople at the Cottage Shoppe had said I'd been coming to the store for quite a while fussing with Drew over some money I thought he owed me." Sheila sounded distraught. "I didn't *think* he owed it to me, I *knew* he did. But I only went there once before you all came with me. I wasn't stalking him, like she said." Sheila swallowed a few times. "The detective kept saying, 'It must have really made you angry, didn't it?' over and over. The trouble is her saying it over and over was making me nervous, and looking nervous is like looking guilty." Sheila put her face in her hands. "I know she thinks I did it."

I gave Sheila Mason's card and told her to keep it with her. I didn't want to freak her out by telling her to call him if she got arrested. I just said he had suggested the less she say the better.

"It's hard. That detective knows how to ask questions so you're saying things before you even realize it."

"What did you say?" I asked, feeling a sense of doom.

Sheila swallowed hard. "I said I might have handled the paperweight that hit him on the head."

"Oh dear."

CHAPTER 13

IT WAS YET ANOTHER OF THOSE COOL AND GRAY mornings so typical for this time of year as I let Blondie and Cosmo out into the backyard. I took my coffee and crochet bag and sat down at the glass table while they ran around. The forest green umbrella was folded down. There was no need for shade. This weather made both the flowers and me feel refreshed.

Peter kept suggesting I sell the house and move to a condo. I wondered if he realized that selling this house would mean he would have to keep his golf clubs, tennis rackets, skis, bicycle and sports trophies at his apartment. It was a moot point anyway, as I had no plans to take his advice. I loved my yard and house.

The gate clanged shut, and I sat up to see who'd come in. Dinah seemed agitated and was winding two scarves around her neck as she walked across the patio. Cosmo ran over and started to bark at her. Blondie merely looked at Dinah. Cosmo seemed to be teaching Blondie a lot of stuff, and I wondered if it would include barking.

"Coffee?" I said as Dinah slid into the chair next to me. She nodded with a grateful smile and took out a pair of her long earrings and began to put them on. Apparently kid-proofing her clothes was only for when Jeremy's kids were present, which made me wonder where they were.

"Do you have something to go with it? Preferably something sweet and decadent."

I mentioned I still had some dessert left over from the dinner party the night before last.

"I bet it would taste better with some of that vanilla bean ice cream."

I laughed as I headed inside.

"Where are the kids?" I asked when I returned with a tray of coffee and the baked apple dessert topped with a generous scoop of ice cream.

Dinah sat back, stretched her legs out and sighed with a definite sense of relief. "The babysitter, again. Jeremy promised he'd be back tonight. I can't believe I let him stick me with them this long." She took out her crochet bag and laid it on the table next to mine.

I set the mug of coffee and plate of food in front of Dinah. "I thought you were kind of getting attached to them."

Before she could answer Morgan came out the door. She was dressed in a creamy yellow leotard and matching tights with some kind of loose short dress over everything. She stopped by the table.

"I'm so sorry I missed the crochet group yesterday," she said with a tinge of guilt. I saw her eyes stop on the dish in front of Dinah and offered her some. She put up her hand in an extreme "no" motion. "I'm off to the studio for a morning class."

"You should eat something," I said, then regretted interfering. She was a grown-up, and besides, there wasn't a chance in the world she was going to listen to me. But I couldn't stop myself and threw in a few more lines of how breakfast was the most important meal of the day.

She headed off, giving me the slightest of hopeless head shakes.

"If she wasn't staying here I wouldn't know about all this." I leaned against the back of my chair, feeling frustrated.

"Welcome to my world. If those kids weren't staying with me I wouldn't know a lot of things I'd rather not know, too. Like somebody never taught them the basics—pick up your toys, go to bed when I say so, and at least try the spinach souffle."

"I knew you were getting attached to them."

"Don't even say that. It is too upsetting to care and then know that Jeremy is going to be the one responsible for them. Did I tell you Mrs. About To Be Ex took off and isn't coming back."

She had already told me that gem, and we looked at each other with understanding. No matter what either one of us said about not getting involved and not caring, we couldn't help it. I asked her if she'd given them any of her famous cream cheese and caviar sandwiches. It took her a moment to remember that gourmet treat she'd made for her own kids. Then she laughed.

Since there was no group meeting this morning and Dinah didn't have a class and I didn't have to be at the bookstore until evening for Romance Night, we were having our own little crochet gathering. I took out my shawl in progress. Now that I wasn't dropping stitches as often and needed to unravel less, the dusty rose rectangle was beginning to resemble a shawl.

Dinah took out her forest green project. I was amazed how much she'd gotten done, especially with small children in the house.

As soon as we started crocheting, Dinah brought up Sheila and the growing case against her.

"We better hurry up with the other suspects," Dinah said. "Sheila's her own worst enemy. Now that they know to look for her fingerprints on the paperweight, they'll probably try to get her to confess. I've seen what the cops do when they get you locked up in an interviewing room. They pretend to be your friend, like they're going to help you if you just tell them what happened. Then they keep pushing, saying things like they know you were at the murder scene and they know you're not telling them the whole story and maybe it was just an accident anyway. And the next thing you know, the person starts saying they did it."

"Where did you see that?" I said, surprised.

"On TV, but it was a reality show," Dinah said. "I'm just worried that Sheila could end up confessing to something she didn't do."

"You're right. I need to find somebody else for Detective Heather to fixate on." The dogs ran in the house, and I shivered. "It's kind of chilly out here."

Dinah agreed, and she gathered up her stuff, saying we were Southern California wimps. "What is it, maybe a bone-chilling sixty-seven degrees?"

Inside, Dinah sat down at the kitchen table. I left my crocheting next to her and went to get a load of laundry, so it could be washing while I worked on my shawl. That was about as close as I got to multitasking.

I carried the load to the laundry room that was just off the kitchen and dropped the pile of clothes on the floor in front of the washing machine. We continued to talk, and I started to load the things in the washer, stopping to check pockets. I picked up a pair of khakis and pulled out one of the pockets. Two balled-up no-show socks tumbled out.

When I did the same to the other pocket a white crumbled ball of fabric popped out and landed on the floor.

"I recognize the socks," I said, picking them up and putting them off to the side to be included in a load of whites. "But what's this?" I leaned down to get a better look.

Dinah got up from the table and came next to me.

We both stared at the crumpled ball of fabric, and I got an ominous feeling.

"Why don't you pick it up?" she said, bending a little closer.

Why don't you pick it up?" I countered.

"It was in your pocket, so you should pick it up." She backed away and put her hands up.

"All right," I said finally and reached for it. I started to smooth it out, examining it as I did. There seemed to be a soft cotton center with a lot of lacy trim, but when I saw the red splotches on it, I dropped it like it was scalding.

"Is that blood?" I said, making a face.

Dinah bent over the half-crumpled ball. "There's this stuff, phena something or other, that can tell you if it is."

"That's great information, but unless you happen to have some in your purse, it's not much help," I said.

"Sorry, I'm fresh out," she said with a chuckle. "We could get a better look at it if it was completely flattened out."

"This must be what I picked up in Kevin's office." I explained how I'd seen something white under the desk and thought it was one of my no-show socks.

"Didn't you say you saw something white and lacy hanging off the drawer in Drew's office when we found him in the soup?" Dinah pointed at the lacy edge. "Maybe it was this."

"Omigod!" I shrieked. "You could be right." Then I thought for a second. "If it was, it wasn't the whole thing.

What I saw looked like a small part of something, as if it had caught on the drawer pull and ripped." I knelt next to the white ball. "Let me see if part of this is missing." I went to put my hand on it but pulled back. While I needed to spread it out, I didn't want to touch it anymore.

I got up and searched Samuel's room for something he had as a kid. Thank heavens Samuel believed in hanging on to his stuff. The pinchy-winchy was stuck in the corner of his closet next to some old robot toys. It was a plastic claw from some cartoon show that came in handy for reaching things on high shelves. It also was perfect for picking up things you didn't want to touch.

I grabbed an edge of the white ball of fabric with the pinchy-winchy and shook it until it opened enough to be recognizable.

"It's a hanky," Dinah said. She reached out to touch it and then reconsidered when her finger got near the red spots. "Though there doesn't seem to be much space for nose blowing."

I laid it on the kitchen counter. The center was small and appeared to be made of thin, white cotton. Most of the handkerchief was comprised of the lacy edging. I checked for missing pieces in the edging, but found it was intact.

"I guess that isn't what you saw."

"No, but I bet it's somehow connected. It seems too coincidental that there was a piece of something similar to it hanging off a drawer handle and this shows up under Mr. Ke—" I rolled my eyes. "Calling him Mr. Kevin sounds way too pretentious—under Kevin's desk."

Dinah agreed. We both studied the edging, and I said I thought it was done with crochet like the doilies on Adele's skirt.

"It certainly looks different than the things we've been making with yarn." Dinah took the pinchy-winchy and picked the hanky up by the corner, eyeing the filigree-like trim. "I can't even see the stitches."

I told her about the steel hooks and thin thread I'd bought when I'd gone shopping with CeeCee for the material for the shawls. When Dinah set the hanky back on the counter, I examined the cotton center where the red splotches were. That's I when I noticed there were some flecks of red stuff on the spots. "I don't think it's blood," I said, pointing. "The flecks look like tomato skin. I bet it's tomato bisque soup."

"Wow," Dinah said. "Do you know what that means?"

I didn't mean to, but I squealed, "Omigod!" again. I knew exactly what it meant. Both the hanky and whatever had gotten caught on the drawer handle had both been in Drew's office when he hit the soup. "It must be soup spatter," I said, feeling a shiver. "And since it ended up in Kevin's office, it kind of points the finger at him."

Dinah nodded yes, and I felt another shiver. "Maybe we should turn it in," she said.

"To who? Detective Heather? And how am I supposed to explain having it?"

"You have a point there," Dinah said, wincing. "She probably wouldn't take it well if she knew we sneaked into Kevin's office."

"I didn't mean to pick it up, but as long as I did, it's our clue. Though it might be better if we kept it on the down low." I stopped to think for a moment. "What if there's something else up in Kevin's office—like that piece I saw hanging on Drew's desk drawer?"

Dinah knew where I was headed. "We've got one good clue. That should be enough."

"But there could be more. We already know somebody in black slacks went up there, too. I'm going back there now before anybody else has a chance to look." Dinah said she saw my point and would go along. But then her cell phone rang. The babysitter had to leave. It looked like I was on my own.

I PARKED THE GREENMOBILE AT THE BOOKSTORE and walked over to the Cottage Shoppe. As I went inside, I noticed a contractor's truck parked out front. A man in jeans and a white tee shirt was walking around the dining room, holding a clipboard and a tape measure. I recognized the footwear from the day I'd been under the desk. It was interesting to see the rest of Mr. Work Boots. I did a double take when I got to his head. It was shaved bald. Was he the illusive bald shopper? I looked closer and realized the man with the Harrods bag had been considerably taller.

I glanced toward the stairway, but there was no way I could sneak up there right now. Kevin was fidgeting around in the dining room and would have a clear view of me on the stairs. Though the tables and chairs had been stacked against the wall, the bar was still functional. Kevin took the lid off a large pot sitting on some kind of warming device. The smell was delicious enough to make my mouth water. When he saw me he offered me a sample.

The man definitely had a way with soup, and the taste lived up to the smell. His samples were generous, too. None of those little cups they give you for water at the dentist. He used coffee cups and provided a spoon. It was some kind of vegetable stew, thick with mini ears of corn and mushrooms and every vegetable I could think of simmering in a flavorful broth. There were also thick slices of sourdough bread and a bowl of foil-wrapped butter pieces.

"We're doing mostly a to-go business now," he said. "But when we finish the expansion it will be very pleasant to eat here." He was all smiles now. I wondered what he'd fought with his brother about and thought of trying to ask him about it. But before I could come up with a strategy, he excused himself and went looking for Mr. Work Boots, who had disappeared into the kitchen. I considered making my run for upstairs then, but someone called to me from the living room area.

"Mrs. Pink, is there anything I can help you find?" Dorothy said. She didn't wait for an answer, instead launching into an explanation about how due to the remodel, the consignment items were being rearranged. I was surprised to see Dorothy wasn't alone and even more surprised when I realized who was with her. So, Trina had come back to work after all. Her dark red hair was done in a stiff style that didn't move as she bent to gather a creamy beige poncho off a chair and put it on the shelf of one of the three lawyers' bookcases with lighted interiors. These had been moved against the wall, apparently to be used as display cases.

All the living room furniture had been moved out except for one of the rockers in front of the fireplace.

Trina appeared very tense. She kept looking over her shoulder and dropping things. It was lucky she was moving unbreakable items. She dropped one scarf, then another. I went to help retrieve them, though not without feeling up the yarn. I recognized the even rows as knitting. Something about the color and style reminded me of the knitted small blanket I'd admired the other day, and I figured it was probably made by the same person. I looked at the tag thinking it might have the name of the artisan, but there was just a bar code.

Dorothy saw me staring at the black lines. "That was one of Mr. Drew's brilliant ideas. The way his aunt did things wasn't good enough for him. He didn't seem to care that she had run a successful business for years by keeping written records of who brought in stuff and how much it sold for. He wanted everything computerized and had begun transferring over to using bar codes to keep track of things." She glanced toward the torn-up dining room. Kevin was busy arranging the soup things. "That man is a soup maniac. Well, he finally is going to get his way."

On a hunch I asked her if that was what the two brothers fought about, and she nodded.

"Mr. Kevin wanted to make this place more restaurant and less consignment shop, but other than computerizing things, Mr. Drew didn't want to spend any money on the place."

"Was there any money to spend?" I asked.

Dorothy checked that no one was listening. "Sure. Mrs. Brooks owned the land and building. Do you have any idea what this lot on Ventura Boulevard is worth? I heard that the first thing the brothers did was take out a large loan on the place. Mr. Kevin wanted to use the money to make some changes to the place so the restaurant area would be bigger. I think Mr. Drew just wanted to pocket the money, even though he claimed to he was going to use it to create an Internet business. I mean, how much can a Web site cost?"

Two women came in and said they were looking for new baby gifts. All I needed was for Dorothy to get occupied helping them and I'd get my chance to run upstairs. Trina was no threat. She seemed lost in her own world and probably wouldn't have noticed me on the stairs if she was staring right at me. But instead of assisting the customers, Dorothy just pointed them to a box of things she was in the process of putting in the case. The women moved over and began to unfold blankets and tiny sweaters, discussing their merits among themselves.

Suddenly Trina flopped in the rocking chair with a loud sigh. "This isn't going to work," she lamented. "I keep seeing poor Mr. Drew with his head in the tomato soup." She started getting worked up just thinking about it, and all the upset led to a case of the hiccups, which she explained, between the clacky noises, was what happened when she got upset. Dorothy noticed the shoppers' uneasy reaction to Trina's outburst, and in an effort to save the sale finally walked over to help them.

Realizing this was my golden opportunity, I offered to get Trina some water. I didn't mention I planned to import it from the upstairs bathroom.

"Would you do that? I think it will help." She got through the first sentence hiccup free, but then every other word was cut in two as she gave directions about the temperature the water should be. I was in the entrance hall when she got to the part about wanting the water in a blue glass as it gave off the right kind of vibrations.

Since Dorothy was busy with the baby-gift hunters and Kevin was tied up in the kitchen with the contractor, I headed for the stairs. Now there was a chain across them with a sign that said "Employees Only." I had one foot over the chain when a voice startled me.

"What are you doing?"

I turned and saw it was Dorothy. Her expression had changed to a scowl. "Going past that chain is trespassing."

I muttered something about getting Trina a glass of water, as I tried to step back over the chain. Unfortunately, my foot caught on it and I fell on my butt with a loud thud. I had a bad feeling the loudness of the noise was directly proportional to the size of my butt, but this was hardly the time to worry about that.

Kevin and Mr. Work Boots responded to the noise, and when they saw me on the floor with my foot caught in the chain, Mr. Work Boots untangled me and Kevin helped me up. His usual pleasant demeanor had gone dark. He pointed at the sign.

"Can't you read?" Then he seemed to catch himself and

his tone softened. "I'm sorry, but the upstairs is off-limits for customers. We've had some problems with people wandering up there."

I really wanted to ask him for more details, like was the person he saw before with the black slacks a woman or man? As if there was any chance he would answer. Instead I just gave him the Trina hiccup story. "And with all your remodeling, I didn't know if there was any place to get water down here," I said, wearing my best innocent expression.

As I got up, Trina came in. To my relief, she still had the hiccups, which gave credibility to my story about looking for a glass of water. Then Mr. Work Boots whispered something to Kevin, after which he became very solicitous, wanting to make sure I wasn't hurt. I assumed Mr. Work Boots had brought up the possibility of a lawsuit. I assured Kevin the only thing injured was my pride. After that I had only one option: leave. It looked as though my first chance at snooping was going to be my only chance. At least I had the hanky. Now to find out what it meant.

Chapter 14

As soon as I got back to the bookstore, I set up for Romance Night and then headed for home. I called Dinah on my cell as I drove.

"It's me," I said when she answered the phone. "There's good news and bad news."

There was a pause before she responded. "Could you hang on a second?" I heard her tell someone to go talk to their father. There was a kid's voice and then a male voice. The voices got softer, and I assumed Dinah was taking the cordless into another room.

"Sorry," Dinah said softly. "Jeremy finally got back, and I was trying to impress upon him that Ashley-Angela and E. Conner are his kids and his responsibility. It's not going well."

In the background I heard the plaintive voices of both kids now wanting something from Dinah. Her voice went away from the phone, but I still could hear her as she sent them back to their father. Dinah rejoined our conversation.

"That man is impossible. And no matter what I say to the kids about going to their father for stuff, they keep coming to me." Dinah let out a loud, frustrated sigh.

"Okay, what's the bad news?" she asked. It was our little game. Whenever we did the good-news-bad-news thing, we always went for the bad news first to get it out of the way.

I told her I had gotten caught before I could get upstairs at the Cottage Shoppe.

"And the good news?"

"I talked my way out of it, and I got some information that makes somebody besides Sheila look guilty."

"Okay, spill," she said. "Anything to get my mind off what's going on here."

I repeated what Dorothy had said about the money the brothers had borrowed on the building and how their arguments were over their two different plans for the store.

"People have killed for less," Dinah said. "It sounds like the only way Kevin was going to get his soup emporium was if his brother was out of the way. Kevin must have brought the tomato bisque up to him. Maybe Drew's head being in the soup was more than a coincidence; maybe it was his attempt at poetic irony. Drew wouldn't agree to the soup, and so it became the cause of his death."

"But I'm not sure how the hanky fits in," I said, cradling the phone against my shoulder as I searched my purse for the house keys. I crossed my yard and opened the back door. Cosmo flew out and started running around the trees. Blondie did a little happy-to-see-me dance and then went out after Cosmo. He was certainly bringing her out of her shell.

"It might help if we knew something about the hanky. Like you said, it doesn't look like it was meant for nose blowing," I said.

Dinah responded with a few noncommittal uh-huhs, and

I heard Jeremy's voice in the background. At least he had finally shown up, but whatever he was saying inflamed her because even with her mouth away from the phone, I could tell she was yelling and heard her quite clearly tell him he better not go out the door or else. It was obvious our conversation was over. I said something about realizing it wasn't a good time to talk, and as I was saying good-bye, she clicked off. I didn't take it as being hung up on. Rather, she was too distracted to talk.

I stuck my cell into my purse and as I was setting down my things noticed the light was flashing on my house phone, which meant messages. Along with an offer of a discount on home repairs and a query from a Realtor interested in listing my house, there was a message from Patricia Bradford. Even on the machine her voice sounded cloying as she asked me to call her the moment I got home. She must want something, I thought, punching in her number.

Patricia didn't have a machine. She had a maid. Before I finished explaining who I was, Patricia came on the phone. She seemed very happy to talk to me. She must want something big.

"We're having some people in for cocktails. It's a little get-together for some of Benjamin's campaign people," she gushed, "and I was hoping you could drop by." She didn't wait for a reply. "Before you worked at the bookstore, didn't you do something in publicity? I was just telling Benjamin you'd be a real asset to our team."

I hesitated. I was flattered by what she'd just said, but I didn't completely trust her. Up until now, Patricia had treated me like a fixture. I was just the person at the bookstore who set up chairs for her demonstration and book signing and was part of the crochet group. "When is it?"

"Now. I mean, sixish. It's business casual. I'd really like you to come." She seemed flummoxed. "Sorry for the late invite. I thought I sent you an invitation, but I found it stuck in my purse."

I didn't buy that story for a second, and even though I was curious about what she wanted from me, I decided to decline since Romance Night started at eight. She read my silence and tried to win me over by reeling off the names of all the people who were going to be there. They were indeed the movers and shakers of Tarzana, and though I didn't actually know any of them, I recognized most of the names, until she got to Byron Nederman.

"Who's he?" I asked. She had said his name in such a glowing tone, I was curious.

"He shares Benjamin's vision for things, and he's been very, very generous. We're glad to have him on the team. I'm surprised you don't know him. He's tall and quite good-looking. I wish Benjamin would ask him where he gets his suits. They always hang so perfectly. But I'm not so sure about the bald look. I know it's in now, but personally I think it makes him look like Mr. Clean."

She kept rambling, but my mind was clicking. This Byron was tall, a good dresser and bald. Could he be the elusive man I'd seen at the Cottage Shoppe?

"Does he shop at Harrods? I think he's just the man I'm looking for," I said quickly, then held my breath waiting for her answer.

As soon as I heard her tone, I realized she'd misunderstood my interest.

"Molly, I know you're single now and probably looking for a new husband. I'm sorry to dash your hopes, but Byron is gay."

"But he's coming to your party," I said, trying to sound casual.

"Yes, Molly, I already said he was. You did hear what I said about him," Patricia cautioned.

"Of course, Patricia," I said, then I accepted her invitation on the chance he was the bald man I was looking for.

She'd said it was business casual. I guessed that was somewhere between the khaki pants and shirts I wore to work and black tie. In the back of my closet was a stash of clothes left over from the business parties I used to attend with Charlie. I found the classic black linen dress I'd always paired with a red blazer. I debated between black heels and ballet flats. The heels won, though I knew my feet would complain.

After a quick shower, a blob of hair gel and some time with a hair dryer, I slipped into the dress and jacket and put on more makeup than I had worn in a long time. The shoes were last along with a pair of subdued gold hoop earrings. I almost jumped when I caught sight of my image in the mirror. Clothes definitely do make the person. I looked formidable and about ten years older.

I saw Patricia's big white house almost every time I went out. It was perched on top of one of the ridges that ran south of Ventura Boulevard and was visible from all different angles. But I had no idea how to get on the street that led up to it. I went all the way to Corbin Avenue and back without figuring out the way in. I had to go home and check my street guide, and even then it was confusing to get through the maze of streets.

I whispered a wow as I finally pulled into the circular driveway that ran in front of the house. Of course there was valet parking. It seemed silly since the whole street was empty, but this was about image not reality. No wonder Patricia was hanging on to Benjamin for dear life. After her struggle as a single parent, she'd struck gold. I wasn't sure where Benjamin's money came from, just that his family *was* Bradford Industries.

A red-vested man opened my car door. He was discreet, but I did notice a slight look of disdain.

A uniformed maid answered the door and ushered me through the entrance hall into the living room, which had a panoramic view of the west San Fernando Valley.

I had heard of people's houses so clean you could eat off the floor, but this was the first one I had seen where you could do surgery. There wasn't a magazine out of place or a smudge on the glass coffee table. Every pillow on the cream-colored couch was perfectly plumped, and even with the twenty-five or so guests there wasn't a stray cocktail napkin or empty glass sitting anywhere. I immediately started looking for my bald guy. But everyone I saw had hair.

A black-haired man set down a martini glass. Almost before it touched the table, a waiter appeared and removed it. A moment later, the same waiter appeared with a tray of drinks and offered me one. They were classic gin martinis with large green olives. I loved the smell of gin but was always disappointed by the taste. I took one of the offered wide-rimmed cocktail glasses, but knew I'd probably not get past a few sips. Besides, I wanted a clear head.

Thanks to *The Average Joe's Guide to Criminal Investigation*, I'd learned to check out every place I went to as though it were a crime scene. Patricia had definitely hired an interior decorator. Everything worked too perfectly. Nobody bought a painting of sunflowers, throw pillows and a vase in such perfectly blending shades of golden yellow by chance.

Though I did like the eclectic mix of furniture. There were some old, unusual pieces thrown in with the contemporary couch and chairs. I particularly liked the throne-shaped green velvet Victorian chair. Working as a table, an antique trunk sat next to an easy chair and made the room more interesting.

I surveyed the crowd for Byron Nederman and came up empty again. This time, though, I noted that everyone in the crowd had a similar look. The men all had short hair and wore well-tailored suits, and the women had over-styled hair, outfits that matched too well, lots of jewelry and red lipstick. They seemed older than me but probably weren't. It was all about the clothes. These weren't a bunch of campaign volunteers who stuffed envelopes or knocked on doors.

Patricia appeared from the center of the crowd and came over and greeted me as though I were visiting royalty.

"Benjamin, honey, look who's here." She slipped her arm around my shoulder and presented me to the other guests. "Everybody, this is Molly Pink. She's the manager of Shedd & Royal Books and More and lead crocheter in that fabulous charity group I joined."

Manager? Lead crocheter? Boy, was she laying it on thick. Adele would be green with envy and probably dressed to match. It was pretty obvious why I got the boost in status as she introduced the others. They were all CEOs and business owners, and giving me a title made me seem like I fit in. But the big question was why?

I tried to pull Patricia aside and ask her about Byron Nederman, but she was already stepping away.

"Just mingle for a few minutes," Patricia said as she made her way to a couple who had just arrived. "Benjamin and I have something we want to talk to you about later."

I took an occasional sip of the martini, nibbled on baked brie and joined a small group standing by the window. I listened for a few minutes and then added something to the conversation. I had learned how to make small talk from the years of going to countless charity affairs, award shows and social evenings where I'd often known no one. Charlie always had clients or potential clients he wanted to talk to at such events. That's the way it was when you were in public relations. You worked the room.

"Patricia and Benjamin have the *look*," the small dark-haired owner of a Ford agency confided in me. "City council is only to get his feet wet. Then who knows? Maybe the White House."

He seemed like the type who had no sense of humor, so I didn't bother pointing out they were already in a white house. But he was right. They did have that look. Old enough to have some character in their faces, but young enough to appear vital and energetic. Patricia had latched onto a comet.

I asked him if he knew Byron Nederman.

"Of course. *Everyone* knows Byron," the man said. I asked if he had seen him, but the Ford agency owner shook his head, though he assured me he'd heard Byron was coming for sure. Then he asked how I knew Byron. I said I'd met him at a sale at Harrods. The Ford guy gave me an odd look and stepped away.

I ditched the rest of my martini only to have the glass whisked away before it even touched the table. I was beginning to get impatient both for the arrival of Byron Nederman and for an answer as to why Patricia was laying it on so thick, and I needed to use the restroom.

Certainly I could do that. I walked back toward the entrance hall, looking for a powder room. I opened a few doors and found closets and noticed a hallway going in the other direction. More doors, and finally one with the right stuff. When I came out I was disoriented. It was that big of a house. Instead of going back toward the living room, I must have walked the wrong way and ended up in the Patricia's Hints room. I knew that's what it was because a cute wooden sign on the door said so.

I was amazed. Not only did Patricia never have a hair out of place, but apparently she also never had any stuff out of place, either. There were shelves filled with neatly labeled boxes and lots of books—some on cleaning formulas and some old ones with illegible spines. She had a testing table, a computer and lots of photos. Boxes of her new books were neatly stacked against the wall. She had a section set aside for yarn arts, as the label read. I noticed the tote bag I'd seen earlier. Next to it was the pattern for it.

My crochet room had started out neatly organized, but with a little time chaos had ensued. I'd start working on something, the phone would ring and I'd leave it on the couch. Then there were the bags of yarn I bought and needed to organize. I had discovered it was fast and easy to buy yarn, but making something was another story.

Patricia clearly was more disciplined. On one shelf she had her shawl project and next to it a clear plastic bag with a some yarn, directions and needles. Adele would have a fit. One of our own still hanging on to knitting. There was also a small wooden chest on the shelf. I slid open one of the drawers and noticed a selection of steel hooks.

"Patricia wondered what happened to you," a male voice said behind me. I flinched in surprise and a little embarrassment. I hadn't meant to snoop; I'd just gotten carried away. I certainly hadn't intended to get caught, especially not by Benjamin.

"I was looking for the powder room and I made a wrong turn." I raved on about the room to try to cover my nosiness. "Patricia is a wizard," I said, gesturing toward all her hints stuff.

Benjamin nodded, but his eyes weren't crinkly and friendly. He was covering it pretty well, but he seemed irritated. "Patricia was looking for you. We want to ask you about something."

I felt nervous and flustered and started to babble. "Is it a good something or a bad something?" I asked, realizing as

I did that I sounded pretty stupid. "Of course, it must be a good something."

I grabbed a photo sitting on the desk. "Are these Kimmee and Demetrius?" I asked. Even if they were his stepchildren, talking about kids always seemed to smooth everything over. They were in Old West outfits, standing next to a stagecoach. "This must be from the PTA carnival the year she did the old-fashioned pictures." I was really rambling now. "It was probably before you knew her. You should have seen all the costumes she brought."

He nodded, and I kept going on about how they'd grown, how fast kids grew, how my sons had just been babies what seemed like five minutes ago and now they were men and so on. He stood in the doorway until I walked out, and then he followed me back to the living room.

"Here she is, honey. I found her admiring your hints room." If he was annoyed, any trace of it had disappeared from his voice. A number of the guests had already left, and I began to wonder if the tall, bald Byron was really going to show. Patricia took me off into a corner. The *we* had turned into her talking to me.

She apologized for keeping me waiting and explained that the couple who had arrived were generous contributors. "Let me get to the point," she began. "We're collecting people now. When Benjamin gets elected we're going to need a much bigger team, and the people who show themselves to be our friends now are going to be the ones we want on it." She leveled her gaze at me. "I'm sure you realize this council seat is just a stepping stone to bigger things."

"I've been getting that impression." I was talking to her but checking the crowd for Mr. Nederman.

"I told Benjamin how underused you are at the bookstore. I mean, with your public relations background, you could be invaluable to us."

Okay, so she was getting to me. Who doesn't like to be told how great and underappreciated they are? She had all my attention now, and for a second I forgot that what I was really after was getting a chance to question the illusive bald guy.

I smiled and listened attentively while she rambled on about what an exciting future lay ahead for the team. Then she leaned in toward me, a sure sign she was getting to the important part.

"Of course, all of that depends on Benjamin getting elected. That's our job right now, isn't it?" She nodded, and I nodded with her. "I need your help on a few little things."

Someone came into the room and called good-bye to her, and she smiled and waved in response. Her face grew serious as she turned her attention back to me.

"We need to change the date of the event."

"Event?" I said, wondering if I'd missed something.

"My book signing for *Patricia's Perfect Hints*, Volume 4. Benjamin's campaign manager suggested moving it up."

I shrugged and said I didn't think it would be a problem. If need be, I'd switch somebody else. Before I could ask her if she had a preferred date, she handed me a piece of paper with a date on it, so I'd be sure to get it right. Okay. Not a surprise since Patricia was such a micromanager.

"And there's something more. I'd like to incorporate Benjamin into the program. Instead of taking someone from the crowd, I'd like to use him for the demonstration."

Again, I told her it was no problem. If Benjamin wanted to be the one she poured red wine on, far be it from me to stand in his way. I started to move away. "At the next crochet meeting, I'll confirm the date."

Patricia put her hand on my arm, stopping my retreat. "There's one more thing. You'd don't mind if we bring along someone to videotape it, do you?"

Whoa. Now I got it. Patricia was good. She had played me like a cello. First, the whole thing about making me sound like I ran the bookstore and raving on about my underappreciated skills and hinting that if I was a good soldier, I'd end up an important part of the team. Then getting me to keep saying yes to little things until she got to what she really wanted.

"That might be a problem. You should really talk to Mrs. Shedd about it," I said.

"You are in charge of events, aren't you? Besides, other people have videotaped their book signings and demonstrations." When I gave her a blank look, she helped my memory. "Don't you remember that Brenda Rochner? She's the author of *The Bagel Solution*. She had both her uncle and her brother there with cameras."

It was coming back to me now. "That's right. Her uncle almost got burned when he went in for a close-up of Brenda dropping the dough circles in the vat of boiling water."

"If Brenda could do it, why can't I?"

"They just showed up with video cameras," I said, realizing Patricia was backing me into a corner.

"So, you're going to penalize me for asking first?" she said with her hand still on my arm.

She had me. What could I say? As soon as I agreed, her face brightened and she made an okay sign with her fingers. When I turned, Benjamin was standing in the doorway.

The next thing I knew, she'd shoved a piece of paper in front of me. I tried to read it, but she kept moving it around so it jiggled and the words were just black squiggles.

"It's nothing important. It just says you said it was okay. Benjamin is such a stickler about doing things one hundred percent right." She handed me a pen and pointed to a line on the bottom. I scribbled my name and she pulled it away.

"Don't I get a copy?" I asked, but Patricia had already handed it off to Benjamin, who promptly disappeared.

"Molly, you're a dear. We really mean it about you being part of the team." She hugged me and kissed the air next to my cheek. "I really appreciate how you came at the last minute, but I don't want to keep you from whatever important thing you tore yourself away from to come."

I was moving before I realized it. Patricia had her arm linked with mine, and we were heading toward the door. She had almost ushered me outside when I remembered I'd had an agenda, too. I didn't have time for the soft-soap technique and had to get right to the point.

"But I didn't meet Byron Nederman yet."

Patricia's expression darkened, and she talked under her breath. "Molly, I told you he's gay. Go to some bar if you're looking to pick up men." Someone came up behind her and she did a complete about-face in the expression department as her eyes lit up with a warm smile. "I'm so glad you finally made it, Byron. We were just talking about you. All good things. Go on in and have a martini. I'll be with you in a minute."

She held tightly onto me as we advanced toward the door. I turned, but all I could see was Byron's back as he walked across the room. He certainly looked like the man I'd seen at the Cottage Shoppe.

Omigod, this was my chance. I pulled away from Patricia's grasp and moved toward him. She was not going to keep me from having my little chat with Byron. As I approached him, I racked my memory for what *The Average Joe's Guide* suggested about questioning someone when you might only have a minute or two. There was definitely something about getting right to the point.

I was going to follow the book's advice, so touched his arm to get his attention. "Byron, it's so good to see you again," I said. "I saw you at the Cottage Shoppe the day Drew Brooks was murdered. I guess you didn't see me. It was just horrible what happened. So, how did you know Drew Brooks? Were you, like, dating?" The man had turned completely toward me by now and was looking at me as though I were totally out of my mind. As I took in his features, I suddenly had a bad feeling—a really bad feeling. So, maybe he wasn't the bald man I was looking for after all.

It got worse when I heard some woman introduce herself as his girlfriend.

Oops!

CHAPTER 15

WHEN I GOT HOME I TRIED TO DISTRACT MY thoughts from the unfortunate incident with Byron Nederman by cooking a quick dinner. Besides, I was still hungry; Patricia's appetizers were really appeteasers, being more about looks than substance. The bits of brie and tiny mushroom puffs were just enough to remind me I'd skipped lunch. And I still had Romance Night at the bookstore to deal with.

I changed into the ballet flats, went into the kitchen and wrapped an apron around the black linen dress. I put some water on to boil for pasta and swirled some olive oil and garlic in a frying pan over a low fire. I took out a bag of cut-up vegetables and a jar of sun-dried tomatoes while I called Dinah to give her an update. I hoped this time she could talk. It turned out she knew Byron Nederman or at least who he was. It seemed everybody knew him but me.

"He owns a chain of health clubs, including the one where Sheila works," Dinah said.

"Great," I said with a groan, making a mental note never ever to run into him again. "As I was leaving I heard Patricia making excuses for me. Something about my being distraught because I'd been recently widowed. I think her whole spiel about being part of the team might be bogus."

"Not necessarily. You do have publicity experience. He's probably going to win, anyway. I think the only other person running is the guy whose wife owns Caitlin's Cupcakes."

Dinah was making me feel better. But just when I thought I had my friend back I heard the sounds of crying on her end and Jeremy's agitated voice.

"E. Conner just poured grape jelly all over the floor. Got to go." As she clicked off, I heard her mutter something about having to get out of there.

As I put the phone back in the charger, a door down the hall opened and Morgan drifted out of her room. She laid some crochet work on the table to show me what she'd created. She had only done the beginning of a shawl, but it was perfect. Not a surprise as I was getting the feeling she demanded perfection from herself. I complimented her on it and dropped some shredded carrots, broccoli florets and sun-dried tomatoes into the olive oil and garlic.

"Want to join me for dinner? I always make too much." I took out a package of angel-hair pasta and dropped it in the boiling water.

She hesitated. I knew the smell had gotten to her. But she shook her head.

"I'm being supervigilant about my diet." She went to the freezer, took out a frozen diet dinner and put it in the microwave. "But we can still eat together. I'll even set the table."

"You know, if you don't eat enough you won't have the energy to give the auditions your all." Then I backtracked and apologized for minding her business.

Morgan smiled. "I kind of like it. My mother is so

wrapped up in her own life she never pays any attention to what I do." She put plates and silverware on the kitchen's built-in table. She was dressed in warm-up pants and a tiny tee shirt. I still didn't know where she was going to find that five pounds she wanted to lose.

But I liked having her around, too. It was almost like having a daughter.

I strained the pasta and mixed it with the sauteed vegetables, then made myself a plate. When I joined her at the table, she couldn't seem to keep her eyes off my dinner, which seemed a lot more appealing than her reduced-calorie macaroni and no-fat cheese with a side of green beans. If I'd had just a little longer, I bet she would have weakened and had some of mine.

As we ate I told her about my debacle at Patricia's party. "My only hope is that I never meet him again." By now I could see the humor in it. Morgan laughed at the story—something I hadn't seen her do before. The way her face brightened, it really was like the sun coming out on a cloudy day.

"How's it going with your murder investigation?" she asked.

"Are you joking?" I asked, checking her expression, which was completely serious now.

"No," she answered. "Why would I do that?"

I went down the list of people who either were telling me to stay out of it, like Barry, or were afraid I'd do something to embarrass them, like Peter or Mrs. Shedd, or who were just hoping I'd do something to give them a reason to arrest me, like Detective Heather. Samuel, I realized, was only worried I might get hurt.

I couldn't believe what she did next. She came around the table and hugged me. "Molly, I think what you're doing is wonderful. You're trying to help a friend."

Fueled by Morgan's support, I told her what I knew and mostly what I still didn't know about Drew's murder. "His brother Kevin seems to have gained the most from Drew's death. Now the whole place is his, and he certainly didn't waste any time starting to remodel. Kevin certainly had the opportunity. I wasn't paying any attention to his whereabouts before the murder. He could have hit Drew, and when he heard Trina coming, stepped into his own office."

I looked up as if a thunderbolt had just hit me. "That's how the hanky ended up under his desk!"

Morgan's confused expression made me realize she didn't know what I was talking about. I had put the hanky in a plastic bag for safekeeping and then put the bag between some cookbooks to flatten the handkerchief out. I pulled the bag out from the kitchen shelf to show her. She wrinkled her nose when she saw the red spots, so I quickly explained my soup theory. She became more animated than I'd ever seen her before, though I was disturbed to notice she'd barely touched her dinner.

"Then you think Kevin Brooks did it for sure?" Morgan's hazel eyes were keen with interest.

"He certainly could have. But I'd still like to talk to the bald guy—the right bald guy. I'd like to know what he was so angry about and why he wasn't anywhere to be found when the police showed up."

Morgan helped me load the dishwasher when we'd finished eating. Then she said she was off to an evening dance class. No matter how I tried to tell her that too much of a good thing like exercise could be bad and suggested instead an evening of romance at the bookstore, she wouldn't budge.

Since Barry hadn't come by, I assumed he was tied up with work so I let Cosmo and Blondie in the yard and fed them. Then I slipped back into my heels and headed for Romance Night.

All was still quiet at Shedd & Royal. I was glad I'd already done all the prep work. Since we always got an extra large turnout, I had put out all the chairs. The black dress, red jacket and heels I was wearing were more formal than what I usually wore for Romance Night and certainly not good for moving stacks of chairs. Tonight was supposed to be extra special. Not only did we have the author of *Gina and Captain Blackhart*, but the cover model was coming as well. I'd seen the book cover, and although bulging biceps and shirts ripped open to expose six-pack abs weren't my thing, the long, flowing black hair and shimmering dark eyes definitely made an impression.

Bob the barista had made plenty of scones, and I brought out the special blend of tea and spices we called Romance in the Night. Our romance authors liked to read an excerpt, and they usually chose something really sexy, which tended to inflame the crowd's appetite. We always sold out of whatever snacks we had.

As people began to trickle in, I noticed right away the crowd was even bigger than usual. From the buzz of conversation, I gathered it had a lot to do with the appearance of "Captain Blackhart." No one was hanging around not wanting to be the first to sit down. The early comers went right for the seats in the middle of the front row. Everyone dressed up a little more for Romance Night, but tonight they'd gone over the top. I'd never seen so much cleavage. They were all ages, from teens on up to granny types.

Dorothy and Trina came in and sat in the third row. I walked over and greeted the two saleswomen from the Cottage Shoppe. Something occurred to me from *The Average Joe's Guide to Criminal Investigation*. There was a whole section about interviewing people but making it seem like informal conversation. Maybe I could find out something about the handkerchief. But, there wasn't any way I could casually ask what Kevin might be doing with a lacy hanky. The only thing I could come up with was to say I was looking to purchase such an item and ask if the store had any.

However, Dorothy and Tina seemed more interested in admiring the covers of their copies of *Gina and Captain Blackhart.*

"Lucky we snatched our copies early," Dorothy said, pointing at the end cap display of the books. The crowd usually waited until the end of the program to decide if they wanted a book. Tonight they were more concerned with making sure they got one. The display was already close to empty.

"We have more in the back," I said. "But back to that hanky I'm looking for . . ." I let my voice trail off, hoping one of them would jump in.

"I don't think we've carried anything like that for a long time," Trina said.

Dorothy thought for a moment. "Ramona Brooks liked that sort of thing. Someone brought in some family heirlooms, but that's the last time we had anything like what you described. Sorry."

Even *The Average Joe's Guide* said the conversation technique didn't always work. Besides, I suddenly had something more immediate to deal with.

Adele chose that moment to make her entrance. Everybody turned as she sashayed toward me. In an effort to look like some pirate princess, she wore a full black skirt, part of which she'd caught in her belt, revealing far more thigh than anyone wanted to see. This was topped off with an off-the-shoulder peasant blouse. She had layered on a week's worth of makeup, giant gold hoop earrings and a bandana tied around her head. The final touches were a big eyebrow-pencil-induced beauty mark and a toe ring on her bare feet. And she was acting as if nothing was strange.

She draped herself across the table set up in the front and toyed with the stack of books. Was it my imagination or did she run her fingers across the lower lip of the picture of Capain Blackhart?

"Pink, since you're helping me out with the horror guy, I thought it only fair I help you out with tonight's program. Besides," she said, looking me up and down, "I'm dressed better and I talk his language." She said the last part in her impression of a sexy growl. Being a woman, I guessed I was not a fair judge, but the voice thing didn't work for me. As for the clothing issue, that didn't work for me, either. My attire was businesslike, while she looked like she was on her way to a costume party. However, I had to admit, it was a crowd pleaser. People were even coming up to her to have their pictures taken with her. I heard some comments about the fun atmosphere. Maybe it was, but I was drawing the line at starting to wear costumes for book signings.

And I wasn't helping Adele with the horror guy, as she called him. I was handling Milton Mindell's extravaganza; she was the one doing the helping. I certainly didn't need her assistance with Romance Night, but she had gone to a lot of trouble with the outfit and it seemed important to her. I shrugged to myself. Why not?

More people had come in, and almost all the chairs were taken. From the buzz of conversation I picked up a comment here and there about the cover model. Kat Wylde, the author, certainly knew what she was doing including him in her presentation. I'd never seen such a big turnout, nor felt such a high level of excitement.

I saw Rayaad waving at me. The cashier was holding the phone and pointing at me and then at it—sign language that there was a call for me. I had a good view of the area right in front of the door as I took the phone and said hello.

"Molly," Dinah said in a whisper so low I could barely

hear her. I held the ear piece closer, trying to hear her while I looked out the window.

"Is something wrong?" I asked, surprised to get a call from her at the store. "Why are you whispering?"

"I'm on my cell at the movies," she said a little louder. I could hear swelling music in the background along with someone trying to shush her. Meanwhile I watched Kat Wylde get out of her Honda. The lights from the walkway spread out into the parking lot, making it easy to see her dusty rose–colored pantsuit. A man climbed out of a Ford Explorer, and by the way he was tugging at his black leather pants, I guessed he had a wedgy. There was no mistaking who he was. I recognized the flowing mane of raven black hair and the unbuttoned billowy white shirt from the cover of her book. All our signage referred to him as Captain Blackhart, and I realized I didn't know his real name.

Kat marched over to him, and they fell into immediate discussion. Sparks were definitely flying between them, but not the hot, passionate kind. Their body language said they were arguing, and it continued as they approached the door.

"Molly, are you still there?" Dinah said.

I apologized and started to explain I sensed a crisis about to happen, but Dinah interrupted me.

"He's here," she said.

"Who's there?"

"The bald guy. The one who had the Harrods bag. He's sitting in front of me with some woman."

"Are you sure? Tarzana seems to awash in bald heads," I said, forgetting my crisis couple for a second.

"I'm sure it's him."

"Did you get his name?"

"You're kidding, right?" she said. "What should I do?"

That was a good question and I didn't have an answer. The author and cover model had moved their argument inside. It was not good for business and I had to deal with it immediately. I told Dinah to keep an eye on the bald guy and I'd get there as soon as possible, then hung up.

Moving briskly, I stepped between Kat and Captain Blackhart and introduced myself, hoping to defuse their argument, but instead I became the referee.

"Would you tell her that I am not just a good-looking face and well-developed muscles," he said. "My understanding was that I was going to get a chance to read some of my poetry."

"And would you tell him that he is supposed to behave like the character in the book."

I had only read selections, but it was enough to know Captain Blackhart was an alpha male, and more interested in being a swashbuckling pirate than settling down. The women in the book were breathless about him, despite his dark moods and who-cares-about-you kind of attitude. He was definitely not a poetry-writer type.

"He's just supposed to read a selection from the book and maybe glower a few times and let the women take pictures with him. And that's it," Kat said.

Hoping to appease Captain Blackhart, I asked him for his real name, which was Eduardo Linnares. I persuaded Eduardo that if he agreed to read a selection from Kat's book and do the photo thing tonight, he could come back and read his poetry another time. I said he'd be guaranteed a spot on Poetry Night. Up until that moment we hadn't actually had a Poetry Night, but it sounded like a good idea.

Then I brought Kat and Eduardo up to the front of the crowd and introduced them, and they took over from there. I had to hand it to Kat; the idea of having him read was brilliant. The book started out as the pirate's diary, and Eduardo's deep voice was perfect for the copy. It was all about being at sea looking for some ships to rob and some women to have his way with. I thought everything was going fine until Eduardo stopped reading and looked out at the crowd. "I don't know why you want to read about a guy like this. He's a jerk."

Kat put her hands over her eyes, and the whole group seemed to suck in their collective breaths in shock. When she recovered, Kat lunged for him. I blocked her, shut the book and announced we'd get right to the signing and anyone who wished to could take a photo with Eduardo. And by the way, there were complimentary scones and tea. That did the trick; the crowd rose from their seats and lined up.

I had discovered that unexpected turns of events and even catastrophes could actually help book sales, and this night was no different. We not only sold out of *Gina and Captain Blackhart*, including the copies in the back, but also had to take orders. We also sold a ton of Kat Wylde's backlist and a lot of books with Eduardo on the cover.

Adele handled the photo line and tried to get in as many of the pictures as she could. Everyone seemed to want a picture of Eduardo kissing them, and he was very obliging. By the time he was done, his poor lips must have been chapped.

When I left the store, the crowd had dispersed and Eduardo was in conversation with Adele. I overheard him say something about how hard it was being a cover model and her saying she understood, but I didn't listen more because I wanted to get to the movie theater to see Dinah and the bald man.

The theater was just down the street. It was a small art theater with three screens that had survived despite the push for fancy stadium seating and numbers of screens running into the double digits. The woman in the box office was just closing when I rushed up, and it was a struggle to get her to sell me a ticket. She must have said six times that the movie was in its last half hour, and there wasn't a later show, and I should go to their sister theater in the city because it still had another showing. She gave me a funny look when I said all six times that I didn't care. Finally, I told her I was meeting somebody and that seemed to satisfy her enough to sell me the ticket.

When I walked in the theater, there was a night scene going on and I couldn't see anything. I hung at the back until it faded into morning and illuminated the screen enough for me to count the rows to find Dinah. It was lucky she had given me directions to find her because from here all I could see was the back of heads.

I heard muttering and groans as I climbed over feet to get to Dinah, who was sitting in the exact middle of the row. As I slid into the adjacent seat, she pointed to the row in front of her. Sure enough, I could see the on-screen sunrise reflected on one of the heads. The woman with him was shorter and had some kind of scarf covering her hair. Dinah offered to share the last of her popcorn, but I was more interested in trying to see his face. I wondered whether he was really the guy I was looking for—perhaps Dinah had just overreacted to the first bald head she'd encountered. The movie went to an underwater scene, making it too dark for me to make out any of his features.

A few short scenes later, the movie ended. Most of the crowd started to leave, but the pair in front of us just sat there as the credits rolled. Apparently they were some kind of film buffs or knew somebody on the crew because they sat through everything from the director and main cast list to the assistant to the transportation captain. We stayed there with them.

When the lights came up, the woman stretched and they got up to leave. The bald guy took her hand, and they walked out of the theater without noticing we were mirroring their steps. I finally got a good view of his face and squeezed Dinah's arm.

"It's him. It's really him," I said in an excited whisper. When I checked out the woman's face, I realized I'd seen her before, but I couldn't place her. That happened to me all of the time; usually they turned out to be customers of the bookstore.

We followed them all the way out to the parking lot, and as soon as they climbed in their big white Lexus, we rushed toward Dinah's car.

"Now what?" Dinah said as she put the car in drive.

"We follow them home," I said.

"And then?"

"I'm still thinking," I answered finally.

Chapter 16

"What do I do now?" Dinah squealed as we trailed them down Ventura Boulevard. The Lexus had its turn signal on.

"We follow them," I said, pointing toward their destination.

"I guess they got hungry," Dinah said as she pulled behind them in the In-N-Out Burger drive-thru line. Ahead they were already ordering, and a distorted voiced repeated back their order loud enough that we could hear.

"Does she really think a diet soda is going to make the burger and fries a lo-cal meal?" I said as they confirmed the order and pulled forward.

"Hmm, a cheeseburger sounds good," Dinah said, eyeing the menu.

I was glad we were in Dinah's car. It was a silver Nissan. I didn't know the model name, just that it blended in with all the other silver compacts on the road, unlike the greenmobile, which never blended in anywhere. We pulled up to the order spot. Dinah decided against the burger; we ordered two coffees, no cream.

They got their food and pulled back onto the main street. We barely stopped long enough to grab our coffees and toss some money at the clerk before zooming after them.

The street was pleasantly empty, which was another of the positive points of the Valley. By late evening, traffic was light on even the major streets. We stayed several car lengths behind them, though I don't think they had any hint they were being followed. I saw the turn signal go on as they approached Vanalden and nudged Dinah to do the same.

The road stayed level for a while, but then as it twisted around began to go uphill. This area of Tarzana was above where I lived. A whole development of houses had been built on pads on the side of the Santa Monica Mountains. Beyond the houses the land was open and belonged to the Santa Monica Mountains Conservancy. When the boys were small, we used to hike along dirt Mullholland and on some of the trails. It always amazed me how we could seemingly be in the middle of wilderness but still just a five-minute drive to Starbucks.

Our couple turned off the main street and we followed. I was a little worried they'd notice us since there was virtually nobody else on the road, so I told Dinah to douse the headlights. I was glad they knew where they were going because I was lost after the second turn. We passed through a maze of streets until I saw a garage door opening up ahead and told Dinah to pull over.

As soon as the Lexus went in and the door lowered, Dinah eased the car forward up the hilly street until we were directly across from the house. Ahead the street ended in a cul-de-sac. I realized that while we were driving I should have been thinking about what we were going to do once we got here because now that we were in front of their house, I had no idea what to do.

"I guess maybe we should just sit here for a while and see what happens," I said. "Ideally, I'd like to talk to him and ask him some questions."

Dinah looked at me and then at the house. "I don't think that's going to happen."

"We might as well have our coffee before it gets cold." I took mine out of the drink holder and sipped it. I usually burned my lips when I tried to drink through one of those openings in the lid, but this time the coffee had sufficient time to cool during our ride and was the perfect temperature. "At least if we could get a name, we'd have something to start with."

"Do you have any ideas how we are going to do that?" Dinah asked.

I suggested we get their street address. "Peter knows about a reverse directory." I squinted at the curb across the street. There was supposed to be a white rectangle of paint with the address printed in black. The way the streetlight was reflecting I couldn't tell whether there were numbers let alone what they were.

"I can't see much of anything from here," I said. "I need the window open." Dinah turned the key without turning on the ignition, and I lowered the window and stuck my head out. It didn't help. I said I'd have to get out. I opened the door quietly and stayed low, moving along the car toward the front. Then I dashed across the street and bent down to look at the curb. Every year someone claiming to be a student or painter looking for work came by and offered to repaint my numbers for a price. Apparently, these people hadn't taken them up on their offer because three of the numbers were worn away enough to be illegible.

There was a wood sign hanging on the small entrance

porch. I'd seen them at the county fair. The wood plaques were ready-made with flowers or birds and then personalized with the address or a residence name like Home of the Belmonts or Casa de Kennedy. From this distance I couldn't even tell if the white writing was letters or numbers. I had no choice but to move closer. I was practically on the bottom step, peering up at it when the lights came on in the room that faced the street.

There was nothing covering the window so I had a perfect view of the bald man and the woman I assumed was his wife coming into the room with their burger meals. I was afraid they had an equally perfect view of me. But since they weren't expecting anyone out there, I thought if I moved very slowly I could work my way into the shadows without being noticed. They put their food on the table and one of them turned on the TV. Meanwhile, I inched away from the pool of light. As soon as I hit the darkness, I skittered across the street to the car and got in.

I leaned back in the seat and let my breath out in a gush. "That was a close one. Any second I thought the guy would look up and see me."

Dinah urged me to take a sip of coffee, though I didn't know why—I was more than awake enough from the adrenalin rush. "Did you find out anything?" she asked.

I mentioned the sign I'd almost been able to read. I glanced across the street. The couple was on the sofa. "They'll probably just eat the burgers and go to bed. If I just got a little closer I'd be able to read it."

We decided to finish our coffee and wait.

"Why were you at the movies alone?" I asked, wishing we'd gotten something to eat along with the coffee. Didn't private detectives always have donuts on stakeouts?

"Jeremy said he had a meeting about some business deal."

"So, Mr. Mom left you with the kids again?"

"Tried to," she said, taking a sip of coffee. "I told him they were his kids and I was going out."

"And?"

Dinah sighed. "He said I was standing in the way of his career opportunities and tried to make me feel guilty. When I didn't budge, he postponed his so-called meeting until tomorrow. When I left he was trying to put them to bed."

"It sounds like the same old Jeremy."

She sighed again. "You're probably right. What was I thinking letting him stay with me?" She set down her cup. "You'd think a woman of my age would have more sense."

"Don't be so hard on yourself. You were just giving him the benefit of the doubt." I glanced back toward the house. The couple was still sitting there; I could see the flickering bluish cast of the television. "Haven't they had enough passive entertainment for one night? Why don't they go to bed and read a book or something?"

"What's that noise?" Dinah said, looking out the windshield. I heard it, too. It was a rhythmic thwack kind of sound and seemed to be getting louder. I pressed my face close to the side window and noticed the flashing lights of a helicopter in the distance.

"I think it's a police helicopter. There's probably another one of those chases that keep showing up on the news. The cops try to pull somebody over and they just take off instead. What are they thinking of? Do they honestly believe they have a chance of getting away when they end up being chased by a helicopter and a whole line of police cars?"

The noise grew louder, and suddenly the area around the car was bathed in an intense white light. I turned and looked over my shoulder to see if the car being pursued had turned on this street.

Just then a knock at the window made both of us jump.

"Open the window, please," a deep voice commanded.

I glanced up at the rearview mirror and saw a line of police cars with their lights flashing pulling up behind us. They didn't seem to be chasing anyone. "You better do it," I said to Dinah.

As soon as the window was open, she stuck her head out. "Is there some kind of problem?" she asked in her most innocent, charming voice.

The deep voice belonged to a patrol officer with a somber expression that didn't lighten up at her comment. Instead he ordered us to step out of our vehicle with our hands on our heads.

We followed his request, and Dinah put on her best blathering act.

"Am I glad to see you," she said. "My friend and I are lost. Do you know what street this is? We were trying to see the street sign, so I could check it on my *Thomas Guide*." She actually pointed her elbow at the street guide next to the front seat. I was impressed that she came up with an excuse so quickly, complete with a visual aid.

I decided to let Dinah do the talking since she seemed to think so well on her feet. I stood outside the car and glanced down the street. It was choked off by black-and-whites with their doors flung open. I had seen something like this only on TV, and in those fictional situations the cops were always crouched behind the doors with their guns drawn. I swallowed hard and wondered if that was what was happening here.

Another officer approached us warily as someone yelled at us to put our hands on the roof of the car. Dinah gave them a dirty look but complied. I slapped my hands down on the cold metal without hesitation.

"Officers, I think there's been some kind of mistake. I don't know who you're looking for, but it couldn't be us," I said, looking over my shoulder. What criminal would be wearing a black dress, red jacket and heels? Lights had come on in most of the houses, and people were standing in the windows; some had even streamed out into the street. I hoped there wasn't anyone who recognized us.

I felt hands get way too personal as one of the patrol officers patted me down. I heard some kind of skirmish going on with Dinah's search. Apparently the cop got all twisted up in the long pink and orange scarves she had draped around her neck. I got a glimpse of the bald man's house. He and his wife were outside talking to several uniforms. There seemed to be a lot of pointing toward us.

"That's them," the bald guy shouted. "They were going to rob us."

I was about to say something about how ridiculous that was, but one of the officers spoke first and asked if he could have a look in the trunk.

We had nothing to hide, so both of us nodded yes. I just hoped Dinah didn't have anything weird like that dismantled mannequin she'd picked up at a garage sale once. One of the officers checked the trunk, and the other shined her flashlight in the car. Apparently there was nothing weird in it, because after a moment he shut it. The officer with the flashlight spent a lot of time around the base of the seat, but eventually she shut off her light.

The officer who had checked the trunk walked over to the bald man. "We didn't find any weapons in their car. Sir, there's no law against them sitting in their car."

"I don't care," the bald man shouted. "Arrest them. Maybe they don't have any weapons because they were just casing the place and waiting for their gang to show up."

We still had our hands on the roof. My arms were starting to feel a little tingly, and I wished I'd gone with the ballet flats. Dinah and I looked at each other over the car. Would anyone seriously believe we were gang leaders?

Another car pulled up, and the helicopter continued to circle, keeping the area illuminated. The uniforms were talking to someone. I hoped it was about letting us go.

"Molly?" a familiar voice said in an accusing manner.

"Barry?" I said, trying to pick him out of the group.

He turned back to his associates. "This is who you thought were gang leaders?" Even in the darkness I could see him shake his head with disbelief. There was a lot of discussion I couldn't hear, but finally somebody said we could take our hands off the car roof.

Barry was next to me now. "What are you doing here?" he demanded.

Telling him we got lost on the way home from the movies didn't work. The movement of his head made it clear he was rolling his eyes even though it was too dark to actually see what his eyes were doing.

"C'mon, Molly. There is no way you have to come up here to get home from anywhere. Besides, the people who called said you'd been sitting here for a while." He looked in the car and pointed at the empty coffee cups. "You two were playing detective, weren't you?" He shook his head with hopelessness.

I stepped closer. "You should tell Detective Heather to check out that guy. He was there the day Drew Brooks was murdered."

"Sure, I'll tell her," he said.

"You will not. You're just humoring me, aren't you?"

He tilted his head and let his breath out. "Maybe a little. Now go home."

He stood there until we got in the car. The helicopter had left, and the police cars were turning around and heading back down the street. Barry waited until we'd put on our seat belts and locked the doors, then he headed back to his car. I saw his partner in the front seat. He appeared to be laughing.

They were still there when Dinah hit the headlights and we drove away.

Dinah dropped me at my car in the bookstore parking lot. When I got home my phone was ringing.

"Mother," Peter said in that tone that came out like an accusation, "are you watching the news?"

"No, honey, I just came in," I said, hoping my pleasant voice would diffuse his mood.

"From where? Jail perhaps?" he grumbled.

While he was talking I had flipped on the set and cringed. Apparently one of the many neighbors on the street had brought out his video camera. The screen showed the police officer standing next to Dinah and me as we put our hands on the roof of the car.

"Tonight, on our *You Be the Reporter* segment, we have a video just uploaded by Richard Beekman of Tarzana. The police detained two women who were suspected of being part of a follow-home robbery gang," the news anchor said over the picture. The camera zoomed in on Dinah and me. Our faces were in shadow, but even so, Peter had recognized us.

"It was just a mix-up," I said, hoping to avoid going into detail. Meanwhile, I kept watching the screen. The video panned past several of the houses as Richard Beekman explained that his neighbor had discovered the pair just as they were about to strike. The neighborhood reporter went on to explain that seven black-and-whites had shown up as well as a helicopter and that no arrests had been made. The video panned back over the houses and pulled in for a clumsy close-up of the bald man's house.

Richard Beekman wasn't the best cameraman and kept

zooming in and out, trying to be artsy. He zoomed in on the entrance to the house. Just when I caught sight of the sign on the porch, Richard pulled out to give a bigger view of the scene. Then he swung the camera to focus on the uniform talking to the bald guy and his wife. They were standing on the small porch, and the sign was right behind the bald guy's head. I leaned toward the TV, trying to see the writing. Then I saw it wasn't an address; it was a name. Bullard. Their name was Bullard.

Peter couldn't understand why I suddenly sounded so happy. "You should seriously think about spending some time with Mason Fields and not hanging out so much with that Dinah. I think she's a troublemaker."

And the calls just kept coming. Samuel was next. Thankfully he didn't hassle me. He was just checking that I got home safely. Got home as opposed to going to jail.

"Morgan was impressed with how cool you were," he said.

"Morgan's there?" I asked. Though he hadn't said it exactly, it was pretty obvious they had some issues. If she was at his place, maybe they were working them out.

Patricia Bradford was next. I went through the details of the story, and then she fired questions. By now, I was pretty tired. It really had been the longest day.

"You didn't mention Benjamin's name or that you might be part of the team, did you?"

Might be part of the team? She'd certainly changed her tune. But did I really want to be on Benjamin's team, anyway?

"Molly, I'm concerned about your judgment. First the whole Byron Nederman encounter and now this."

I knew I should let it lie, but I couldn't help it. "You're the one who told me Byron was gay."

"I was just trying to circumvent what happened from happening."

Patricia was taking this Mrs. Politician thing too far. "I wasn't boyfriend shopping. I know you said you didn't see the bald man at the Cottage Shoppe the day Drew Brooks was murdered, but he was there and the time before, too. I thought Byron Nederman was him. It doesn't matter anymore because I found the right bald guy."

I heard Patricia suck in her breath. "The guy on the news? You think he's the one who hit Drew on the head? Why?"

"Maybe Drew Brooks tried to cheat him, too," I said. "That's why I'd like to talk to him—but under the circumstances it's going to be tough."

"I think it's nice that you want to help Sheila, but you should stay out of it. Leave it to the police. Everybody on the team has to be squeaky clean," Patricia said before hanging up.

And then there was quiet. I turned off the TV and sat on the couch, worn out from the day and yet wired. It wasn't every day I had a helicopter hovering over me.

I heard the scratch of a key in the front-door lock. It started to turn, then stopped. Next the phone rang. It was Barry.

"Good move not using the key," I said. "That's for dog care only." I went to the front door and let him in. "Though I still don't think calling at my door counts as calling first and making arrangements." I said it before I really got a look at him. Whatever he'd done after he'd left me must have been rough because he looked all done in. His tie was gone and shirt collar open.

"I know. I know I shouldn't have followed the bald guy home," I said, beginning his lecture for him, but he held up his hand.

"That's not why I'm here. It's about the other night." He hadn't sat down and began to pace. "I wasn't about to say anything when you and Dinah had your hands on the car roof. Remind me later to get back to that." He ran his hands through his neatly trimmed dark brown hair.

"I can deal with the Hefeweizen, and your sons. I can deal with your inability to commit. I understand you need time and space." He turned and his eyes flashed. "But I can't deal with Mason Fields." His usually calm voice had grown in intensity. "You seemed awfully glad to see him. What's going on?"

"I was glad to see him because I wanted to ask him about Sheila. She's been a wreck ever since she realized her fingerprints were on the paperweight that knocked Drew out."

Barry stopped. "They are? Are you so sure she didn't do it?"

I made a grrr face. I was getting tired of everybody saying that. "I'm not interested in being some swinging bachelorette. But you have to understand you don't own me."

Barry seemed less than happy with that last part. "So what exactly is going on with you and Mason?"

I tried rolling my eyes to show how ridiculous he was being. "Nothing." There was no reason to mention that Mason kept asking me out to dinner.

Barry stepped closer, lifted my chin and looked at me intently. "So, there is no relationship between you and Mason Fields?"

I hesitated. I wouldn't call it *no* relationship, but then it wasn't really anything, either. But only the *no relationship* answer would give Barry any peace.

"There's nothing," I said while Barry watched me intently. Then I got what he was doing. Mr. Cop never turned off.

"You're doing that thing with the eyes, aren't you?" I asked. I'd read about something called kinesics in the *The Average Joe's Guide*. Most of the time people looked in one direction if they were telling the truth and the other if they were lying. I couldn't remember which direction my eyes had gone, so I quickly began to flip them back and forth.

Barry caught on to what I was doing. "It's too late," he said without a smile. "We detectives are fast. It looked to me like you're confused."

"Okay, so maybe there's not exactly nothing." Then I felt bad for saying it. "But I haven't done anything about it, so far."

Barry glanced around the living room. "Where's your houseguest?"

"Not here," I answered. I'd done enough explaining for one night. I stood up as though I was going to walk him to the door, but he stood his ground.

"What's so hot about Mason?"

"I don't want to talk about it anymore. Wouldn't you rather lecture me about not playing detective?" I took a step toward the door but ended up walking right into Barry's arms.

"I don't want to talk about anything, either," he said, holding me close. "I'd rather do something," he said, tugging at my buttons as he began to kiss me like he meant it.

Chapter 17

When I awoke, someone was kissing my face. I thought Barry had stayed over, but when I opened my eyes, I saw that it was Cosmo. He was standing on his short little legs, licking my face as a way to tell me he wanted to go out. Blondie still slept in her chair. She had never wanted to stay on the bed. But Cosmo declared it his spot from his first overnight stay. He slept nestled next to me with his head on my arm. Barry'd had to bribe him with chicken treats to get him out of the room. Barry said it made him feel strange to have an audience. Blondie just stayed in her chair with her paws over her eyes.

I smiled contentedly and hugged the pillow. For a moment I missed feeling Barry's warmth next to my bare skin, but then I was relieved. I had a lot of things to do, and his presence would have slowed things up.

I showered, got dressed and made coffee. Apparently Morgan had come back during the night because she came into the kitchen, following the aroma. I ground it fresh and the fragrance alone perked me up. There was never a problem getting Morgan to drink coffee, but she passed on my offer of cereal and half-and-half as though I'd just offered her cooties and cream. She had some low-calorie stuff she called cereal—I called it puffed cardboard. Then she added water. Yuck.

An hour later I was heading toward the event area in the bookstore and distressed to see most of the chairs were still there from Romance Night. In my hurry to pursue Mr. Bullard, I'd forgotten all about cleanup. The crocheters must have found the worktable and set it up.

"Dear, even my special makeup wouldn't have helped you last night," CeeCee said as I laid my things on the table and pulled out a chair. What with Barry's special visit, I'd almost forgotten about my appearance on the news. "You certainly lead an interesting life," CeeCee added. "You always seem to be ending up on the news."

"It wasn't planned," I said. Then I explained that Dinah and I had just been trying to find out who the bald guy was so I could pass along the information to Detective Gilmore.

"I told her she ought to stay out of it," Patricia said to CeeCee. Then she turned to me and shook her finger like an annoyed parent. "You're just going to get yourself in trouble."

I glanced back toward the bookstore. "Where is everybody?" Then I felt a sense of panic. "Where's Sheila? The police didn't—"

"Not so far," CeeCee said. "She called me sounding upset and said she was running late. And Adele said she'd be late, too. She said she had some important meeting at Le Grand Fromage."

As I took out my partially finished shawl, Dinah walked up to the table. She pulled a pile of papers out of her leather tote and set down a cup of coffee. "I've got to get this all graded by this afternoon. I just want to get some of them done. Then I'll take a break and work on my shawl."

"The whole group seems to be falling apart," Patricia said. She handed CeeCee another knitted shawl. "I know, I know, it's not crocheted, but I'm sure the recipients won't mind."

CeeCee slipped it in her bag. "As long as Adele doesn't see it, no problem. The way things are going I am glad for any kind of shawls. This is terrible. We made the commitment to the shelter, and now everyone seems otherwise occupied." As CeeCee spoke, she continued working on her rust-colored shawl. Her fingers were flying as though on autopilot. The edges of her shawl were perfectly straight. Somehow she never got caught in the stitches of despair.

"Am I ever going to be able to crochet like that?" I asked, watching her hook move across a row at lightning speed.

"It takes practice, dear," CeeCee said with just the slightest edge to her voice. "Instead of watching me—" She gestured toward my dusty rose–colored work in progress. Of course she was right, and I began to move my hook across the row. Ever since Adele had showed me how to use the plastic stitch markers, I hadn't lost any stitches. I glanced at the edges and was relieved to see they were straight.

Patricia seemed preoccupied. She didn't even seem to hear our conversation. She was finally crocheting, though I suspected there were knitting needles hidden in her bag.

"There's just so much to do," she muttered.

"Did you say something, dear?" CeeCee asked, turning toward her. The distraction didn't slow her progress. It was as if there were little brains in CeeCee's fingers.

"Sorry, I was talking to myself. There is just so much to do to get Benjamin elected. Did you see the window at Caitlin's Cupcakes? Her husband Victor Ditner is Benjamin's chief opponent. The whole window is full of cupcakes that say "Vote for Victor." Even his name sounds like victory." Patricia appeared disgruntled. "Have you seen the price of the cupcakes? People should realize Victor's an elitist."

"Cupcakes?" CeeCee repeated. Her hook slowed a little as her face softened. "I love cupcakes. The closet I've come to eating one lately is crocheting pincushions that look like them. I've never tried Caitlin's." Then her voice trailed off as she looked down. "They sound wonderful, but I have to get rid of these pesky five pounds before we go into production for my show again."

Apparently the mention of cupcakes had cut through Dinah's concentration because she looked up from her paper grading.

"You know, some people think it's all about portion control," Dinah said. "A cupcake would seem like the perfect answer to how to have your cake and diet, too."

"I like the way you think," CeeCee said.

Just then Sheila staggered in and pulled out a chair. Her hair was askew and her face sagged with exhaustion. She looked in need of something to revive her, and my immediate reaction was to offer to get her a coffee and some of Bob's cookies of the day. Today's were almond-butter cookies and again, he'd used one of my recipes.

When I came back with a mug and a plate with enough cookies for everyone, she was talking.

"That Detective Gilmore just won't let up," Sheila said, leaning back and closing her eyes. "She said I'm a person of interest." She started to tap the fingers of her right hand against the table but then used her left hand to stop them. She was jittery in her seat as she quickly took out the shawl she was working on. There was certain franticness as she began crocheting. It was all about keeping her hands busy.

At least she didn't have to worry about her stitches becoming knots. CeeCee had noticed that ever since Sheila had come under the continued scrutiny of Detective Heather, her stitches had become permanently too tight, but CeeCee had come up with a solution. She'd made a revised pattern just for Sheila that let her use a Q-size hook. It looked like a baseball bat for a GI Joe doll, and no matter how tense Sheila got, she couldn't do tight stitches. She was working in a deep plum acrylic worsted, and the shawl was almost half done. It was great that Sheila was turning her tension into something positive.

"She keeps taking me into the police station to talk to me. Do you have any idea how creepy it is to sit in one of those interview rooms? Again and again the same questions about why did I threaten Drew Brooks. Wasn't I so angry when I finally confronted him that I had to do something when he refused to pay me what he owed me?" Sheila stopped crocheting. "She keeps saying, 'Do you want to tell me what happened?' And that she understands it was an accident. Who knew he'd fall in a bowl of soup and drown like that? She has me so confused I almost think maybe I did hit him with the paperweight. Detective Gilmore said it was the one shaped like a globe. I know I picked it up twice. My hand fit so perfectly around the bottom of the pedestal."

"Shush," I said instinctively. It was just like Dinah said. "Don't even think about it. You haven't said anything like that to her, have you?" I suggested that if it happened again, she should say she wanted a lawyer and call Mason. Sheila rejected the idea, sure that asking for a lawyer was like saying she was guilty.

"I'm working on finding out who really did it. Until then, though, don't let her put words in your mouth," I said, reaching across the table and touching her hand.

It didn't seem fair that Detective Heather was so focused on Sheila when there were other possible suspects, but I knew what she was doing. Barry had mentioned once that detectives thought they had an uncanny ability to "just know" who the guilty party was. And Detective Heather had decided it was Sheila. I knew I'd better hurry and figure out who the real murderer was because soon Sheila was going to crack.

Under the circumstances I wondered if coffee had been such a good idea. Maybe some herb tea with a sedative effect would have been better. But the coffee seemed to work. Kind of like giving uppers to hyperactive kids calmed them down. She came over and gave me a thank-you hug. "You guys are like my family," she said, almost in tears.

"Ladies," CeeCee said, "let's not forget why we're here." She held up her rust-colored shawl. Throughout everything she had kept working. Patricia gave her a dirty look. I didn't think she liked being upbraided. With the exception of Dinah, who was still working on her school papers, we all began to seriously crochet.

I had to pay attention to my crocheting and be sure to mark the right stitches with the plastic pins, but I still kept my eye on the goings-on at the bookstore. It was relatively quiet in the morning and seemed unlikely there'd suddenly be a rush, but just in case, I was ready to help Rayaad.

During one of my surveillance glances I noticed a woman in exercise wear coming in the door. She had on a baseball cap that threw a shadow over her face, but something about her seemed familiar. There was nothing unusual about that—we had lots of repeat customers—but I just couldn't place her. She stopped just inside the entrance, and the way her gaze moved around to the various sections of the bookstore, she was obviously looking for something. She took off the baseball cap, and then I realized why she looked so familiar: She was the bald guy's wife.

I pushed back my chair and moved across the bookstore, putting on my best can-I-help-you face. Actually, I was more interested in getting information than giving it. There was a slight problem. As soon as I said, "Can I help you?" her face froze in horror and she began to back away.

"Omigod, it's you again," she said loud enough to cause people in the vicinity to glance up from their book browsing and stare. "Are you some kind of stalker?" She reached in her purse and pulled out her cell phone. She pushed three numbers, and I didn't need to see them to figure out what they were. She glanced back toward the event area, and her expression got even more upset when she saw Dinah.

"What are you, some kind of gang of crocheters?" Mrs. Bullard was about to hit the send button on her phone.

"No," I yelled and reached for her cell. She pulled her arm away and the small phone went flying. When it landed, she dove for it and I started to talk really fast. "We're not a gang. We're real crocheters. I'm not stalking you. I work here."

She picked up the phone and eyed me warily while keeping her finger over the send button.

I quickly offered a complimentary cup of our coffee of the day and some of our cookies. That seemed to help. "I guess a stalker wouldn't offer snacks," she said, pushing the clear button on her cell phone before she slipped it back in her purse.

As we went into the café, I introduced myself and she did the same, saying her name was Pixie. It had to be a nickname. Who would really name someone that? She didn't have a pixie sort of look, but she wasn't the opposite, either. You know, like someone called Tiny who is really a giant. She was short and on the round side with a certain earthy quality. Maybe it was the raspy voice. But what I noticed most was her hair—not the color, which was kind of an ash blond, but the style. She had a short wedge cut. It reminded me of someone, but I couldn't place who.

Once she had her drink and cookies, we sat down at a table by the counter. She took a sip of her coffee, held up her cup and smiled at Bob. "My compliments to the barista." She fluttered her eyelids just enough for me to figure out she was a flirt; Bob fell for it big time.

"Maybe we overreacted last night," Pixie said, finishing off a cookie. "But Arnold's an orthodontist, and we've had a few problems. Occasionally there's been a disgruntled patient whose smile doesn't turn out quite as they envisioned. It certainly isn't his fault. The man's a perfectionist. Nobody works harder or cares more about their patients. Even more so now that our kids are away at college. He's started keeping evening hours several nights a week to make it easier for his patients who work. Of course, it makes it harder for me. He doesn't want me going out places alone. He's the jealous type, you know."

I was a little surprised by his profession. It was certainly not what I'd have chosen if I were guessing his occupation. Bob came over and offered her a sample of a new frozen drink he was trying out. She accepted, took a sip, then raved it was delicious and said he must be some kind of drink genius. Bob seemed to grow visibly taller with the compliments. I had to admire her style. She wasn't particularly attractive, but she had a way with men. I'd never seen Bob so animated, and he only reluctantly returned to his station.

Before I could get to my information gathering, she brought up the reason she'd come to the bookstore. "I just have to get a copy of that new book on Princess Di. What section would it be in?" She didn't give me a chance to answer but went off on what a fan of the late princess she was. Suddenly, I got the hair. It was the style Diana had when she married Prince Charles. "I should have been there for her funeral," she said, explaining she wanted to go to London then so she could pay her respects. "I just know we would have been friends if we'd met. I would have been simpatico with her."

I wasn't sure if that was the correct way to use the word, but I got her meaning. Apparently, Pixie had finally gotten to London. She spent a long time describing her visit to Kensington Palace, where Princess Di had lived, and she raved over the display of her dresses. Pixie and Princess Di would have made an odd couple, with Diana's tall boyish figure and Pixie's shorter roundness. She moved on to the tribute at Harrods. The mention of the famous department store reminded me of Arnold and his shopping bag.

"Did your husband sell some things at the Cottage Shoppe?" I blurted it out before I realized how out of context it was and that it might give her pause to rethink the stalking thing.

"What?" she asked, looking at me oddly. I said her mention of the store had triggered my memory and I recalled seeing Arnold at the Cottage Shoppe with a Harrods shopping bag and wondered if perhaps he'd sold off some items.

She blinked a few times. "You must be mistaken. Arnold's never been in that store."

Okay, either she was totally lying or she didn't know about something Arnold had going on. I was going to go with lying. Maybe it was because she answered too quickly and seemed too sure he'd never been in the store.

She stood, ending our conversation, and asked where the book she wanted was. I walked her into the bookstore and pointed toward our new releases section before heading back to the event area.

When I rejoined the crochet group, they were all working in silence. It was like the break in traffic on the freeway, only temporary. A moment later everyone started talking.

I'd barely settled in when Adele appeared from her meeting—and she wasn't alone.

Chapter 18

After all the talk about Caitlin's Cupcakes, I was anxious to try the place. Dinah finally pulled her head out of her papers when the crochet group ended, and I talked her into coming along.

It was on Ventura just across a side street from the Cottage Shoppe and had taken over the spot that used to be a Persian restaurant. Just as Patricia had said, there was a display in the window of red, white and blue frosted cupcakes arranged to represent an American flag. "Vote for Victor Ditner" was written across them in gold frosting. The cupcakes were obviously a hot item. We had to practically get in line just to take a number. When it was finally our turn, Dinah picked a banana cupcake and I chose a carrot one.

"Fruit and vegetable," I joked as I gathered up the small plates and Dinah took the coffees. All the tables were taken, but we found a couple of empty stools at the bar that ran along the side window.

"Give Adele a mile and she turns it into a road trip," I said to Dinah. "Mrs. Shedd says she can help with one book signing and suddenly she thinks she's running things."

Dinah appeared confused. "Did I miss something during the group?"

"I think so. I think you might have missed a whole lot of stuff. What was with the paper grading?"

Dinah sighed. "I forgot how much time two little kids take, three if you count their father." She looked frustrated. "I was going to do the papers this morning, but there was just one disaster after the other. Jeremy keeps saying just another day or so and he'll have everything straightened out and they'll be on their way. I should never have taken them in, but he knows how to get to me. He reminded me that E. Conner and Ashley-Angela are my kids' half siblings. I don't know why, but somehow that makes me feel connected to them." She shook her head as if trying to clear it. "So, tell me what I missed."

"Where to begin?" I said. "Did you notice that Adele showed up with someone?"

Dinah shook her head, and I told her the someone was none other than Eduardo Linnares, the cover model from Romance Night. All crocheting had abruptly stopped with his arrival; Dinah had been the only one not to stare with her mouth open. He was almost too good-looking, like some kind of statue come to life. He'd lost the theatrical outfit and wore well-fitting designer jeans with a navy blue polo shirt, and had his flowing black hair tied in a loose ponytail. He carried a cup of coffee and had a smile so magnetic it practically gleamed. While he made conversation with CeeCee, and Patricia, Adele pulled me aside.

I swallowed back a smile when I caught her outfit. This was Adele's idea of business wear. She'd paired what looked like men's dark gray trousers with a white shirt and a black crocheted vest. The white shirt was unbuttoned enough to give a hint of cleavage, and she'd finished off the outfit with a purple-and-yellow-striped men's tie with the knot just below the first closed button. Her just past chin-length hair was usually a wavy light brown, but she'd given it a mahogany rinse and forced it into a severe straight style. Her eye makeup was so heavy she looked like a raccoon.

"Pink, you have to go with me on this. I told him he could have his own evening at the bookstore. We'll have a display of all the books with him on the cover. Then he can talk about being a cover model and read some of his poetry." Adele avoided looking directly at me so she wouldn't have to see my expression.

I was speechless for a moment. "You should have talked to me first. Mrs. Shedd said you could help me with Milton Mindell's thing because he's a children's author. Nowhere did she say you could start setting up events on your own." I kept my voice low to keep it just between the two of us. "I told him he could read his poetry on Poetry Night."

"Poetry Night?" Adele said.

"I just started it," I answered. "I can do that. It's my job to arrange programs and set up author events. And my job only—except if Mrs. Shedd wants to do something like invite the crochet group here."

Adele knew what she'd done was wrong, but that didn't mean she would back down. The worst part was it wasn't a bad idea. I had no doubt advertising an evening with Eduardo would bring in a lot of people and sell a lot of books. We could even arrange for customers who bought something to have their photos taken with him. I wasn't quite clear what was in it for him, but from our standpoint, it would be a money maker.

"What did you say to her?" Dinah asked, taking a morsel

of her banana cupcake with just the right amount of vanilla buttercream icing.

"The only thing I could, really. I said this one time I would go ahead with her idea, but I was still in charge of the event, which meant I make all of the arrangements."

"How'd she take it?"

I rolled my eyes. "Fifty-fifty. She was relieved I went along with it but not happy that she didn't get to run the show. Then she wanted some kind of credit for getting a new member in the crochet group."

"Who?" Dinah asked between bites.

"You really didn't notice who joined?"

Dinah shook her head.

"Eduardo," I said, watching her do a double take and then giggle. "That was my first impression, too. I thought he was joking, but he was completely serious. It turns out he already knows how to crochet. Go figure."

He had charmed CeeCee and listened attentively as she explained our shawl project. He thought it was a great idea and took a copy of the pattern and started working on one. Within a few minutes Patricia was pitching him on joining the Benjamin Bradford bandwagon and coming to her book signing.

"You sure can't judge a book by its cover," Dinah said and I laughed. She thought I was laughing because she'd used a cliche.

"It's true," I said. "He is definitely more than just an extremely handsome face and well-built body." I needed a sip of coffee to cut the sweetness of my minicake. "If you missed all that, you must have missed Pixie, too."

"Pixie? Who's Pixie?"

"Pixie Bullard, the bald man's wife," I said. "She was the short woman with the Princess Di hair who I was talking to in the café."

Dinah shrugged with a blank expression.

I gave her a brief rundown on Pixie's calling Bob a drink genius and her obsession with Princess Di. "She came to the crochet table to show me she'd found the book she wanted. She was practically standing next to you. I certainly envy your power of concentration."

"I don't," Dinah said with a perturbed expression. "So, what happened then?"

"Once she saw CeeCee, she forgot about me."

"Ms. Collins, it's such an honor to meet you," Pixie had said in a hushed tone. "I've been a fan since you did *The CeeCee Collins Show*. And now you're on top again. I absolutely adore your reality show *Making Amends*."

CeeCee sat a little taller in her seat and her eyes sparkled as Pixie continued. "I've watched every episode. The show when the truck driver came by his aunt's house and admitted that he was the one who'd broken all her heirloom china when he was a kid and then blamed it on the cat was really powerful."

She started to mention another episode, but then she saw Eduardo and her eyes widened and her mouth opened.

"Is this a dream or what? You're Captain Blackhart," she said in a breathless voice. Being a gentleman, Eduardo stood and took her hand as he asked her name. With her free hand, she reached up and touched his chin. "The book cover didn't do you justice." She let out a raspy giggle. "It's lucky my husband isn't here. He was jealous when he saw me admiring the book cover. He'd be nuts if he saw me actually talking to you. I don't know why he gets so jealous."

When she heard Eduardo was going to have his own evening at the bookstore, she flashed a seductive smile and said she'd be sure to be there. Adele had glowered through the whole encounter.

When I got to the end of the story, Dinah had an amused

smile. "And she wonders why her husband gets so jealous. It sounds like she was flirting with the book cover. I can't believe I missed all that to grade some atrociously written freshman compositions. They're starting to write papers in instant-message language. Things like *cme2nite* and *ur mybff lol.* So, that's everything?"

I smiled at my friend. "I saved the best for last. You won't believe what Pixie said when I asked her about Arnold being at the Cottage Shoppe."

Dinah leaned closer, and I repeated how she'd said he'd never been in the store. "I'm sure she was lying. She answered too quickly and with too much certainty," I said. "I think she was trying to cover for him."

"If she's covering for him, it must mean . . ." Dinah's voice trailed off.

"Right. It could mean she knows he killed Drew. But we have no proof or even a motive. Detective Heather doesn't even believe he exists," I said.

"We need to question her some more. Maybe we can do something out of your *Average Joe's Guide*. Wasn't there something about playing good cop, bad cop?" Dinah asked. Two women sat down on the stools next to us. Dinah moved her stool closer to mine.

Some activity outside the window caught my attention. "Whoa, what's going on there?" A truck had pulled into the parking lot behind the Cottage Shoppe and was in the process of lowering a temporary storage container. A man came out of the back door, and as soon as the container was off the truck, he opened the door on it. When I glanced at the store building, I noticed a new banner had been placed on a window announcing the store was open during remodeling. And the Cottage Shoppe sign had a temporary addition underneath it that read "And Kevin's Kitchen."

"Kevin's Kitchen is catchy," Dinah said, following my gaze.

A man in work clothes came out of the back door carrying big pieces of what looked like plaster and threw it in a Dumpster.

"I don't think the name being catchy is the point. It's all the changes so soon after Drew's death." I thought back to when Charlie died. I had been stunned, out of focus and too numb to do anything beyond the basics. There is no way I could have been buzzing around the way Kevin was. "It gives you pause to think."

The door opened on the cupcake shop and CeeCee came in. I could tell by her fluttering eyelids and smile that she was savoring the sweet smell of the place. She stopped in front of the display case and gazed at the rows and rows of cupcakes.

Before she had a chance to choose, Caitlin apparently recognized her. She pointed excitedly at a series of celebrity photos on the wall, and I gathered the shop owner wanted one of CeeCee.

It seemed like every restaurant, dry cleaners, office supply store and dog groomer had photos of their celebrity customers on the wall. Most were eight-by-ten publicity shots, but the most coveted were the personal ones—the ones taken with the owner. I nudged Dinah, and we watched CeeCee go into action as Caitlin's assistant came out with a digital camera. CeeCee put her arms around Caitlin as though they were best friends. CeeCee was a pro and posed to show off her best side. When they finished, Caitlin offered CeeCee a complimentary cupcake. Before the peanut butter delight was even on the plate, the assistant had returned with a print of the photo.

It still amazed me. "Remember the old days when you had to take film in?" I said.

Dinah nodded in agreement. "And the things you can do on a computer, like take the red eyes out or make a color photo look like an old-fashioned one. You can erase wrinkles, gray hair, even the ten pounds the camera puts on."

CeeCee looked over the picture and shook her head; I think she was hoping for some of that erasing. But in the end Caitlin slipped it into a frame and hung it on the wall. When CeeCee saw us, she brought her cupcake over and sat down.

"Next time I just bring in my own publicity shot," CeeCee said, looking dismayed. "I know how to present my best side, but when the photographer isn't a professional . . ." She gave us a knowing nod. She glanced down at her cupcake, which had a happy face made out of peanuts on the maple buttercream frosting. "I'm going with your portion idea," she said to Dinah before cutting off a piece and spearing it with her fork. Then she smiled at the taste of the cupcake and pronounced it delicious.

"If you think that's good, you'd love Molly's special cupcakes," Dinah said.

"Dear, you make cupcakes? If they're anything like your other bake goods, they must be fabulous."

I smiled modestly, even though I had to admit the cupcakes Dinah was talking about were great. CeeCee ate another piece of cake, wiped her mouth demurely and went back to talking about my baking.

"I just remembered. Weren't you going to come over so I could show you how to do thread crochet? And didn't you mention something about bringing over some goodies? Maybe it could be those cupcakes." She had a twinkle in her eye. "Why don't we make it tomorrow?"

Dinah nudged me and held up a paper napkin. It took me a moment to figure out she was trying to remind me of the hanky. Dinah pointed her head toward CeeCee and nodded. Of course, CeeCee with all her crochet knowledge might be able to help me figure out where the hanky came from.

We agreed on a time and then went our separate ways. Dinah had errands and a class. CeeCee had a production meeting about the upcoming season of her show. And I had to get back to the bookstore. But before I did I decided to make a side trip to the Cottage Shoppe.

The bell tinkled over the door as always, but inside everything was in flux. Kevin was dreaming if he thought it was going to be business as usual. Dorothy looked around at the confusion and appeared overwhelmed.

"What's going on?" I asked, approaching her.

"A mess if you ask me, but Mr. Kevin won't listen to anyone." She gestured around the place. "I mean, would you want to browse around here now?"

I could see her point. Having everything pushed together took away the charm. Plus there were loud and annoying workmen sounds coming from the kitchen area.

I followed her through the living room into the alcove that had held the children's things. There was a box sitting on the floor with odds and ends sticking out. I pulled out something round with nobs on it.

"Those are some new things someone brought in yesterday." She sighed. "At least they priced the things themselves, though I don't know where we're going to put them."

I asked her what I was holding, and she smiled. "It's called a yarn swift."

The name didn't help, and then she explained that when you had a hank of yarn that needed to be rolled into a ball, you hung it around the swift and wound the ball. "It kind of takes the place of a friend's hands," she said, holding hers out to demonstrate how the friend version worked. I looked farther into the box and noted quite a bit of yarn and some other supplies and asked her who had brought the things in.

"Sorry, but I'm not allowed to tell. With our handicraft items it's usually not a problem, but the people that bring in antiques or things from their houses, well, they don't necessarily want their neighbors to know they're selling things."

Of course. I got it. Selling things implied you were hard up, and nobody wanted to admit that. I was impressed by her knowledge about the yarn swift. "You have to know about a lot of different stuff."

She smiled. "I've picked up information along the way, but we rely on the sellers to explain what they've brought in." She took something else out of the box. "I would have thought this was just a lamp, but the seller explained it was originally a kerosene lamp that had been electrified and the glass shade had actually come from another lamp and is a Tiffany." Then Dorothy showed me the price tag on it. I swallowed. It was pricier than I expected.

"So, you just take the seller's word it's a Tiffany shade?"

Dorothy shrugged off the question. "Personally, I'd call it Tiffany style since there aren't any markings to authenticate it."

Kevin walked through then and seemed glad to see a customer. It was odd how he had the same even features as his brother, but on him the smile was pleasant whereas on Drew it had appeared contemptuous. "I'm glad to see somebody realized we're still open," he said in a friendly voice.

The back door was propped open and obviously the alarm had been disengaged. The man I'd seen from across the street came inside and pointed at the stack of boxes near the door. "Are these for the Dumpster or the storage container?" he asked.

Kevin leaned over and thumbed through what looked like files. "Put them in the storage unit for now. Eventually, we'll probably shred them." He turned back to me. "My aunt was certainly a copious record keeper." Then, changing the subject, he asked, "Did you come in for soup?"

He led me into the dining room. The furniture was piled against the wall, but there were big metal pans on the heating device on the bar. "We only have a limited selection for now," he said, lifting the lid on one and letting the savory fragrance fill the air.

He seemed a little agitated as he glanced toward the door. Although he didn't say it, he was obviously worried about business. He wanted me to taste the soup and suggested I might mention how good it was to the bookstore customers.

Finally I couldn't hold back anymore. He seemed too collected for someone who'd just lost his brother and in such a sudden, violent way. "You're certainly holding up well, under the circumstances," I said, trying hard to hide my sarcasm.

He flashed me an angry look. "I'm sorry about my brother, but he brought on what happened himself. And that's exactly what I told that lady detective." A bus rolled by on Ventura Boulevard, shaking the whole place. Kevin faced me directly. "My brother was a bully. We had equal ownership, but like always, he took over. I didn't agree about cutting the two clerks' salaries and taking a bigger cut from our consignment people, but he did it anyway. I want everyone to know all that is over with now. I told that to the detective, too."

"And the remodel plans?"

Kevin grimaced. "The detective asked about that, too.

Drew was against them, okay? More than against them—he just said no. The day before he died he told me we were doing an Internet store that was going to bring in a bunch of money."

When I asked him for details, Kevin gave me an odd look. "Why do you want to know?"

"It might have something to do with who killed him," I said.

Kevin seemed uncomfortable with my remark. "Did you come in for something in particular?"

"Well, actually I did," I said, realizing he'd just offered me the perfect opening to find out about the handkerchief. I gave him the same story I had given Dorothy and Trina at the bookstore about looking for a certain kind of hanky for a gift and then described the one I'd found, all the while watching for his reaction.

Either he was an Academy Award–caliber actor or he really had no idea what I was talking about. I was going with the latter.

Adele was hiding in the children's department when I got back to the bookstore. It was a sweet area decorated with carpet depicting cows jumping over moons and furnished with little chairs and tables. She was sitting on one of the child-size chairs as far in the corner as she could get.

As soon as she saw me, she started talking about Eduardo and how wonderful he was and what a great program he'd put on. Her eyes had that dreamy look, and I suspected she thought she'd found Mr. Right. But I also suspected that she hadn't noticed that he talked to each of us as if we were the only woman in the world who mattered. I wasn't sure what to say to her. Even with all her barbs, I hated to see her get hurt. But leave it to Adele. In her usual manner she went right for the offensive.

"Okay, Pink, I'm not angry that you almost made a scene with Eduardo. I understand that you were upset it wasn't your idea and all. I won't mention it to Mrs. Shedd."

All I could do was roll my eyes.

Chapter 19

I HAD HOPED DINAH WOULD COME WITH ME TO CeeCee's, but she was planning on confronting her ex, had appointments with the students who'd failed their assignment because they'd written their papers using instant-message shorthand and had an evening class to prepare for and teach.

As promised, I'd made my special cupcakes, and they were sitting on a paper-doily-decorated plate and covered with plastic as I walked to CeeCee's. Her house was a little far for a walk but too close to justify driving, and anyway I needed the exercise. As soon as I got a couple of blocks from my house, the terrain was different. That was the thing about the area of Tarzana south of Ventura Boulevard. The lay of the land kept changing. My street was on a gentle upward slope, and the lots were wide and level. But just a short distance away there was the steep ridge Patricia's house was perched on. CeeCee's house was situated farther back, near the bottom of Corbin Canyon. There was a deep ravine behind it, and the front was like a miniforest, giving the stone cottage-style house a mysterious, very un-sunny Southern California appearance. I expected to see Hansel and Gretel or Cinderella show up any minute.

She'd warned me about the front gate. Now that she was a name again, she'd started locking it and had an intercom installed. As she talked through the speaker, I could hear barking in the background. Maybe barking wasn't the best description. It was more like wild yipping. She was still working out the kinks in her security system, so it took a few tries to coordinate her buzzing to unlock the gate and me pushing it open.

I passed a trio of hummingbirds hovering around a red nectar feeder as I walked up the pathway. The door was open a crack, and she ordered me to wait while she scooped up "the girls." She opened the door enough for me to come in, and three sets of eyes focused on the plate in my hand.

"Oh, how wonderful, dear. Your cupcakes are cheese-cakes." She kicked the door shut and let Marlena and Tallu-lah loose. The tiny Yorkies did a thorough investigation of my shoes and ankles. Now that I had Cosmo and Blondie and a double dose of dog scent, they went nuts. CeeCee re-lieved me of the plate, which was disposable. I made it clear the cupcakes were all hers to keep.

"Tony's going to love these," she said, lifting the plastic and drinking in their creamy vanilla aroma. Tony was her boyfriend, though she thought calling a veteran soap opera star with white hair a *boyfriend* kind of ridiculous. Actu-ally she didn't like any of the variations, either, like *man friend*, *just friend*, *significant other*, or the more direct *lover*. When she had to give him some kind of definition, she'd settled on calling him *her guy*.

She didn't like the title *widow*, either, which I could

completely relate to. It conjured up images of women wearing black veils and sensible shoes and tearing out their hair or something. Her late husband had been a world-famous dentist, and they'd had no children. She said with both of their careers, they'd just never had the time or emotion. The closest she had come were "the girls" and their predecessors.

"Tony's working," she called as I followed her to the dining room. Tony Bonnard, aka Dr. Kevin McCoy, was a pillar on the long-running soap opera *My Family and Friends*. And like CeeCee, he hadn't let his celebrity status go to his head.

The house smelled of fresh paint, and I noticed boxes piled against the wall when I glanced down the hall that led to the bedroom wing.

"I'm doing some remodeling," she said as if reading my mind. The interior had been a replica of the set of her old hit sitcom, *The CeeCee Collins Show*. "It was beginning to look tired. I decided it was time to move on with something fresh," she said with a dismissive wave. I was glad to see she was leaving the dining room furniture as is. I liked the dark wood trestle table. A long ecru runner ran down the table, and a royal blue ceramic bowl of oranges sat in the center. The walls sported a pleasing shade of peach with white trim.

CeeCee had already brought out a ball of white thread and some steel hooks. She reminded me that the thread was called bedspread weight and that it was the most common kind used for thread crochet. I had brought along the supplies I'd purchased; I took out my thread and steel hooks, picked one from the bunch and looked at it. The end was so tiny I could barely see the hook, but then the thread appeared very thin, too. I had my doubts about being able to learn thread crochet. I had my doubts I'd even be able to see the stitches. I just wanted to get her talking about handkerchiefs.

A woman came out of the kitchen, startling me. CeeCee handed her the plate of cupcakes and said something to her in Spanish. Another change—CeeCee had household help now. There seemed to be a lot of conversation back and forth and CeeCee leaned toward me. "I'm emceeing a charity event tonight." She smiled and went on about how now that she was back in the limelight with the reality show, everyone wanted her to do a charity event. This one was a personal favorite of hers. "They help seniors who can't take care of or afford their pets." She touched my arm. "You know, dear, it feels good to be able to give back."

Underneath CeeCee's overdone blondish, reddish pouf of hair and the jewel-colored velour outfits was a tender heart. When the original leader of the crochet group died, it was CeeCee who had carried on the idea of making projects for different charities. She was always making a lap blanket or a baby sweater for someone.

"I'm afraid I don't have as much time as I thought," she said. "I have a stylist, and hair and makeup people coming over to help me get ready for tonight."

I sat down and fingered the runner on the table with new interest, wondering how it was made. It had a gridlike background and a design of butterflies and flowers.

CeeCee saw my interest and commented, "It's not real. They tried to make it look like filet crochet, but the background is machine made and the design is closer to embroidery." She showed me how someone had created the design by running rather thick cotton thread over and under the grid.

"Filet crochet? It sounds like something to eat."

"Dear, I'm afraid that comment isn't any more original than your yarnoholic one. I've heard people call it filet of crochet or a crochet filet and joke about it being a crochet steak." She laid a book of crochet instruction open on the table and pointed to a photo of a white dove in what looked like the middle of a grid.

"That, my dear, is the real thing." She pointed out how the open spaces were made by doing chain stitches and the filled-in areas were just double crochets. There didn't seem a lot of room for error, and CeeCee said the design had to be drawn on graph paper first.

I gazed at the photo for a long time as CeeCee read the instructions out loud. "That isn't exactly what I had in mind," I said, thinking it looked nothing like the hanky.

"I thought you could try all different kinds of thread crochet. But if you're not interested in filet, we'll do something else." She set down the book. "So is it doilies you're interested in?" she asked, picking up a thin hook and making a slip knot with the fine thread. She quickly did some chain stitches and joined them in a ring, and then her hook moved so fast I wasn't sure what she was doing until she explained the pattern called for a bunch of single crochets in the ring. She pushed some supplies my way and told me what she'd done and said to do the same.

"That isn't exactly what I had in mind, either," I said.

"Fine. Then just make a foundation chain of say twenty, and then turn it and do a row of single crochets just for the feel of the thread while you tell me what you did have in mind."

I tried to follow her instructions, but it was not easy. The thread was so thin it was hard to manipulate it, and the hook—I spent most of the time picking it up after it slipped out of my hand.

"I was thinking about trimming something," I began. "You know how there are those little linen hand towels with crochet trim, or even terry hand towels? Or a handkerchief.

Yes, that's what I want to know about. Maybe a small square of cotton with a lot of this doily kind of stuff as trim."

CeeCee gave me an odd look. "A handkerchief? Molly, what you're describing sounds lovely, but you don't want to defeat yourself when you're just learning." She pushed an instruction sheet titled *Simple Washcloth* across the table to me. "This is perfect if you want to try something simple to get the feel of working with the thread. Then you can try a handkerchief."

CeeCee's simple washcloth was no help for my hanky dilemma, except to give me some appreciation of how difficult that lacy trim must have been to make. I decided to prod her further. "But if I *were* to make a handkerchief, how would I make some fluffy filigree kind of trim?"

"Why are you so fixated on making a decorated hanky?"

I wasn't ready to tell her the real answer, so I changed the subject to talking about hankies in general. She put up her hand to stop me.

"Why not just focus on what you're doing?" She touched my hook, and I looked down at my work. It was a mess. She unraveled it, did the foundation chain for me and gave it back, urging me to practice with the single crochets.

My shoulder blades were achy by the time I got to the second row. I felt tense and frustrated from trying to work with the tiny hook. CeeCee moved my hands down and my head up while telling me that staring directly at it would strain my eyes. I was thrilled when she suggested we take a cupcake break.

"You have to get used to it," she said in a reassuring manner. I wondered if that would happen in this lifetime.

She gestured for me to stop working and called Rosa to bring in the tea and cupcakes.

A few minutes later, Rosa appeared with an elaborate

tray and put it on the table. CeeCee thanked her and winked at me. "It's nice to have help again. I could burn water," she said with her trademark tinkly laugh.

CeeCee's late husband had been brilliant about teeth and a moron about money. When he died she found out he'd gone through all their money. She'd had to start all over, and it wasn't until the reality show that she'd finally started getting ahead.

I'd dropped some deep purple pansies from my garden around the edge of the cupcake plate to add a little color. I'd learned during all the years Charlie worked in PR that presentation was everything.

"I think this whole concept of portion control is just the thing." CeeCee moved her gaze around the cupcakes and then picked the biggest one. "It's all about not eating too much of anything."

Now that CeeCee had help, she'd gone all out with the tea. The tray held a dark blue pot covered with a blue and white cozy, a silver tea strainer and two white bone china cups. There was also a pitcher of cream, a small honey pot, a bowl of sugar cubes and even a half lemon all gussied up with a cheesecloth cover. Rosa had brought in plates and silverware separately.

As CeeCee poured, I took a cheesecake. What can I say, I like my own baking. I was still wowed by the mixture of the creamy vanilla top over the buttery graham-cracker-crumb crust. I'd originally called the recipe Baby Cheese-cakes, but with all the hoopla about cupcakes, I renamed the recipe Cheesecake Cupcakes.

No need to worry about portion control for me. One was quite enough. The tea was a nice accompaniment. I loved coffee, but every time I had tea, I was amazed how it made my insides feel calm and serene.

The two Yorkies positioned themselves on the chair

behind CeeCee. They each stuck a head under her arm and started yapping as they stared at her plate.

CeeCee gave them each a bit of cheesecake, telling them it wasn't good for dogs. They didn't seem to care and were instantly back for more.

The handkerchief was in my purse. I'd hoped there would be a casual way I could bring it out and show it to CeeCee, but it didn't look as though that was going to happen. So, I just took out the plastic bag and set it on the table.

"Do you have any idea what this is?"

"So, that's why you were asking all the handkerchief questions," CeeCee said, glancing at the bag with the hanky inside. I had wondered what to do about cleaning it. The red stains were kind of icky, but if the hanky was evidence they might be important. In the end, I'd left it as is, only flattening it out. The fabric still had wrinkle marks, but at least it wasn't squished into a ball anymore.

CeeCee wrinkled her nose in distaste, and I knew she was noting the red marks. "It looks like a hanky in need of a bath." She pointed at one of the spots with the metal hook. "Is that blood?"

"More likely tomato bisque," I said.

CeeCee's eyes widened. "Where did you get it?"

I was hoping she wouldn't ask, but in case she did I'd already worked out an answer. It was basically the truth without all the details. I said I'd picked it up by mistake at the Cottage Shoppe.

"Do you think it was in the room when that Brooks person died?" CeeCee didn't wait for me to answer. "It's some kind of clue, isn't it?" She picked up the plastic bag and began to examine the hanky. "I'd say the trim is definitely thread crochet. I'd guess it is old, since nobody carries something like this these days. It reminds me of a prop I had in a period piece I did at the beginning of my career. They gave me a hanky to hold in my hand, saying the lacy edge made my hand movements more dramatic." She set the bag back down. "I'm afraid that's all I know. You should show it to Sheila. Remember, she's studying costume design."

I hadn't thought of that, but it was a good idea. I put away the hanky, and CeeCee gave me some directions for making a coaster with thread. The doorbell rang, and CeeCee made it clear our time was done. "I know you're busy, dear," she said, leading me to the door.

As I walked out, a woman pushed a rack of clothes in. She was followed by a small brunette carrying a makeup case and a man dressed all in black with a blow dryer stuck in his belt. Apparently CeeCee's stylist brought a crew.

CeeCee was right. I was busy. After stopping home to change and take care of the dogs, I had to set up for Patricia Bradford's book signing. And I had a feeling it was going to be a bumpy evening.

CHAPTER 20

THE BOOKSTORE WAS IN CHAOS WHEN I GOT there. Patricia's people seemed to be everywhere. Someone was taking out the regular chairs I had set up, and someone else was bringing in better-looking ones from a rental truck out front. A woman was rearranging the top sellers' table, taking off what was there and filling it with stacks of *Patricia's Perfect Hints*, Volume 4. I'd expected a person or maybe two with a video camera, not the film crew that was setting up, complete with lighting and screens to soften the glare. More of her people were pushing bookcases out of the way and creating an event area in the middle of the store.

This was way beyond what I'd agreed to. To make it worse, Adele was watching it all and taking notes. I tried stopping the progress of the chair people to no avail. I found the guy in charge of the camera crew, but he told me to talk to Patricia. Eduardo was hanging around near Adele and taking it all in. I certainly hoped that Adele wasn't promising him a production like this.

I was at the front of the bookstore when a small bus pulled up. One of Patricia's people flew past me and rushed outside to greet the passengers as they disembarked. It was like the Noah's ark of the politically correct. An elderly Caucasian couple got off first, followed by a pair of prosperous-looking African-Americans, two Hispanic teens, Asian twins, an arm-in-arm couple of gay men and finally, two hand-holding brunette lesbians.

Patricia and Benjamin came across the parking lot. Even from a distance, it was obvious they both were wearing stage makeup. When they reached the front of the bookstore, the bus passengers were arranged around them and a still photographer got it on film.

How could I have been so dense? They were filming this to use it as part of a campaign commercial. The crowd moved inside, and I dodged the parade of chairs to get to Patricia.

"You're going to have to tone this down," I said. She was all smiles as she reminded me it had all been spelled out in the paper I'd signed. Now I understood why she'd made it impossible to read when she'd given it to me to sign.

"Don't worry, it'll be fine," she said in an artificially warm voice. "Look, Benjamin, here's Molly." She pulled me into their little circle.

"We can't thank you enough," Benjamin said, greeting me. "It's good to have you on our team." Benjamin turned his head toward the camera and put on a sincere smile while he shook my hand and put his other hand on my shoulder.

I could just imagine the caption: *Benjamin Bradford takes time from his busy schedule to comfort widow.*

I let out a sigh and realized there was no way I could undo this circus, but maybe there was a consolation. People seemed to be attracted by the film crew. Maybe they were curious, or maybe they thought it was their chance to be part of history, but passersby kept coming in. And once they got bored watching the group from the bus be arranged and rearranged in the front rows, they browsed the rest of the bookstore. I noticed a constant line at the cashier. A surge in sales might smooth things out if Mrs. Shedd found out about the filming, which I'm sure she would, courtesy of Adele.

By the time Patricia's program was to begin, all the seats were filled and there were even people standing. It seemed odd to have everything set up in the middle of the store, but by then I was just going with the flow. I started walking toward the demonstration table to do my introduction, but Benjamin got there first. He took the microphone off the stand and began addressing the crowd while two men with large cameras on their shoulders videotaped him.

"Let me tell you a little about my wonderful wife. Before we married, she was a single parent and she'd told me how hard it was to keep it together for little Kimmee and Demetrius. Her book of hints is testament to her ingenuity and creativity." He was laying it on pretty thick, and I tuned out so as not to go into sugar shock. I checked out the crowd and noticed a lot of regulars, but was surprised to see Pixie had come in.

As I eased my way toward her, Bob came out of the café holding some iced drink with a lot of whipped cream. He presented it to her and hung around waiting to see her reaction. She was more interested in Eduardo, who was leaning against a bookcase behind Benjamin and the demonstration table, so he was facing the crowd. She took a sip of the drink and threaded her way through people until she was next to the cover model. Bob followed her like a puppy dog. I made a mental note to give him more compliments on his work. I hadn't realized he was so needy.

By now Benjamin had segued into his campaign pitch

and he'd rolled up the sleeves of his dress shirt. I'd seen enough of these campaign things to know they would probably just use the visual of him looking hardworking and concerned and mix it with a voice-over.

I glanced toward the front of the bookstore as more people came in, but one person in a blue doctor's jacket grabbed my attention. Dr. Arnold Bullard. I started toward him. This was my big chance to talk to him and I wasn't going to miss it. I'd already figured out what to say to trap him. It was Basic Sales 101. You didn't ask somebody if they wanted to buy something or not—you asked if they wanted it in red or blue. I was going to use the same logic with him. Instead of asking if he'd been at the Cottage Shoppe, I was going to ask him if he was there to buy or sell something.

As I got closer, I noticed he'd stopped. Patricia had taken the spotlight and was beginning her spiel. He watched intently for a moment and then began to move around the edge of the crowd. I trailed behind him and when I'd almost caught up realized I might have been mistaken about who he was watching. Pixie was talking to Eduardo and Bob was next to her.

"Excuse me," I said, trying to get Arnold's attention. Fat chance that a jealous husband was going to be distracted by me when his wife was in the middle of two men.

Patricia was at her grand finale. She threw the red wine on Benjamin's white shirt and held up the bottle of special spot-dissolver potion, mentioning the recipe was in the book. This was her big moment. When she got the wine to disappear, the audience always gasped in surprise and applauded enthusiastically.

Bob put his hand on Pixie's arm, no doubt asking for her verdict on the drink. Pixie suddenly saw Arnold, and as he got closer, she put up her hands as if to stop him from doing something.

I sped up and tried to block Arnold, but it all happened too fast. There was some yelling—something about "paws off my wife" and Pixie screaming, "Don't!" And then I heard the sound of a fist hitting a jaw. Bob had stepped back, and I saw that Arnold's fist had landed on Eduardo's face.

Pixie started shouting. "Stop, Arnold! Stop before you do it again!"

Then all hell broke loose. In a flash, Benjamin's handlers rushed him out the door, leaving Patricia at the table, still holding the magic-potion bottle.

If I were her, I'd think twice about tying up with a man who left me out to dry when stuff hit the fan. But it was none of my business. I wondered if Eduardo would hit back, but Pixie hustled Arnold outside before he had a chance.

I was left facing the crowd. Adele came up behind me. "Pink, you better do something."

I had an idea, didn't know if it would work, but figured it couldn't make things worse.

I grabbed the microphone. "We're trying something new here at Shedd & Royal. I hope you all enjoyed our first evening of performance art."

My words hung in the air for a moment as all eyes stared at me. Then someone said, "So you mean that was all planned, kind of like *Tony and Tina's Wedding*?" And I nodded, recalling the interactive play.

Suddenly everyone got it and applauded.

"YOU DIDN'T," DINAH SAID. ON MY WAY OUT I'D called her on my cell to give her a recap. "I miss everything," she said with just a tiny whine in her voice.

"I did," I said with a laugh. "And despite everything, it turned out to be a good night. Even without her grand finale, Patricia sold out all her books. People thought Bob was part of the show and complimented him on his acting as they bought drinks and cookies. Adele got an ice pack for Eduardo. A cover model can't very well go around with a bruise on his chiseled jaw. And all I want to do is go home and collapse," I said before clicking off and getting in my car.

Chapter 21

I OPENED THE BACK DOOR, GLAD TO BE FINALLY home. But when I walked into my living room, I jumped. It wasn't just that the room seemed in disarray. It was who was on the couch. Barry and Jeffrey were asleep sitting up. Jeffrey was leaning against his father's tall frame, and there was a dog on either side of them. Blondie, who never cuddled for long, was nestled against Jeffrey. Cosmo was drapped across Barry's lap with his legs in the air.

Once I got over the shock of seeing them, I started to get annoyed. This was taking it too far with the dog thing. Barry must have been sleeping with his eyes only half shut, because he awoke before I could take another step in the room. I supposed it was from years of getting calls at odd hours and having to function, but he was immediately alert.

I was about the make my comment about the dog care, but he stopped me.

"Now, don't worry, Molly," he said, which was like a green light in my worry department. If there wasn't something wrong, why would he even need to caution me? He extricated himself from Cosmo and sat forward. He had way past a five o'clock shadow on his face, his tie was pulled lose, but he was still wearing his suit jacket. Without Barry to lean against, Jeffrey fell into a prone position behind his father.

I glanced around the living room again. Something had gone on. Things had been knocked off the coffee table, and an easy chair had been moved along with the table next to it.

"Sorry, they had to move that to get the gurney in." He got up and started picking up the books and doodads that had fallen and putting them back on the coffee table.

"Gurney, like in the thing they roll you into an ambulance with?" My voice sounded a little hysterical. "Who went to the hospital?"

Thanks to his job, Barry was an expert at giving bad news. First he got me to sit down and take a few breaths to calm myself, then in an even tone he told me what happened.

He and Jeffrey had just pulled up to spend some time with Cosmo when the ambulance arrived. "I was afraid it was you and practically broke the door down," Barry said. "When we came in, Morgan was passed out on the floor and Samuel wasn't handling it well.

"The paramedics wanted to know what happened, but Samuel kept walking in circles, muttering something about her being dead." Barry saw me go pale and touched my arm. "She's not dead. Remember, I said not to worry. I wouldn't have said that if she was dead." He went on about Samuel barely holding it together and how he'd taken over and told Samuel to sit down with Jeffrey. The gist was that Morgan had passed out, probably from not eating. She had come to and said she was fine, but when she tried to stand, she collapsed again. "I told Samuel he better man up and take care of her."

My mother protector came out and I told him again that Samuel was still having a hard time with Charlie's death, and seeing his girlfriend sprawled on the floor probably brought it all back. Before I could ask about Morgan, Barry said he'd already checked with the hospital and some of her levels were low and they were keeping her overnight. "Samuel called her mother in Phoenix, and she's coming to take her back there. He said he'd come by and pack up her things."

"I'd say that's taking care of things pretty well," I said a little too defensively. I sank into the chair as the weight of the evening and the adrenalin rush from the news sunk in. Barry asked if I needed something.

"No, just a few minutes to collect myself." Then I told him about my evening at the bookstore. He shook his head with disbelief when I got to the punch part. "You really should tell Detective Heather she ought to check out Arnold Bullard. He obviously has a problem with impulse management, and he was angry at Drew Brooks. He could have easily smacked him on the head."

"What was Bullard so angry at Drew Brooks about?" Barry asked.

"I don't know."

Barry put his hand on my shoulder. "You're staying out of it, right?"

I just looked at him. His cell phone rang, interrupting us, and his face grew stern. Phone calls this late usually weren't good.

"Greenberg," he answered; he clenched his jaw a few times while he listened. When he hung up, he announced he had to go to work. He straightened his tie and ran his hands over his hair as if that would make him look shower fresh. He bent over Jeffrey to awaken him. "I'll drop him off at home on the way."

I'd been concerned about Jeffrey being at their place alone at night so much and Barry had told me he had an arrangement with a neighbor. If Jeffrey needed anything he could go there. I knew I should let it go, but he looked so peaceful and as much as I knew I should stay out of it, it bothered me to think of him home alone all night.

"He can stay," I said, hoping I wasn't making a mistake. Isn't that how it had started with Cosmo?

THE NEXT MORNING THERE WAS A NOTE NEXT TO me. It said, "Thank you. Please consider this the advance notice you are always asking for. Jeffrey and I would like to take you out to dinner at the restaurant of your choice." He'd signed it, "Love, B." I read it over and smiled. How could you not melt for a guy who would sign a note *love*?

The couch was empty, the blanket neatly folded on the pillow I'd put under Jeffrey's sleeping head.

I showered and got dressed and did some chores around the house. Considering my previous night, I felt amazingly refreshed. I packed up my crochet goods and made sure the plastic bag with the hanky was in my bag. I was going to show it to Sheila.

The bookstore was in better shape than I'd expected. Patricia had been truthful about one thing: She made sure things were put back where they belonged. Rayaad said a crew had been waiting when she opened the bookstore. They had moved everything back, picked up stray coffee cups and even put the best sellers back on their table. The only person not happy about it was Adele. It gave her one less thing to tattle on me about.

As I approached the event area, I heard Adele telling everyone at the crochet table about the previous night's *performance art*.

"Pink really called it that," she said. I was relieved that she'd dressed semicasual today after all the business attire and crocheted ties. She wore black leggings with a brick red baby-doll tunic and a bunch of beaded necklaces. She finished it off with a print scarf wound around her head. Adele went on about how Eduardo had been an innocent bystander and had gotten punched for no reason. "I'm going to make sure nothing like that happens at the Milton Mindell signing," she said, her voice full of self-assumed authority. I hoped Mrs. Shedd realized she'd created a monster when she said Adele could help with the book signing.

I almost didn't recognize CeeCee. The stylist had dressed her in loose gray slacks, ballet flats, a white silk blouse and a black sweater—probably cashmere—tied over her shoulders. Her hair was now a natural shade of brown and had been poufed into a style that practically covered her face. The feather bangs were so long they were in her eyes. She looked good in a Lauren Bacall sort of way, but not like the CeeCee we were used to.

All eyes were on me as I set down my things, then came the torrent of questions about the night before. CeeCee wanted to check my work to see how I was coming along and wanted to know why Patricia and Dinah were AWOL. And what had happened to the ballet dancer I'd brought?

I started at the end first and told them about Morgan passing out from not eating and that for now she'd gone home with her mother.

"I should have talked to her," CeeCee said. "Maybe if she'd heard about my portion control plan, things would have been different." I wanted to explain that you had to eat something to be concerned with portions.

Even with all her book sales, Patricia had left in a huff after her event. The evening hadn't gone the way she'd wanted, and I think she blamed me. For all her talk about how wonderful our project was, I wondered if she'd ever show up again. In any case she'd given CeeCee several knitted shawls on the sly, so she'd really done her share. I had a feeling I was no longer part of the team.

Dinah was another story. She had a legitimate reason for her absence. She'd called me in a frantic state. The kids were throwing up, and it had been a long time since she'd dealt with that kind of cleanup and needed advice. Under the circumstances she couldn't leave them with a babysitter or take them to child care, and Jeremy had been gone when she woke up. Too bad Patricia wasn't there. She probably would have had some good hints on the cleanup.

My gaze met Sheila's and she smiled wanly. No drumming or tight stitches, she seemed to have turned all her nerves inward. That made me more uneasy than her finger tapping. With all the tension and nerves roiling around inside her, building up heat and energy, I feared she would suddenly explode. I hoped I was wrong. She appeared to have a rhythm going, and I watched the ball of golden honey–colored yarn jump as she finished a row of stitches

Eduardo was sitting near Adele, though I suspected she thought he was sitting *with* her. Who would have guessed that he would be one of those flying-finger-type crocheters? He'd already brought in a completed maple-colored shawl, and in the time it took me to get my stuff arranged, he'd produced two more rows of stitches on the olive green one he was working on now.

I did a row on my shawl, then I brought out the plastic bag with the hanky and showed it to Sheila. "Do you have any idea what this is?"

She picked up the plastic bag and examined the contents. "It looks like a handkerchief," she said.

I rolled my eyes and explained I knew it was a handkerchief. "I was hoping you could give me some information about it, like when it was made."

She paused and took a few long breaths. "I'm trying something new for my anxiety. When I get tense I count to five as I inhale and then do the same when I let the air out. It's supposed to do something to fool your vagus nerve.

"As long as I never hear from Detective Gilmore again, I'll be fine," she said with a sigh. She turned the plastic bag over a few times and looked closely at the filigree-like edging around the fine cotton center. "It might be Victorian," she said. "No, change that to First World War." She turned it over again. "I'm really not sure. The class I'm taking now is geared toward designing wardrobes for robots and space creatures." I saw her do her breathing move, and when she let all the air out she asked where I'd gotten it.

"She found it at the Cottage Shoppe, dear," CeeCee blurted out. "Molly, didn't you say you thought it was connected with the murder?" She gestured toward the red spots. "That's not blood. It's tomato soup."

Sheila's breath turned shallow, and she dropped the bag as though it were a scorching poker.

I put my head down in dismay. So much for keeping its origin a secret. When I looked up, the whole table was staring at me again.

I went through the story, saying I'd picked it up by mistake. I told them the whole no-show sock thing but left out that I'd been under Kevin's desk at the time. Where was Dinah when I needed her? She could corroborate my story. Her ex ought to be at her house cleaning up after his own kids. This situation was worse than if she'd met a new guy and was caught up in that infatuation fog that made you forget all your other friends.

"Pink, you're losing it. Isn't that called shoplifting?"

Adele said. She had moved her chair so close to Eduardo's they knocked into each other.

"It's not shoplifting if the thing you pick up is crumbled up and has soup on it, and most of all, isn't for sale," I said, giving Adele the evil eye. I reached to get it back, but Eduardo asked if he could look at it.

He turned the bag over, examining it from all angles. "This looks like Irish crochet." When he saw my quizzical expression, he explained he was a McGurk on his mother's side, and he went on to tell us a bit about his family. Eduardo had a deep, melodious voice and a charismatic smile. He could have been telling us the history of dirt and we all would have happily listened. Luckily, the story he told was much more interesting.

"My Gran Maeve wanted to pass on the knowledge of Irish crochet, but we were a family of boys." His blue eyes sparkled with good humor. "I was the last to come along, and she realized there weren't going to be any girls to teach, so I got the gift."

Eduardo pointed to the wide scallopy edging of the handkerchief. "This isn't what most people think of when you mention Irish crochet. Most of it is made of motifs like flowers and leaves, sometimes around cord to give it more of a three-dimensional appearance. My gran taught me how to baste the motifs to some fabric like muslin and then join them with Clones knots or picot filling stitches." He looked down at his hands and chuckled. "I'm afraid that even with all her lessons I was never that good."

His Gran Maeve had told him about the history of it as she tried to teach him how to do the fine work. "The craft was created during the great potato famine and saved many families. It was based on Venetian lace that had been available only to the very rich people. My ancestors created a new craft and made money to feed their families. And for the first time the not-so-rich were able to have lace. But the work was so beautiful that royalty and the very wealthy wanted some of it, too. Queen Victoria owned some, and Queen Mary's coronation dress was rumored to have been made of it."

I asked him if he had any idea of the value.

"I saw something like it in a shop for six hundred dollars."

"For a hanky?" I exclaimed and he nodded.

CeeCee shook her head, and her feathered bangs flipped up and down in the resulting breeze. She reached up to push them out of her eyes but then reconsidered and let them be. "That was all very interesting, but nobody's hook is moving. We made a commitment, remember?"

I took back the hanky and we all got to work. Adele looked at my shawl and let out a "tsk-tsk." "Pink, you really need to work on your speed."

I just rolled my eyes.

THE MORE I FOUND OUT ABOUT THE HANDKERchief, the more I believed it was the key to everything. But I still didn't know how it had landed in Kevin's office. When I took a break in the afternoon, I headed down the street to the Cottage Shoppe to see if I could find out.

The inside of the store was more in flux than the last time I'd seen it. The for-sale items had even less space.

Dorothy finished a phone call and walked over to me.

"Things look different around here," I said, gesturing toward the entranceway and the dining room.

"You don't have to tell me." She shook her head with dismay. "Mr. Kevin has gone nuts with the restaurant idea. Want some soup? Even with all this upheaval, he's making it every day." She shrugged and put up her hands. "People say it's good."

"I guess the important question is, is it selling?"

"Surprisingly yes, though it's almost all a to-go business. Who'd want to eat in there now?"

I nodded in agreement. Tables had been set up next to the heavy plastic sheet hanging where a wall used to be.

"I know you looked at this before," she said, pointing to the basket of yarn supplies. She took out the yarn swift and opened it. She set it on the floor, picked up one of the hanks of yarn and then showed me how the swift worked. She was quite the saleswoman, though she almost got her arm caught in it. "It works better when it's attached to a table or something," she said, indicating the clamp on the bottom. "We're offering a deal on the swift and the yarn," she added in her best sales voice. "It's likely to go fast."

I wasn't there to go shopping, but I was tempted. I thought of all the yarn I had already, but the swift was intriguing. Finally, she offered to put them on hold for me. It was an offer I couldn't resist, and she said she'd stick them in the storage container with a note on it.

I asked her where Trina was.

"She quit. She said she couldn't get past the trauma of finding Drew," Dorothy said. "It's been better for me, more hours, and Mr. Kevin has been taking up the slack."

I picked up some tea towels with a layer of crocheted trim on the bottom. Now that I had the name of what I was looking for, I thought it might make a difference.

"You mentioned having some heirlooms a while back. I wondered if any of them were Irish crochet," I said.

She thought for a moment and her face brightened. "Yes, that's what the stuff was called." She thought some more. "I don't know if you ever saw the display room upstairs. It's where Mr. Kevin's office is now. It was such a pretty room. Mrs. Brooks used to keep all the really nice stuff up there. The walls were a soft ecru color and made a nice backdrop for the mahogany furniture. She used an old chest of drawers to display antique linens. She always kept candelabra bulbs in the wall sconces so the light was soft. There was an old washstand with a pitcher and washbowl, too." Dorothy was getting all misty-eyed. "It was so different when she was here. So much nicer. She loved the business and this store. Mr. Drew just cared about making more profit, and Mr. Kevin is dead set on making this some kind of soup emporium."

She was getting off the subject, so I asked her again about the heirloom items.

"They were in an old-fashioned suitcase. You know, no wheels or handles. I think it was leather and had decals from different places stuck to it. Mrs. Brooks used the suitcase to display them in the room upstairs. There were some pieces I think she called Irish crochet. I think she even tried to show them to me. I just remember some lacy stuff she was oohing and aahing about. To me it all looked like doilies, which I don't care for. There were other things, too. Some candlesticks, I think, and a silver tea set."

"But was there a handkerchief? Something with lots of trim?"

She gave me an odd look, then apparently remembered I'd said I was looking for a hanky for a gift.

"I'm sorry, but all those things sold. Too bad we don't still have the brochure the seller provided. It probably listed all the items. I think it had the whole story about where the things came from and some photographs."

I asked for more details, but she shrugged. "I can barely remember *Gina and Captain Blackhart* and I read that last week, so I certainly can't remember the details of something I looked at maybe once, eight months ago."

I asked her if she knew who the seller was.

She seemed to be tiring of my questions and said in a dismissive manner, "Mrs. Brooks dealt with the person directly and never disclosed who it was."

Dorothy seemed relieved when someone came in wanting soup and left me to help them. I headed back to the bookstore, disappointed that I hadn't gotten more information.

I spent the rest of the afternoon going over a checklist for the Milton Mindell event and putting up the signs announcing it. It was a pleasure not to have any input from Adele—she had the afternoon off.

When I'd finished at the bookstore, I went to the grocery store. I'd received a frantic call from Dinah. She was stuck in the house with the kids and she was losing her mind. This from a person who could whip freshmen into shape in a semester. I would have cooked something and brought it over, but there wasn't time. Dinah sounded on the edge.

I picked up garlic-roasted potatoes, rotisserie chicken, and salad for Dinah and me, and rice, soda, crackers and that liquid stuff for kids so they wouldn't get dehyrdrated. Then I picked up some kids' movies and a couple of toys, scented candles and both salts at the drugstore and headed to Dinah's. She greeted me with a hug as if she were a shipwrecked sailor and I had just showed up with a lifeboat.

The throwing up had ended, and the kids were feeling better. "Just enough to be really annoying," Dinah said. I could hear them in the other room playing the same *Tommy and His Tootle Boys* DVD over and over. It amazed me how kids who could barely blow their own noses had no problem operating video equipment.

I gave Dinah the scented candle and the bath salts I had gotten at the drugstore and told her she needed a nice bath. I would take care of things in the meantime. She still had the rescued-sailor look as she headed off to her bathroom.

I replaced the *Tommy* video with a new one. Personally, I was against electronic babysitters except in an emergency, but this clearly was one. I finished the cleanup, threw in a load of laundry and sprayed the house with odor remover. It got rid of the acidy, old-cheese smell from the kids being sick and replaced it with a fragrance that was like elevator music: pleasant, but you couldn't place what it was.

Dinah came out of the bath looking refreshed and relaxed. I'd set the table, and we all sat down. Dinah ate with gusto, but E. Conner and Ashley-Angela refused to eat the rice or saltines. Finally, I gave them regular food and hoped for the best.

"What would I do without you?" Dinah said as we went into the living room after we'd eaten. The kids took the toys I'd gotten them and went to rewatch the video I'd brought. Knowing they probably would watch it multiple times, I'd picked one about wildlife with a soothing-voiced narrator.

Dinah wanted to know what she'd missed at the crochet group. She was stunned when I told her what Eduardo had said about the hanky.

"Six hundred dollars?" she repeated.

"Who'd have thought a handkerchief could be worth so much?" I also told her about my trip to the Cottage Shoppe.

"So what do you think it all means?" The zest had returned to Dinah's manner.

"We still don't know where the handkerchief fits in, and we still have a whole list of suspects. After Arnold Bullard punched Eduardo, he moved up on my list—maybe right to the top. He was there around the time Drew got killed, angry about something, and he certainly has an impulse control problem. Then there is Kevin. Drew tells him no way on the soup shop, and as soon as he's dead, Kevin goes ahead with his plan. And I have to tell you Trina's quitting, saying she couldn't get over the trauma, seemed a little too convenient. She is the one who was standing over him when we all rushed in. She might have thought if she was out of sight nobody would count her as a suspect. That might work with Detective Heather, but not with me. I'm keeping her on my radar."

I leaned back in the dining room chair. Outside it was getting dark and the temperature was going down. I pulled on the sweater I'd had tied around my waist. "But I keep going back to Arnold Bullard. We know he was angry at Drew Brooks about something. And we know he acts on his anger."

"But we don't know why he was so mad at Drew."

I felt disheartened. "That's exactly what Barry said when I suggested Arnold Bullard looked guilty."

"Barry?" Dinah repeated. She knew how I kept taking a step back and then he would try to take two steps closer. There was so much to tell as she'd been out of the loop.

When I left, the kids were asleep and Dinah was sitting with her feet up, grading papers.

The lights were on at my house when I got home. Barry was sitting on my couch again. This time awake. I didn't have to see my eyes to know their expression had darkened. Helping with Morgan was one thing, but just being here whenever—I don't think so. I started to say something to that effect, but he held up his hand. "Don't say something you'll regret, Molly," he admonished. A shiver went down my spine. His face had that shut-the-blinds kind of blankness. It was his cop face. The one he used when he confronted people with bad news.

Chapter 22

"I WANTED YOU TO HEAR IT FROM ME," BARRY said as he stood up and held on to my arm. "Dr. Arnold Bullard is dead."

I felt the starch go out of my body and my legs turn rubbery. Barry had done this sort of thing many times before and was ready when I slumped against him.

"But he was one of my chief persons of interest," I said. "I was sure he might have killed Drew Brooks. All I needed was the motive." I stopped talking, realizing I'd said too much already. Barry was one hundred percent against me "playing detective," as he called it. I personally didn't think there was any playing involved. I just wanted to find out who did it, so Detective Heather would stop hounding Sheila.

"I know," he said.

"What?" And here I thought I was being so discreet, he'd never get it.

"I am a detective," he said with a slow smile, "a real one, remember? And I can figure things out." He gestured toward the couch, and we both sat down. "That's why I came to tell you in person."

"Okay, Mr. Real Detective, are you going to tell me what happened?" I said. His face had softened into the Barry face I was used to. It wasn't full of expression, but it was worlds away from his blank, bad-news cop face. I supposed over time he'd learned to shield his emotions as a way of protecting himself. It had to be horrible to be the one who had to break the news that a loved one was dead. Barry wouldn't talk about the emotional part of his work. He also didn't talk much about his past. Even though I wanted to know the dirt about his ex-wife, I thought it was honorable that he didn't bad-mouth her. He kept saying that all that mattered was now. I didn't totally agree about that and chipped away at him until he had begun to let things slip out.

One rainy night, he'd told me why he became a cop. It had to do with his parents owning a convenience store that kept getting robbed and the cops never finding the culprits. It made him want to be one of the good guys. Another time he told me the way he dealt with the dark parts of his job was by remembering he was speaking for a victim who couldn't and trying to bring some peace to the victim's family. Then to lighten the somber mood he'd added, "And of course, I get to drive fast and carry a gun."

Now, he sighed with resignation and said, "I'll tell you what happened, if you promise not to get involved."

I didn't answer, which I guessed he realized was the same as not agreeing to his bargain. He grimaced and clenched his jaw a few times, then gave in and told me anyway.

"Pixie Bullard got worried when Arnold didn't show, and she went down to his office and found him slumped on his desk."

"Was it a heart attack or did someone . . ." I started to ask, afraid he was going to leave the story at that.

"It looks like foul play," Barry said. "There was a paper bowl of soup on his desk, like he was eating it. There were also two expelled bug bombs. The office still smelled of insecticide when the first officers arrived. They called the haz-mat crew."

"So the bug bombs did him in?"

"Don't know for sure yet, but it's certainly a possiblity. The soup is being tested, but I'm guessing they will find something in it—some kind of sedative or knockout drops. Nobody would sit there and inhale bug bombs."

"What kind of soup was it?" I asked.

He seemed surprised by the question. "Southwestern corn chowder, but I don't think it makes a difference."

"Then it's your case?" I asked, and he gave me a withering stare and shook his head.

"Someone remembered that you had been caught stalking Bullard. And that he threw some kind of fit at the bookstore. I can't take a case if my girlfriend is involved. If you keep it up, I may never get a case again."

"Who did get it?"

"I'll give you one guess," Barry said.

"Detective Heather, right?" I said, and Barry nodded. But then something struck me as strange. He knew an awful lot about it despite the fact it was not his case, so I asked how he'd gotten the information.

"I was talking to Heather and she filled me in."

"You were talking to Detective Heather?" Instantly I had an image of her white blond hair and well-fitted suit. No doubt as they were talking she was doing the hair twirling thing and touching his arm. Personally, I thought it was very unprofessional.

"We work together, remember?" There was a flicker in

Barry's dark eyes. Mr. Detective knew he'd hit a nerve and he went for it. Even though I knew what he was doing, I went nuts anyway.

"You know, Molly, the way you keep not wanting to commit to anything, even a trip to Maui? Well, some guys would appreciate the attention from someone like Heather, who just happened to mention that Maui was her dream romantic vacation destination."

I was stuck on the image of her in that fitted suit and this ridiculous question popped into my mind: Where did she carry her gun? Barry laughed when I asked him.

"She has this special underwear holster," he said, then laughed harder when he saw my look of horror. "Not that kind of underwear. You *wear* it *under* your clothes. By the way, she told me; she didn't show me."

Cosmo woke up and headed for the back door, and Barry got up to let him out. "You can ask her about it yourself," he said over his shoulder. "She wants to talk to you about what happened at the bookstore and why you were sitting outside Bullard's house."

Great.

When Barry came back from letting the dogs out, I offered to make some scrambled eggs. He smiled and nodded hungrily, but then his cell rang.

"Greenberg," he answered in his all-business, even tone. The slight downturn on his lips told me it was work.

"Rain check," he called, heading toward the door.

Jeffrey called shortly after. It was hard for him to admit it, since he was trying to be such a man, but there were noises and he was scared. I couldn't help myself. Like I said, when it comes to animals and children, I'm a total pushover. I went over to get him and left a message on Barry's cell.

Jeffrey seemed a little embarrassed but looked relieved when he saw me. He was thirteen and still had that soft unfinished look, though he tried to hide it by gelling his hair into a spikey style. He was wearing jeans and a polo shirt and had grabbed a jacket. I suggested he bring along his pajamas and said he was welcome to sleep at my house.

Both Cosmo and Blondie were happy to see him and followed him into Samuel's old room, which had recently been vacated by Morgan. I turned on the lights and told Jeffrey to make himself at home. He took me up on the offer of a snack. I think he and Barry lived on pizza when they were on their own. Jeffrey ate the scrambled eggs, toast and fruit with obvious hunger. I sat at the table with him while he ate, and he told me about the latest in his acting career. He'd gone on a casting call for a commercial and made it through the first cut.

"Next time, I think they're going to tape me. It would be so cool if I got it." He set down his fork. "Then maybe my dad would see I'm serious." I listened and nodded. I thought it was going to take a lot to get Barry to accept Jeffrey's aspirations. And he'd never accept his son changing his name to Columbia. Jeffrey was yawning by the time I gave him some vanilla ice cream with strawberries on top. As soon as he finished, I suggested he might want to go to bed. He nodded and got up. Before he walked away he turned back. "Thank you," he said, coming back to hug me. I ruffled his spikey hair and hugged him back and wished him good sleep.

I didn't hear anything more from him, so I guessed he'd gone to sleep right away. By now I was too wired to sleep. Between the news about Arnold Bullard and my surprise guest, my mind wouldn't quit.

I found the Trader Joe's plastic shopping bag with my shawl in progress. Then I dialed Dinah. It was late, but we had long ago agreed that no hour was too late if either of us needed to talk.

"Arnold Bullard is dead?" Dinah repeated after I'd told her what Barry had said. She'd sounded sleepy when she answered but was completely alert once I told her about the tall bald orthodontist. "But he was so high on our list of suspects. Now we'll never know why he was so angry at Drew or if he's the one who killed him."

"I know," I said. "And now there's no way to get Detective Heather to consider him a serious suspect, which means she's still going to focus on Sheila."

"Have you told Sheila yet?"

I said I was going to do it in person in the morning. Sheila was in such a fragile state I was afraid of how she might take the news. "There's no chance we'll get to see the murder scene this time." I'd told Dinah what Barry had said about it, but hearing a description of the scene wasn't the same as actually seeing it.

"It sounds like someone wanted to get rid of a pest," Dinah said, then yawned.

"But who? And isn't it strange how soup played a part in both Drew Brooks's and Arnold Bullard's deaths?" I told her what Barry said about there probably being some kind of knockout drops in the Southwestern corn chowder.

Dinah yawned again. "Did Barry say where the corn chowder came from?"

"Are you kidding? I can't believe he told me about the possible knockout drops."

I looked down at the shawl. I'd done several rows while we were talking, but somehow the pattern made of double crochets and spaces, which were supposed to look like tiny windows, had gotten screwed up so that there weren't any open spaces in some spots and in others they were so big they resembled sliding glass doors. When I finally hung up, I looked over my work and realized I had to tear out all I'd done. It made me so grateful for the ease of unraveling crochet. As I redid the rows, I kept thinking about what Dinah said. Where did Arnold Bullard's soup come from?

I held up the shawl and realized it was big enough to lay on my shoulder and get an idea of how it would feel when it was finished. Even though it covered only one shoulder, the effect was comforting. Someday, when it was finished, it would offer comfort to somebody who really needed it. Knowing that made me feel proud of what I was doing. At the same time, I was thinking about the soup and the only expert I knew in making it. As soon as the Cottage Shoppe opened, I was calling Kevin.

In the morning, while I was making coffee, Samuel breezed in the back door. Before I could stop him he went in his old room. A moment later he was back. "Why is there a kid sleeping in my bed?" he asked incredulously.

Barry showed up about then, and I left them all to work it out.

As soon as I got in my car, away from prying ears, I called the Cottage Shoppe. Kevin answered.

After exchanging hellos with him and reminding him who I was, I went right to the point. "What kind of soups did you have yesterday?"

"Why do you want to know?" There was caution in his voice. Then he sighed and went on talking without waiting for an answer. "Look, I heard about Dr. Bullard. There was nothing wrong with the ingredients in my Southwestern corn chowder."

"Then it did come from your place." I tried to downplay my surprise, but I was practically high-fiving myself. Wow. I even impressed myself at how easily I'd found out where the soup came from. I was good. And then Kevin gave me even more.

"Dr. Bullard was one of our first to-go customers. He worked evenings a lot and needed something to give him a pick-me-up that wouldn't tire him out. Soup was perfect."

I didn't want to bring up the fact that it hadn't exactly worked that way this time. "So then, he got the soup himself yesterday?"

Kevin's tone made it clear he thought it was a ridiculous question. "No. His wife got it for him."

Pixie got it for Arnold? While I was digesting that fact, Kevin realized he'd been talking too much and asked the purpose of my call. I didn't want to make him feel bad and inquired about the current soup offerings. I noticed there was no Southwestern corn chowder or tomato bisque. I guessed a death connection was a no-no in the soup sales department.

I put the soup issue on the back burner of my mind for the moment, determined to figure out what it meant later. I had to get to work, but I had to talk to Sheila first.

The women's gym where she worked was at the other end of downtown Tarzana. I wondered if Sheila had already heard that her best chance of getting out of Detective Heather's spotlight of interest was dead. I walked through the glass door into the bright plant-filled lobby and threaded my way through the women in black stretchy pants and sneakers who were coming and going.

I got the answer before I even spoke to Sheila. Detective Heather was standing at the reception desk talking to her. I was still getting used to Detective Heather's sleek new hairstyle. The old curly do had made her look a little ditzy even though she definitely wasn't. The new style gave her an ice-queen look of authority, which she turned on me when I came in her line of sight.

"Mrs. Pink, don't move. I need to talk to you."

Sheila looked close to tears. "Molly, I didn't mean to tell her. It just sort of tumbled out."

Before Sheila could finish, Detective Heather was in my face. "Okay, where's the handkerchief?"

I closed my eyes and groaned. I should have realized Sheila would crack under pressure. Detective Heather abandoned Sheila and suggested we go outside. I followed her through the doors, and then she turned on me. "Are you aware of the terms *withholding evidence* and *obstruction of justice*?"

I looked around helplessly.

"Barry's not going to rescue you this time."

What could I possibly say? Maybe the truth.

"It was just a mistake," I began. "Do you know what no-show socks are?" I felt a tiny bit of relief when she nodded. "Well, then you know how if they slip off your heel, they get all crumpled in your shoe." Detective Heather looked impatient and annoyed. What happened to that inscrutable detective expression she was supposed to have? "That's exactly what happened. Well, it was really only the left one that got jammed under my arch."

"Do you suppose you could get to the point?" Detective Heather had obviously heard enough details of what happened with my socks and recognized it for what it was—a stall while I hoped one of us would disappear.

"I took off the sock and put it in my pocket, and when I saw something white on the floor, I thought my sock had fallen out and picked it up."

Detective Heather leveled her gaze at me. "Where exactly did all of this take place?"

I was hoping she wouldn't ask. I tried to sound nonchalant when I told her it was in Kevin's office.

"Was he present?" She took out her notebook and started writing. She seemed surprised when I said yes. Of course I didn't mention I was under the desk and he had no idea I was there. It was my version of the don't-ask-don't-tell rule.

"And I suppose when you realized what you'd picked up, you thought you'd use it in your own investigation."

She had caught me, and I sighed. "Something like that." I looked to see if she was going to pull out some handcuffs from her purse. Instead she just glared at me.

"You'll have to turn it over to me."

I nodded and offered to bring it down to the station. "I'll have it to you by this afternoon."

"No. We'll go to your place and get it right now." She led me to her Crown Victoria and gestured toward the passenger seat. It was not a fun ride.

When she pulled in front of my house, she leaned toward me. "I know I mentioned withholding evidence and obstruction of justice, but I think I left out tampering with evidence. Do you have any idea how much trouble you're in if it turns out that handkerchief is evidence?"

I didn't think she expected an answer. What exactly qualified as tampering anyway? Oh dear. I'd touched the hanky, the pinchy winchy had touched it, and once it was in the plastic bag, a pile of books had flattened it.

And I'd been worried about her asking me about Arnold Bullard?

The dogs were obviously not expecting me home so soon. Cosmo had turned over the trash and was working his way through the contents. When he saw me, he took off across the house, leaving a trail of coffee-ground paw prints. Blondie, who always stayed in her chair when I was home, had relocated to the top of the couch and was surveying the action on the street. It was a slow morning—just a guy with a canvas sack distributing coupons for pizza. Blondie abandoned her post as soon as she saw us, and as she scurried across the house she did something she never did—barked at Detective Heather.

I got the hanky and surrendered it to Detective Heather.

She turned over the bag, examining it. By now it had smoothed out with only an occasional wrinkle. She looked closer.

"If that's blood, you're really in trouble," she said.

"I'm pretty sure it's tomato bisque soup." I debated whether I should say more, like how I thought the soup got on the hanky, but I was afraid it might annoy her more, and she looked pretty close to the edge in that department. But I took a chance and mentioned having seen a piece of something like the handkerchief hanging off the drawer handle on Drew Brooks's desk. "Your CSI people probably got it."

She glared at me in response. I thought she was going to leave after that, but she took out her notebook. "What do you know about Arnold Bullard's death?"

I didn't know what to say since all I really knew was what Barry had told me. My silence didn't sit well with her.

"The bookstore is just down the street from Dr. Bullard's office. Maybe you decided to take a little walk and check up on him. There was a call about you stalking him before."

I should have just kept quiet, but when she brought up the stalking issue I thought if I explained it might make it better.

Ha!

I put all my cards on the table. "I thought Dr. Bullard was definitely a suspect in Drew Brooks's murder. He was very angry about something, and he was there the day of the murder. I thought if I got some information and passed it on to—"

"You'd get your friend off the hook," Detective Heather said, interrupting me. "I don't think so. If your mishandling of this handkerchief messes up my case, you are so in trouble." She glanced around the room. Barry had left his jacket on the couch. She picked it up. "I'm seeing him later. I'll just give it to him then."

I guess there was no way to keep her from mentioning the handkerchief issue to Barry. She started to leave, but I realized my car was still at the gym where Sheila worked. I hated to do it, but I had to ask her for a ride back.

CHAPTER 23

"I'M SORRY," SHEILA WAILED AS I NEARED THE crochet table at Shedd & Royal. Thanks to Detective Heather's side trip I was late. And judging by the surprise on everyone's faces, nobody expected me to show. My guess was that Sheila had told them what happened and they thought I was on my way to jail. I laid my bag on the table and collapsed in my chair. Dealing with Detective Heather had left me drained. I looked around and saw that Patricia had come back and was actually crocheting. She was acting as if nothing unusual had happened with her book signing, but she gave me a dirty look. No doubt it was for my run-in with Detective Heather. The odds of my becoming part of Benjamin's team were dwindling.

Adele was sitting next to an empty chair, continually looking toward the door. I didn't have to ask what that was about. I knew she was waiting for Eduardo.

"I was so worried," Dinah said after getting up to hug

me. As soon as she sat back down, she began crocheting at warp speed, apparently trying to make up for lost time.

Adele finally gave up staring at the door and looked my way. "Pink, I don't want you to worry if you end up going to jail. I can handle the Milton Mindell thing alone just fine." I rolled my eyes at her remark and turned my attention to Sheila.

"I just want to know how the hanky came up in conversation," I said. Sheila's eyebrows were so close together they looked almost fused. Her eyes were big and sad.

"I'm so sorry," she repeated. "You're the last person I wanted to get in trouble after all you've done. Detective Gilmore started asking me about Arnold Bullard. I gave her all the reasons you said he might have been the one who killed Drew Brooks. When she told me he was dead, I kind of lost it and I guess I started rambling. I thought she was going to try to pin his death on me, too."

Sheila had to take a few deep breaths to calm herself. "Then I mentioned the white lacy stuff you saw hanging on the drawer, and when she wanted me to describe it, I said it looked kind of like the hanky." Sheila stopped again and regrouped. "She wanted to know what hanky and before I realized what I'd done I'd told her. I know I wasn't under oath or anything, but she kept saying I should just tell her the truth and that I'd get in more trouble if I withheld information. I should have just kept quiet. How much more trouble could I be in than being a suspect in a murder?"

Surprisingly, Sheila said it all without once drumming her fingers—or anything else. She lowered her head and asked me if I could forgive her. Of course, I did. The hanky disclosure had put me in a bad spot, but who could blame Sheila when Detective Heather kept chipping away at her?

"Can we save this for later," CeeCee said. "Obviously,

Molly is fine. When there's too much talking, there's not enough crocheting"

"That's just what I was going to say," Adele chimed in. She'd been so enamored with Eduardo lately, she'd almost forgotten that she was always vying with CeeCee for the position of group leader.

I took out my shawl, but I was having a hard time concentrating. I kept stopping and staring into space. The threats Detective Heather had made about withholding evidence and obstruction of justice suggested there could be handcuffs and jail involved. My cell phone went off, making me jump. Before I could even say hello, Barry started yelling.

"Molly, are you crazy? Withholding evidence? Why didn't you say something to me?"

I stepped away from the group. I didn't want an audience. "I didn't withhold evidence deliberately. And it might not even be evidence." Detective Heather sure hadn't wasted any time in telling Barry. "I didn't say anything about it because I thought it would put you in an awkward spot."

"Well, it has." Then he wanted to know where and how I got it. I told him the no-show sock story, but he knew enough to keep pressing until I explained exactly where I'd found it and what I'd been doing. I couldn't see him, but I was sure he was hitting his forehead with the heal of his hand.

"Maybe I better call Mason Fields," I said. I had already been thinking about doing it. Mason got his celebrity clients off from really serious charges like murder—withholding evidence would be small time.

The anger in Barry's voice changed to something else. Maybe frustration that he couldn't fix this, but Mason could, and worry about all the time I might spend with Mason discussing it. The picture of them trying to outdo each other barbecuing at my house came to mind.

"No, don't call him. At least, not yet," Barry commanded. "Just please tell me, is that the only thing you had?"

When I said yes, Barry sounded relieved and made me promise never to keep anything like that from him again.

"I hope I never have anything like that to keep from you," I said.

His voice softened and he thanked me for having Jeffrey over. Then he made a big deal about making plans for an actual advanced planned date.

It wasn't until later, when Dinah and I were ensconced at Caitlin's Cupcakes, that I thought about Pixie and the soup. Could Pixie have been involved in her husband's death?

Dinah had insisted on treating for drinks and cupcakes, which, after what I'd gone through, almost counted as medicinal. Dinah seemed more relaxed. She said she'd worked things out with Jeremy and he was taking over the care of his children, so she hoped all of them would be leaving soon. "I want my old life back."

I brought up my phone call with Kevin, and Dinah's smile faded and her eyes widened. "Oh dear. Pixie got the soup."

I told Dinah I'd already come up with a plan. "I'm going to call her, give her my sympathy about Arnold and offer to bring over some food. Then while she's eating I'll tell her I know she got the corn chowder for Arnold." Another hint from *The Average Joe's Guide*. If you said you already knew something incriminating, the person you were talking to was likely to just break down and tell you the whole story.

"I'd come with you, but I need to pack up the kids' things. I don't want to give Jeremy any excuse to delay their departure."

"It's probably better if I go alone anyway. That way I

can just concentrate on her." Dinah told me to be careful, and I assured her I wasn't going to eat anything there or let Pixie hang around behind me with anything heavy in her hand.

I finished up my afternoon at the bookstore. I spent most of the time finishing the preparations for Milton Mindell's book fiesta. Adele kept strongly suggesting changes, and I kept explaining that this was how Milton wanted it.

"Pink, that's old thinking. I'm sure Milton would appreciate some fresh ideas," Adele said, interrupting me.

I sighed with frustration. "I don't think so. He's very specific about how he wants his events handled, and that's how we're going to do it."

Adele stormed off with a "humph."

Returning home, I decided to make up for the fact that I hadn't done much cooking lately. After putting a big pan of vegetable and cheese lasagna in the oven, I made a nice salad of baby lettuce with paper-thin cucumber slices, shredded carrots and a buttery avocado, ready to be topped with homemade dressing and a sprinkling of blue cheese and walnuts. I mixed up a batch of cookie bars and put them in the bottom oven. Then, while everything was cooking, I called Pixie.

I told Pixie I knew the kind of state she was in and explained about Charlie. Instead of asking whether I could come over, I simply announced I was. She seemed grateful, particularly when I mentioned bringing home-cooked food.

I cut a big hunk of lasagna and put it in a disposable pan. A plastic bowl with a cover became the receptable for some of the salad; I kept the dressing and toppings on the side. The serving of cookie bars was generous, too. There would be some for now and some for later. The rest I put in the refrigerator and then left a note on the counter for Barry—in case he showed up to do his doggie-dad thing.

To get to Pixie's I drove up the winding streets I'd been through once before. The cul-de-sac seemed quiet and dark compared to the last time I'd been there. Inside the house the lights were on, but the curtains were drawn on the big window that faced the street. I loaded up the containers of food and crossed the street. It took a while for Pixie to open the door. I almost thought she wasn't going to answer. When she did, she looked drained and numb. Even her Princess Di hairstyle looked flat.

"Come in," she said in a worn voice. I started to walk in, but she nodded toward my shoes. There was a mat by the entrance with several pairs of shoes on it. I understood the reason for the no-shoe policy when I went inside. It reminded me of the Arctic—everything was white, from the thick white carpet to the white brocade sofa covered with furry white throw pillows. Even the glass coffee table didn't interfere with the blinding brightness. Pixie looked like a bit of clear water in her baggy royal blue sweats.

The scent of the food reached her, and I heard her stomach gurgle. She probably hadn't been eating and was starving even though she didn't feel it. I suggested making her a plate of food. She started to say no, but her stomach gurgled again and she agreed. We passed through the dining room, which looked as though it was probably used only on Thanksgiving. The kitchen was a little less white, and there was a table with a lone coffee cup. I set down the food and without asking for permission found a plate and silverware.

Pixie was on autopilot; she sat when I told her to and began to eat when I suggested it. The food must have hit a nerve because she began to eat in earnest, as though she was starving. Color came back to her face and she looked up. I had already decided to let her get comfortable with me before I confronted her with the soup issue.

"This is really good. Where'd you get it?" She named several groceries in the area known for their hot-food counters. When I said I'd made it, she stopped midbite, amazed. "You even made the lasgana?" I nodded, and she went back to eating.

I put the rest of the food on the counter. No reason to put it away yet. I thought she might be going for seconds.

I sat across from her and told her again how sorry I was for her loss.

"You didn't really know him, but he was a good man." Once she'd started talking the words tumbled out. I knew the drill. She was staying strong for her family, but now with me she let it all out.

She finally got to the present, and I was just about to bring up the soup when she brought up Detective Heather. "She's acting like she thinks I could have done it. Don't you think that is ridiculous?" I didn't say anything, but I'd picked up enough from Barry and *The Average Joe's Guide* to know that the first person to consider in a murder investigation was a spouse.

Pixie sighed and then repeated what she'd told Detective Heather—that Arnold had made a few enemies with his temper. "I told her about Arnold punching Captain Blackhart, though I couldn't give her his real name." By now, she'd almost finished with the plate of food. It seemed to be making her feel better. She thanked me again.

"I'm sorry I lied to you before," she said, picking at the last of the lasagna.

Her comment certainly got my attention, but I didn't say anything. It was something else I'd picked up from *The Average Joe's Guide to Criminal Investigation*. The section on questioning suggested not talking, because the party being interviewed would be uncomfortable with the silence and keep talking to fill up the void, often saying more than they meant to. Pixie could have been an example in the book. It took only a few seconds of dead air to get her talking again.

"I'm sure Arnold was at the Cottage Shoppe the day you thought you saw him." She put her head down. "I was just trying to protect him. I thought he might have killed Drew Brooks. He was certainly mad enough."

Even if it was against the book's advice I couldn't help myself. I asked why he was so angry.

"Who wouldn't be after what happened? Imagine not wanting to give him a refund."

She was speaking out of context and I wanted the whole story. "What exactly happened?"

Pixie had gotten up on her own and gone to check the package of food. She closed the aluminum foil around the lasagna and put it in the refrigerator, but took two cookie bars and came back to the table.

It had all started with her devotion to Princess Di. "Someone had brought in some family heirlooms and when Arnold read the brochure and saw that the items had belonged to a distant relative of Princess Di's, he wanted to get something for me."

The something turned out to be two somethings and hearing what one of them was made my mouth fall open. Arnold had bought a decorative hanky with a lacy crochet trim and a large Irish crochet collar. When I looked perplexed at the second item, Pixie explained that the word *collar* didn't do the item justice. "It was long and very decorative, almost like a scarf. The brochure had a picture of Lady Ratcliffe wearing it, and there was a photo of the family house outside London. Arnold wanted me to know the history of the collar and hanky and paid extra to get the brochure.

"They cost plenty, too, but my Arnold knew what it

would mean to me to have something from a family member of Princess Di's." She sighed and brushed the cookie bar crumbs off her lap. "I almost wish we'd never gone to the U.K. Sometimes ignorance is bliss."

She went on to explain how she'd taken the collar with her on their trip. Even though it was a collector's item, she liked the idea of wearing it to its original home. And Arnold wanted to show off that he'd bought her something so valuable. They had even found the family house and stopped in for tea in a nearby town. Arnold had bragged to the owner that the Irish crochet collar around Pixie's neck had belonged to Lady Ratcliffe of Palladium House. He'd even shown the owner the brochure.

"She laughed at us and said there was no Lady Ratcliffe and Palladium was the style of the house, not the name of it. Then she referred us to a shop that sold antiques. The shop owner said the collar wasn't even real Irish crochet. He was pretty sure it was made in China. Arnold didn't take it well. He was angry for being embarrassed and felt taken advantage of. He'd bought the items when Mrs. Brooks was still running the show, but he expected her nephew to make good on them.

"The first time Arnold went in there, Drew said absolutely no, but then out of nowhere he contacted Arnold and said he had changed his mind and if Arnold brought in the items, he'd give him a refund."

"Didn't that seem strange to you?" I asked.

"I didn't think about it. I just wanted Arnold to stop being so angry. He took it way too personally." She made another cookie bar stop and came back to the table. "When he went back, Drew gave him the refund. At least, that was what Arnold said. But when Drew turned up dead, I began to wonder. . . ." Her voice trailed off.

She took a bite of her cookie bar and swallowed it. "But

then the other day Arnold said he was going to get me a real antique piece of Irish crochet. I figured he was going back to the Cottage Shoppe."

I asked her if she still had the brochure that had come with the original items.

She said it ought to be around and went to look, but came back empty-handed. "I didn't think Arnold took it back with the items, but maybe he did." She shook her head a few times. "I thought I saw it in his home office."

I asked her about the picture of the woman wearing the piece. She shrugged and said it was just a reproduction of one of those old sepia-tone photos. All she remembered was that it was very formal and the woman had her hair piled on her head and she had her arm resting on the top of an old-fashioned Victorian chair. "I'm afraid all I really looked at was the crocheted collar. It felt like reaching back in time to see it on her and then hold it in my hand. I'm sure Arnold paid more attention to her face, being an orthdontist and all. He was always checking people's bites and commenting on how they would benefit from orthodontia." Her face crumpled at the thought of him.

I had gotten so involved in her story I'd forgotten about the whole soup issue. She was finished with the food and also finished talking. Her worn look had come back, and I realized I was running out of time. I'd just have to confront her about the soup.

As she walked me to the door, I grabbed my chance.

"I know you were the one who got the corn chowder for Arnold."

She blinked back some tears and appeared shocked. "I don't know who told you that, but they're wrong."

Chapter 24

Something was definitely fishy. Someone wasn't telling me the truth, but who? I rushed to the Cottage Shoppe the next morning on my way to the bookstore. I wanted to talk to Kevin personally. I figured face-to-face I'd have a better chance of figuring out whether he was telling the truth. I had to wait while he took care of a phone call and dealt with a workman, but I was finding it hard to contain my impatience. I suddenly understood Sheila's tapping as my foot began to do it on its own while I listened to the workman ask where to put something since there wasn't any more room in the storage unit.

"I just have a quick question," I said, knowing I was interrupting. But Kevin gave me a dirty look and continued dealing with the workman. Who cared if he was going to get rid of a box of files in a little while so there'd be room for the boxes next to the workman?

Finally, the man walked away and I got to talk to Kevin. "Who got the soup for Dr. Bullard?" I asked.

"Didn't you hear me the first time?" Kevin said. "Like I told Detective Gilmore, Mrs. Bullard got the soup for her husband."

He certainly looked like he was telling the truth, but so had Pixie. They couldn't both be right. Unless . . . "How did she order it? Did she come in and pick it up?"

"No, no. It was a phone order. Dorothy took the call. We have Mrs. Bullard's credit card on file. Then Dorothy took it over to him."

Maybe Kevin and Pixie both were telling the truth after all. I suddenly wanted to talk to Dorothy very badly, but she wasn't in yet and I couldn't wait around.

It was Milton Mindell day.

Most of our events were in the evening, but since Milton's fans were kids, we always held his events on Saturday mornings, and no matter how hard I tried to have all the loose ends taken care of, there were always things hanging. Things Adele would try to take care of and probably mess up if I wasn't there. I practically jogged down the street.

Kids and their parents were already lined up outside the bookstore when I arrived. Milton's appearances were more than events, they were extravaganzas. Large posters of his latest book, *The Zombie Next Door*, hung on the front windows, beckoning his loyal readers. As I walked inside, I passed Milton's Horror Helpers bringing in the tent so the program could have its proper dark setting.

I caught sight of Adele, who looked like a beatnik mortician. She wore a midcalf black knit skirt over black-and-white-striped tights. On top she had on a long black tunic with about six strands of shiny black beads. She'd topped off her ensemble with a black beret. And she'd gone the raccoon route with her eye makeup again. She looked askance at my usual khaki slacks and white shirt. To deal with the morning chill I'd added a long black vest. "Pink, I have a cape if you want to make your outfit more event appropriate." I didn't have time to answer.

The event was so popular we had to give out numbered tickets for places in the tent and the guarantee of a signed book. I gave half the tickets out in advance and the rest the day of the event. The beginning of the line outside was for the people with tickets and the back section for those hoping to get one. I could tell there were already more people in the line than I had tickets remaining.

I knew when Milton arrived by the rising noise level in the line. Then the door whooshed open and he made his entrance. He was about five feet two, dressed in black, of course, with a pompadour hairstyle that had been sprayed until it wouldn't dare quiver. He was flanked by two similarly dressed people of indeterminate sex who immediately left his side to fuss about the placement of the tent—some feng shui thing about the right energy flow.

After greeting Milton, I realized something was missing. Well, really someone. Adele. I found her hiding in the children's section.

"Geez, he gives me the creeps," she said. I considered telling her to stay put, but she'd already started following me, holding on to my vest.

Milton's eye's brightened when he saw Adele. "I like your outfit," he said in his squeaky voice. "Maybe you want to be in the tent with me." He reached toward Adele, but she looked totally freaked out and clung to me as I walked across the store to give out the tickets.

Dinah stopped me with the two kids in tow. "You have to give me tickets for them," she said.

I glanced at the line outside. Several mothers figured out what was going on and gave me dirty looks. I didn't dare hand her tickets, but I also couldn't let my friend down. I promised to get her in the tent at the end. I expected some remark from Adele, but she was too busy being my shadow. From across the store, Milton smiled at her and waved.

"I thought Jeremy was picking up the kids," I said.

Dinah's expression went to upset and she stepped closer to me and out of earshot of E. Conner and Ashley-Angela. "It's a long story. No, it's really a very short story. Jeremy left, alone. He's up in Seattle supposedly locking in a job. He said he just has a hotel room and there's someone who could babysit the kids, but he thinks the person might have an alcohol problem. Clearly he knows how to manipulate me. But it's just temporary. He's got thirty days. Then either he picks up his kids or I'm bringing them up there."

I told her everything would be all right and sent them to the café for Bob's special spider juice punch and shortbread fingers. I suggested Adele help in there, too. I was relieved when she let go.

As soon as I started handing out tickets I knew there were going to be problems. The people at the end of the line were already getting antsy. Just then a woman came up and took my arm. "You're Molly Pink, aren't you?" she asked. I nodded, and she explained the cashier had told her I was in charge of the crochet group.

"Not in charge, just one of the soldiers," I said with a smile. She introduced herself and explained she was director of the Women's Haven and had stopped by to pick up a book. "I also want to thank you in advance for the shawls. You have no idea what this will mean to the women, knowing somebody cares enough to make them something. God bless you for thinking of them," she said before leaving.

The next mother in line was glaring at me for not attending to the tickets. Before I could start handing them out again, Mason Fields showed up with a little blond boy in tow who he introduced as his grandson. The same mother started muttering threats under her breath. Mason pulled me aside and asked if I could get his grandson in the tent. I made a big point of shaking my head as if to say no, while I told him to go in the café and wait with Dinah and I'd sneak them in.

I was glad Jeffrey was too old to appreciate Milton. With everything going on I didn't need some kind of confrontation between Barry and Mason.

Two of the Horror Helpers came out and invited the first twenty kids into the tent. I was about to hand out more tickets when Pixie stepped in front of me.

"I found this on the copy machine," she said, holding out two pieces of paper. She looked a little better and thanked me again for the food. Bob saw her and waved for her to come in. "You're busy. You can look at it later and then give it back to me," she said before heading toward the café. I started to look at the pages, but a mother in line tapped me on the shoulder.

"Are you going to hand out those numbers, or what?" the angry mother said.

"Sorry," I said, tearing off more tickets and handing them out. The Horror Helpers invited the next group into the tent. As I suspected, I ran out of tickets before I ran out of people in line.

"This is ridiculous," a mother wearing a bandana said. "I want to speak to the manager." The other people in line heard her and started chanting the same thing.

"What's going on?" a voice asked in the midst of the commotion. When I turned I saw that it was Dorothy. "I just wanted to pick up a coffee," she said, regarding the squirming kids with distaste.

Ignoring the annoyed parents in the line, I blurted out, "I need to talk to you about who ordered Dr. Bullard's soup." Was it my imagination, or did her eyes narrow?

There were more complaints from the line as Dorothy

pulled away. "Kevin's alone at the store. I have to get back so he can clean out something in the storage unit. Can't talk now."

She was gone before I could stop her. I wanted to run after her, but I had to deal with the restless stragglers first. I rushed the overflow to the kids' department. As expected, Adele was hiding there. I introduced her as one of Milton's extra special helpers and said she would not only read a portion of the new book to them but would also get them complimentary spider punch and shortbread fingers. Her outfit was a big hit. I left before I saw how the reading went.

Then, when no one was looking, I slipped E. Conner and Ashley-Angela, along with Mason's grandson, in the tent. Mason and Dinah had found a table and were talking. Bob was talking to Pixie; his body language said he was offering his sympathy and hers said she was taking it, along with a creamy-looking drink.

I leaned against a bookcase and took a deep breath. So far, so good. I'd been so preoccupied, I'd forgotten I was still holding the two pages Pixie had handed me. At first, it didn't even register what they were. Then I realized they were a copy of the brochure she had mentioned. The title on the front was *Palladian Estate Heirlooms*. There was a picture of one those large English houses that looked like it probably had no heat. Because it was only a copy, the picture quality wasn't great. Below the photo was the story of the house and the family that had lived there. Lady Sara Ratcliffe was described as Princess Diana's third cousin. Though Lord Ratcliffe was mentioned, the only family photo was of Lady Sara. It appeared to be a copy of an old sepia formal portrait. Lady Rafcliffe wore a long dark dress and was standing next to a chair, her hand resting on it. There was a lacy thing around her neck and down the front of the dress, which was obviously the collar Pixie had talked about. It resembled a long scarf. I could see enough detail to recognize that the piece I'd seen on Drew Brooks's desk drawer handle came from it. Her hair was piled on her head in one of those old-fashioned styles, but since the focus was soft and it wasn't a close-up, it was hard to make out her features. Dr. Bullard was good if he could see she had an overbite.

I looked closer at the face and covered the stylized hair with my hand. At first I didn't believe what I was seeing. I stared so hard I had to look away to refocus my eyes. When I turned back to the picture, there was no mistaking who it was. And then all the pieces began to fall into place.

The picture was enough to convince me I knew who had killed Drew for sure and probably Dr. Bullard. But it probably wouldn't be enough for Detective Heather. Ah, but then a thought crossed my mind. Hadn't someone mentioned the meticulous records Ramona Brooks kept when she was the owner of the Cottage Shoppe? A sheet listing the seller of the Ratcliffe Estate items would be the piece that tied everything together.

And I even knew where the files were. I'd overheard Kevin mention putting them in the storage unit. I considered calling Detective Heather and telling her about Ramona Brooks's records. But hadn't Dorothy just said something about Kevin clearing some stuff out of the unit? I had to get that Ratcliffe Estate file now.

Even though I was in the middle of Milton Mindell's event, I couldn't take the chance that the records would get shredded before I got the sheet I needed. I dashed to the children's section and told Adele I had to step out for a few minutes.

"Pink, you can't go," she wailed, looking at the kids sitting around her. Obviously my plan hadn't worked so well; the kids were fidgeting and punching each other. She got up and stepped close to me.

"You wanted to be in charge, well, consider yourself in that position for ten minutes or so," I said. "It's important. I know who killed Drew Brooks, and if I don't get the proof now, it will be gone." Adele demanded details of where I was going, and I pointed toward the Cottage Shoppe. "There is something I have to get before Kevin Brooks has a chance to throw it away. If you have any problems Dinah will help."

Adele sighed and marched back to the kids, asking if anybody wanted another round of spider punch.

I was almost jogging when I passed Dinah and Mason in the café. I turned as I kept moving and told Dinah I had found the answer to everything and was going for the proof. She started to get up to come with me, but I waved her off. I thought something might be developing between them and I didn't want to interrupt it. Besides, all I was going to do was slip into the storage unit and find a file. I started to jog down the street, but it morphed into an outright run.

I rushed past the Cottage Shoppe, barely catching a glimpse of Kevin stirring some soup while Dorothy helped a customer.

The doors to the storage unit were closed but, thankfully, not locked. I pulled one side open and slipped in. It was a full-service container and had a light. I walked down the narrow walkway between tall shelving units, quickly checking both sides for a box of files. The shelves were jammed with stuff from the store. On the upper shelves I saw pots and pans, the espresso machine, and giant glass jars of tomato products along with one-gallon plastic jugs of brown liquid. The yarn swift and the skeins of yarn Dorothy had put aside for me were sticking out from an eye-level shelf. The lower shelves held plastic containers of merchandise from the store and cleaning supplies, but nothing that looked like a box of records.

My heart was pounding from the running and anticipation as I reached the spot at the back where the shelving ended. The whole area was filled with boxes, and I began to tug at them so I could get them in the light and see their contents. The first two I opened contained cookbooks and more merchandise from the store. And then I opened one that made me gasp. It was filled with the paperweights that had been on Drew's desk. Apparently they hadn't been such big sellers after all. All the complimentary coffee and tea things had been packed up in one box, and another had rolls of banner paper and templates to do the sign lettering.

I was beginning to think I was too late and that my next stop would have to be Dumpster diving, but then I flipped the top off a box and saw what looked like file-drawer dividers. When I pulled the box into the light, I saw they were monthly dividers. I randomly pulled a sheet from the middle and read at it.

Ramona Brooks had used a fountain pen to write up in her remarkable penmanship the description of a set of silver serving pieces and a bone china tea set. It listed the seller, the date the serving pieces had sold and the price. She'd written in the date she paid the consignee and gave back the tea set, which didn't sell. Whoever had said she kept meticulous records was right. I sent out a silent thank-you.

All I had to do was locate the sheet for the Ratcliffe Estate heirlooms. Since the files were arranged chronologically rather than alphabetically, I thought I was going to have to go through the whole box. I tried to remember if there was any clue as to when the items had been in the store to narrow down my search. Hadn't somebody said something about when the time changed? Hoping I was right, I thumbed through October. This was taking longer than I'd expected, and I was getting a little frantic as I ruffled through the pale green pages. And suddenly there it was.

As soon as I saw *Ratcliffe Estate Heirlooms*, I knew I'd found the sheet I needed. My eye went down the page as my breath grew ragged. Below the list of items I saw the name of the seller in Ramona Brooks's perfect blue ink. Bingo, I had my proof. I was still holding the copy of the brochure Pixie had given me. That along with the sales sheet and Pixie's story ought to be enough. Detective Heather would see who had a real motive to kill Drew Brooks, and then she'd leave Sheila alone. I pulled out the sheet and as I turned to go, a shadow fell across the page.

"What's your hurry?"

I slipped the sales sheet and the brochure behind my back and looked up, having already recognized the voice. "Patricia, what brings you here?"

"I stopped by the bookstore to drop off some autographed copies of my book. Adele was in quite a state. She said you were off getting something that proved who killed Drew Brooks. May I have it, please?"

I held the papers tighter. "I was mistaken—there wasn't anything. I need to get back to the bookstore. The Milton Mindell event and all." I started to take a step toward the door, but the overhead light reflected on something in Patricia's hand.

"I don't think so." She raised her hand a little so there was no mistaking the small blue handgun.

"I thought Benjamin was antigun," I said, looking at the compact but lethal weapon.

"He is—but I'm not. At least, for me. These days you've got to protect yourself." She moved the gun a little closer. "Now hand me the paper." When I didn't comply, she looked annoyed. "Molly, Molly, Molly, why couldn't you just mind your own business?"

"I don't know what paper you're talking about. I was looking for something I had put on layaway at the store." I pointed at the yarn swift, but as I did the papers slid out of my hand and landed on the floor.

Patricia bent down quickly and scooped them up. When she looked at the copy Pixie had given me, Patricia nodded in an annoyed fashion. "So Dr. Bullard made a copy of the brochure. Well, it doesn't matter anymore." While she was distracted I tried to edge around her and head for the door, but she blocked me and pointed the gun at me.

"There wouldn't have been any problem if that orthodontist hadn't demanded a refund. How could you understand? You've never been a single parent wondering how you're going to keep your children in private school." She set the papers on the shelf and sighed. To my surprise she lit a cigarette and blew out the smoke.

"Yeah, I smoke, so go on, give me a lecture." She took another drag. "I was working two jobs and selling off my jewelry, but it still wasn't enough. I had to do something to get money for the kids' tuition. At first I thought of crocheting some things and selling them."

"But I thought you didn't crochet."

"Are you kidding? Me, queen of the crafter, not crochet? The hardest thing was pretending I was having trouble. It's kind of like if you're an opera singer and you have to sing bad. I was watching one of those antique shows on TV and noticed that who something had belonged to affected its value. That's when I got the idea for Lady Ratcliffe. At first I thought I'd make the pieces myself, but it was too time consuming, even with my skill. I found a place online in China that would create items to my specifications. They attached machine-made motifs to a ready-made backing for pieces like the collar and used machine-made trim for the hankies. Once I got them, I washed them in weak tea and rinsed them in fabric softener to age them, and I was ready to go.

"I made up a whole story for Mrs. Brooks about how I was distantly related to Lord and Lady Ratcliffe and had some family heirlooms that I wanted to sell. I showed her the brochure I'd created. All I needed was a wig and a costume and I became Lady Ratcliffe. It's amazing what you can do with a digital camera and a computer photo program. Once she read the story and saw the photo of Lady Ratcliffe wearing the Irish crochet collar, she believed the whole lot were real heirlooms. She didn't even notice my resemblance to Lady Ratcliffe. If she had, I would have just said it was because we were distant family.

"I guess all the buyers believed the brochure, too, because the items sold. And I might add, nobody but that unpleasant orthodontist complained or tried to return their heirloom."

I was trying to think of a way to get out of there. Between the gun and the confession about making fake antiques, I didn't feel optimistic about the odds of her just taking the papers and leaving. I looked around the storage unit for some kind of help. If only I'd taken my cell phone.

Now that Patricia had started talking, she kept going. "When Bullard demanded the refund, Drew got curious and went through his aunt's records. When he saw how many other pseudo heirlooms were in the batch and that none of them had come back, the greedy so-and-so got an idea. He gave Bullard the refund to get back the Irish crochet collar and handkerchief so he could use them to blackmail me. Can you believe he threatened to go to the media and tell them what I'd done if I didn't keep providing him with fake antiques for his new Internet store?

"Benjamin would have dropped me like a bomb. I couldn't let it come out. After struggling on my own with the kids I'd hit the jackpot with him. He's rich, actually a nice guy, and he's going to get elected. I couldn't let that rat Drew ruin it for me." She let out her breath. "It feels good to finally talk about it." She looked at me and her eyes seemed kind of crazed, though she still didn't have a hair out of place, nor a speck of lint on her black slacks. Black slacks? It must have been her slacks-covered legs that Kevin saw on the stairs.

"I didn't intend to kill Drew, you know. I just wanted to knock him out so I could get the crocheted pieces. I figured that without the items there was nothing he could do. By the way, it may look easy to knock somebody out, but it isn't. I had to smack him a whole bunch of times. How was I supposed to know he'd fall in the soup?"

Apparently when she'd heard Trina coming up the stairs, Patricia had slipped into Kevin's office. Well, now I knew how the handkerchief got there and how the lacy piece had ended up hanging off the drawer handle. Patricia had ripped the collar as she made a hasty exit. She didn't seem to care that Detective Heather had the hanky now, since the only thing that could connect her with the fake heirloom was the paper in her hand and me. I felt a strong uh-oh go off in my head. Maybe she didn't plan for either the papers or me to get out of there.

She dropped the cigarette and stamped it out, reached in her purse and pulled out a huge roll of silver duct tape with a cutting edge attached. "You have no idea how many things you can do with this stuff. I never go anywhere without it—I'm doing a whole chapter on it in my next hints book." She secured the roll under her gun arm and pulled a long piece off with her free hand, snapping it off against the sharp edge. She wrapped it around my wrist and then pulled it against the other one, binding them together. "You can roll it up and use it for shoelaces or hair ties and even do an emergency repair on a hem."

She ripped off another piece and kneeled in front of me.

She put the gun down and quickly tried to wrap the tape around my ankles. Seeing the gun on the floor, I attempted to kick it away. She grabbed it back and pointed it at my head.

"I don't want to shoot you, but I will. Although, I think I've come up with a better all-around solution." She surveyed the small space crammed with stuff. "This place is a fire trap." Having secured my legs together, she dropped the gun in her purse and stood.

I hadn't realized she'd cut another piece of tape until she was about to stick it over my mouth. I felt light-headed at the prospect and thought by talking I might be able to keep her from doing it.

"Before you do that, I'd like to ask you a question." I was using as many words as possible since as long as I was talking I didn't think she'd slap the tape on me. "The question is—well, maybe it's actually a couple of questions."

Patricia looked impatient and I realized I better get to the point or she'd put the tape on me just to shut me up.

"Why kill Dr. Bullard?"

"Who said I did?" she said with her eyes flashing. Then her expression changed to a thoughtful one. "It was perfectly done, wasn't it? But I had a chance to plan, unlike with Drew.

"Dr. Bullard recognized me at the book signing. He got in touch with me and started to lay into me for causing him and his wife embarrassment. I knew he could be trouble when he mentioned he still had the brochure I'd made up." Patricia smiled. "I'm good. I really am. I told him I was oh, so sorry about the whole thing and wanted to make it right. I said I had the real piece of Irish crochet I'd used as a model for the fakes and wanted to give it to him. I asked if he'd give me back the brochure so I could put the whole thing behind me." She shook her head with disbelief. "He said yes. I actually don't think he would have ever turned me in, and he never mentioned Drew's death, so I don't think he connected it with the fake antiques. All he cared about was having something real to give his wife. But I didn't have any authentic Irish crochet to give him. So, I had to get him out of the way."

Patricia didn't seem to feel any remorse about what she'd done. But she did seem pleased with the perfection of her planning. She'd arranged to meet Bullard in his office in the evening. "I pretended to be his wife and ordered the soup and had it left in the reception area. When I arrived, it was there waiting. I dropped a roofie in it. They are way easy to get hold of," she said as an aside. "I said he must be hungry after a long day and offered him the soup as a goodwill gesture." She snorted out a laugh. "He actually thanked me for it and said he'd missed lunch. A few spoonfuls and he was out cold. I grabbed the brochure, set off the bug bombs and I was out the door."

She looked at her watch. "I really must be going." She lit another cigarette. "My, I am surprised they store something as flammable as this," she said, pouring some citrus cleaning liquid on some rags and dropping them on the floor.

"Sorry I don't have another roofie." She found the box of paperweights and took out the one shaped like the bust of Teddy Roosevelt. "I think I have it down now. I should be able to knock you out with only a few smacks." To demonstrate, she swung her arm with the paperweight a few times. I flinched and tried to move. She got ready to do it in earnest, but then the cigarette fell out of her hand and hit the rags, and they began to smoulder.

She glanced down for a moment and gasped at the growing flames. But still, she stepped toward me with the Teddy Roosevelt bust poised. Any second now, it was going to fade to black for me. I was helpless with my hands and feet taped together. Behind her I could see the yarn swift on the edge of the shelf. I couldn't do anything with my hands or feet, but I still had my shoulder. With all the power I could muster, I threw my shoulder against the shelves. They made a rattling sound and shook. At first I thought it hadn't done any good, but as the shelves vibrated, the yarn swift toppled off.

As it fell, it opened, revealing an inner structure like that of an umbrella.

The rags were really beginning to flame, and Patricia coughed and squealed. She threw down the bust and took a step back to escape. As she did, she stepped right into the yarn swift and her foot tangled in it. Panicking, she tried to break free, but the more she tried to pull out of it, the tighter it became. She tried to walk with it on her foot and lost her balance. Frantically she reached for something on which to steady herself. The only things to grab at were the shelves. I had merely tapped against them, but Patricia grabbed them full force, and as the big unit began to totter from side to side, everything on them began to shake, rattle and then roll off toward her.

I was feeling pretty panicky myself as the enclosure started to fill with smoke. Trapped by Patricia and the shaking shelves, I started to cough and choke.

The jars of tomato products slipped off the top shelf. They missed Patricia but crashed on the floor, spattering both of us with blobs of red. The plastic gallon jugs of brown liquid came next. One after another they fell over, rolled off and hit Patricia on the head. She was right. It wasn't that easy to knock somebody out. It took three of them smacking her on the head before she finally crumpled. And as the jugs finally hit the ground, their plastic caps broke off and the liquid poured out. I cringed, afraid of an explosion. But as I smelled the onion scent I realized it was soup base. It poured over the burning rags, dousing the flames.

I didn't waste any time getting out. Patricia still had the gun in her purse and her head wasn't in a bowl of soup. She could come to. I tried to jump over her, but instead I fell on her and had to twist myself around to get my legs faced in the right direction. I hopped toward the door and finally outside—and collided with Adele.

"Pink, I have to talk to you," she said, throwing her arms around me. "You won't believe what Eduardo did. . . ." Then suddenly it registered that I had my hands and feet bound together and globs of red stuff all over me.

"Is something wrong?"

Chapter 25

"Eduardo showed up with his girlfriend and her kids. He wanted me to get them into the tent," Adele wailed. "I feel so betrayed." We were sitting on the curb waiting for the police. We must have made an odd sight, she in her mortician beatnik look and me in my white shirt and khaki pants covered in blobs of tomato stuff. I thought *betrayed* was a bit much since the extent of their relationship seemed to have been one coffee date to discuss his bookstore program and several incidences of being chair neighbors. Adele knew how to squeeze every ounce of drama out of anything. Still, I comforted her and told her there was somebody out there who was much better for her.

"Pink, you're so right. There is somebody out there who is way better." She went to hug me, but stopped when her eyes rested on the red blobs.

It had been Kevin who called 911 and cut me free of my duct-tape restraints. And not without a certain amount of pain. He'd looked up from his soup making, seen me through the window and rushed outside.

In the event Patricia came to before the cops arrived, I'd found the roll of duct tape in her purse and, after pulling the yarn swift off her leg, wrapped her ankles and wrists. I wondered if she would think it was such a great hint when she was the one wearing the duct tape. It was my second run-in with duct tape, and I hoped never to see the silvery stuff again. I made sure her purse with the gun in it was out of her reach.

I heard sirens in the distance and as they grew louder, I prepared for the onslaught. Moments later, amid a lot of flashing lights and noise, a fire engine, rescue ambulance, several black-and-whites and a black Crown Victoria pulled up in front of us.

Detective Heather got to me first. Her eyes took in a red speckle on my shoulder, and she waved the paramedics over, but I stopped her, explaining it wasn't blood. She started to snicker when I said it was tomato stuff, but her expression changed when I brought her to the storage unit, explaining Patricia's phony antique scheme and how all the pieces fit together to show she was the one who killed Drew Brooks and Arnold Bullard. I also mentioned she had confessed to me and then tried to kill me.

"Don't believe her. She tried to kill me," Patricia yelled. She'd come to and was sitting up, kicking her feet, and even with her wrists taped she was trying to grab at the shelf unit. She struggled to pull herself up, but everything that hadn't fallen the first time started to fall now. For the first time since I'd met her, Patricia had a hair out of place. She was a mess.

And when she heard Detective Heather tell her she was under arrest, she kept yelling they'd gotten it all wrong. A uniformed officer pulled off the duct tape and replaced it with real handcuffs. Patricia screeched and said she needed medical attention for the tape burns as the cop led her toward one of the cruisers.

"We're even," Detective Heather said as she watched Patricia get in the backseat of the police car. "I'll forget about the hanky tampering. There won't be any obstruction of justice charge, either." Our eyes met for a moment and I detected a flicker of respect. Then she turned away to make sure the storage unit was wrapped in yellow tape.

Another plain car pulled up. The door flew open and Barry jumped out. I saw him take in the scene, and his gaze stopped on my shirt. I knew he was looking at the red spots. His eyes flared with emotion and betrayed his bland cop face as he double-timed it across the street.

"Tomato sauce," I said, pointing at the largest spot when he got within earshot. He rolled his eyes and I saw his shoulders relax. He seemed to let his breath out, too. Then he asked if I was really all right.

When Barry was working he never gave hugs or did anything personal. But this time he stood next to me so that my shoulder rested against him and he took my hand and squeezed it. Detective Heather looked over just then. I saw her lip quiver when she spotted Barry's hand holding mine.

"Omigod. I have to go," I said, pulling away. "I left Milton Mindell at the bookstore." Messy clothes and all, I took off down the street.

As I walked into the bookstore, the kids were just coming out of the tent. Two boys took one look at me and started pointing with happy horror faces. "Eww, it's Rhonda the Zombie." I gathered it was a character in the latest book, because other kids started saying the same thing.

I glanced toward the table of presigned books and Dinah waved. She was already collecting tickets and handing out books. I blew her a kiss.

Then I remembered the overflow kids I'd left with Adele.

Worried that she'd abandoned them and they were taking apart the children's section, I rushed over. Mason was just escorting Milton Mindell to the center of the group. When Mason saw me, he looked concerned and stepped away. Not that the kids noticed. They were looking at Milton like he was some kind of rock star.

I told Mason it was tomato sauce on my shirt and then immediately began to thank him for helping out. "How did you do it?" I said, gesturing toward Milton and the kids. Milton had always been a stickler about only dealing with the kids in the tent.

"Are you really okay?" Mason asked, touching a dollop of tomato and rubbing it between his fingers. I nodded and his face relaxed into a grin.

"I think after what I did you owe me," he said. "If you want to know how I wrapped Mr. Mindell around my little finger, you'll have to have dinner with me. Of course, you might want to change first." I realized I'd been wrong about there being something starting up between Dinah and him. Later she told me all he'd done was ask her about me.

I sensed somebody behind me, and when I looked over my shoulder I saw that Barry had caught up with me. When he saw Mason, he glared at him. Mason nodded and saluted Barry with a little raise of his eyebrows. It was the barbecue all over again.

Chapter 26

"It was a nice idea to make an event out of presenting the shawls," CeeCee said as we stood outside the Cottage Shoppe. The storage container was gone, and now that the remodeling was done, a permanent sign for Kevin's Kitchen had been added. For tonight the whole place was closed for the private party. It was just going to be the women from the shelter, the Tarzana Hookers and a few guests. Kevin had made a special buffet of his soups and homemade breads, and I had provided the cheesecake cupcakes for dessert. The plan was that after everyone had food, we'd hand out the shawls.

"Where's the rest of the crew?" Sheila asked as she joined us. She sighed. "I can't believe how good it feels to know that Detective Gilmore isn't going to pop out of the bushes with any more questions."

"Do you think my stylist is right?" CeeCee turned, model fashion, to show off her sleek outfit. She'd given up trying to lose the five pounds once her stylist told her that the right clothes could make her look as though she had. We both gave her a thumbs-up, and CeeCee asked about dessert.

Dinah arrived breathless with E. Conner and Ashley-Angela in tow. "They'll be good, I promise." She threw me a hopeless look. "Jeremy called again with another stall, and the babysitter didn't show." Then she sighed. "I'm afraid he's never going to pick up his kids." I didn't want to say anything, but I'd been thinking the same thing.

"Ladies," Eduardo said, taking a place next to CeeCee. His long black hair was loose, and he'd dressed in slacks and a sport jacket. He had asked me several times why Adele was acting so strangely. He appeared to have no idea he'd done anything wrong because, I gathered, he'd only thought they were crochet partners. I covered by saying that was just Adele.

No one could accuse Adele of being subtle. She joined the group with a snap of her black cape, which she'd worn over a purple silk dress. She made a point of ignoring Eduardo as she said in an extra loud voice that her boyfriend William was picking her up.

Only I knew who William really was. After the episode with Eduardo, Adele had rethought her date with Koo Koo the Clown, aka William Bearly, and decided she liked him after all. He'd been thrilled when she called him, or at least that's what she said. Adele threw me a panicked glance after she mentioned his name, apparently afraid I would give away his other identity. I said nothing. Her secret was safe with me.

"Why are you all standing out here?" Mrs. Shedd said. I'd invited her but didn't know she was coming until she showed up. All she knew about Milton's fiesta was that it was a huge success moneywise. Adele had conveniently forgotten she'd been afraid of Milton and had run off when she'd gotten upset over Eduardo. She took lots of credit for the horror author's success and had convinced Mrs. Shedd she should work with me on any events that were kid related. I guessed I could live with that.

Mrs. Shedd took the lead, and we all followed her up the stairs into the store. Soft light glowed out from the windows and it looked inviting.

Benjamin Bradford was in the entrance hall acting as greeter. Actually he had come up with the idea for the shawl presentation and had Bradford Industries sponsor it. He had several motives. The Women's Haven really was his pet charity—he'd spent time with his mother in a place like it and it was his way of saying thank you. He wanted to do something good to counteract all the problems his wife had caused. Well, soon to be ex-wife. He'd filed for divorce almost before they finished fingerprinting Patricia. She had been charged with two murders, and one attempted. Because of the charge, she wasn't given bail and had plenty of time to crochet while she waited for her trial. And Benjamin still hoped to get elected and recognized the shawl event as a good publicity opportunity.

It was the first time I'd been in the store since the work was finished. Mr. Work Boots had done a good job and the place looked great. Kevin was rushing around making last-minute adjustments in the restaurant area.

"Come in, come in," Kevin said as we approached the redone dining room. Several long tables had been set up, and a buffet had been arranged on a dark wood built-in sideboard. Overhead the wrought iron chandelier had been dimmed.

The women from the shelter arrived along with their director, and we intermingled as we found seats. Everybody wanted to sit next to Eduardo and he solved the problem by moving around. He really was so much more than a handsome face; he had that ability to make people feel good. He also invited everyone to come to his poetry reading at the bookstore.

Kevin knew his way around soup, and everyone had multiple bowls. He had added some salads and stuffed mushrooms to the buffet, too. He was no slouch in the bread department, either.

"I'm so glad you're all here," Benjamin said getting up to the front of the room when everyone was finished eating. I noticed a photographer and man with a video camera had come in and were capturing the moment. Benjamin finished his remarks by announcing it was time for the Tarzana Hookers to give out their handiwork.

We came up one by one and handed out the hugs of comfort shawls we had made. After each of us had wrapped a shawl around a recipient's shoulders, we gave the women a real hug. The women from the shelter all said how much it meant to them—the physical feeling of being wrapped in something soft and warm and that someone had cared enough to make it for them.

By the end there wasn't a dry eye.

Afterward, Kevin showed off the sales area. "Dorothy talked me into keeping it half restaurant and half store." He took us into the living room and pointed to the alcove and room beyond that were devoted to consignment items and handicrafts. "I'm glad that Trina decided to come back to us," he said as we admired the items. He pulled Sheila aside. "I just wanted to make sure that your check was for the right amount. I don't want to take a chance losing your scarves and blankets. They are big sellers."

"Blankets?" Adele said, getting into the middle of it.

"You haven't seen them?" Kevin picked up a soft heathery red blanket off the arm of the rocker.

"But it's knitted," Adele sputtered, touching it like it was made of worms.

So Sheila was the one who'd been making the blankets all of us had admired. She was full of surprises, but not good ones, according to Adele, who was going on about how she couldn't believe one of our own was a closet knitter. Koo Koo arrived just in time and collected her.

"Am I too late?" a soft voice said behind me. I turned as Morgan came toward me and hugged me. She was holding out a completed lavender shawl. The gauntness was gone from around her eyes and she looked happier. She pulled me aside and explained she'd come back a couple of days before. The time with her mother had helped, and she'd seen a professional.

"Thank you for letting me stay with you." She sighed deeply. "I finally faced the real problem. It might not be the five pounds that's kept me from getting the parts." She said she wasn't giving up, that she was just going to go to auditions with a new attitude. She still hoped she and Samuel could work things out.

She looked down at the shawl in her hands and at the empty dining room. The women from the shelter had already left in their van. "I don't know what to do with it."

I said I thought I knew someone who needed it. I looked toward Dinah. The kids were asleep on the floor in the Kids' Korner. "Do you think we should give this to Patricia?" I asked her.

Dinah nodded. "She's going to need all the comfort and hugs she can get."

WHEN I GOT HOME BARRY AND JEFFREY WERE giving Cosmo a bath. Blondie came out and looked at me as if to say, "What's going on?"

"Good question," I answered out loud. No matter what I said about not wanting to make a commitment, Barry and Jeffrey had become a part of my life.

But what about Mason?

He was holding me to the dinner I owed him after saving me at the bookstore. He'd suggested a restaurant in San Francisco with a weekend around it. I'd countered with a beachfront eatery in Malibu, dinner only.

Mason wanted what I wanted—a casual relationship. Someone to go places and do things with, no strings, no pressure to make it permanent. That was appealing. And I liked Mason. I really did. He was funny, and yes, there was a spark when he touched my hand. The dinner was coming up the next weekend. But still, I hadn't figured out what I was going to tell Barry.

Then I walked into the kitchen and opened the refrigerator. All during the shawl ceremony I'd been thinking about doing something. I would never stop missing Charlie, but in my heart I knew it was time to let go. I took out the amber bottles of Hefeweizen and touched one of the cold bottles to my warm cheek. My eyes welled as I lowered it and flipped off the top. For a moment I hesitated. Then the yeasty smell filled the air as I began to pour the liquid down the drain. When the last one was empty, I dried my eyes and dropped the bottles in the recycle bag before I turned off the light.

Hugs of Comfort Shawl

EASY TO MAKE

Materials:	About 930 yards of worsted-weight yarn such as Vanna's Choice or Red Heart. K hook or size needed for gauge.
Finished size:	About 18 inches by 72 inches
Gauge:	3 stitches = 1 inch 4 rows = 1½ inches
Stitches:	Single and double crochet (sc - single crochet/ dc - double crochet)

Chain 53. Turn.

Row 1: Chain 1 and sc in each chain across. Turn work.

Row 2: Chain 1 and sc in each sc across. Turn work.

Row 3: Chain 1 and turn work; sc in each sc across. Turn work.

Row 4: Chain 4 (counts as first dc and chain 1), dc in third stitch from hook, *chain 1 skip stitch, and dc in next stitch,*. Repeat from * to * across. 27 dc and 26 spaces made.

Repeat Rows 1-4 approximately 47 times, until the shawl measures approximately 71 inches.

Repeat Rows 1-3 once.

Finish off.

Note: When making Row 1 the first time, single crochet stitches will be made in the chain stitches. When repeating Row 1, the single crochet stitches will be made in the double crochet and chain stitches in the preceding row.

Molly's Cheesecake Cupcakes

MAKES 18

Crust
1¾ cups graham cracker crumbs
¼ cup sifted powdered sugar
¾ stick butter, melted

Line muffin tins with paper baking cups. Using a pastry blender, mix the graham cracker crumbs and powdered sugar. Pour in melted butter and blend. Distribute in the paper-lined cups and press down firmly.

Filling
½ cup sugar
1 8-ounce package cream cheese, softened
2 eggs, beaten
2 cups sour cream
1 teaspoon vanilla
Pinch of salt

Mix sugar and cream cheese until well blended. Add 2 beaten eggs and beat well. Mix in sour cream, vanilla and salt. Spoon into prepared crusts.

Bake at 350° for 25 minutes. Take out, spread on topping (see below) and bake 10 minutes more. Chill before serving.

Topping

1 cup sour cream
2 tablespoons sugar
2 teaspoons vanilla

Mix all three ingredients together.

A CROCHET MYSTERY FROM

Betty Hechtman

BY HOOK OR BY CROOK

Meet the happy crafter who believes every mystery should be unraveled...

Molly Pink's crochet group has a new mystery on their hands when they find a paper bag with a note that speaks of remorse, a diary entry on the sorrow of parting, and a complicated piece of filet crochet that offers an obscure clue in pictures. They immediately set out to find the owner of the bag, but things get even more complicated when they find the talented crocheter—murdered by a box of poisoned marzipan apples. Now they must pick up the stitches before a killer creates a deadly pattern.

penguin.com

M559T0809

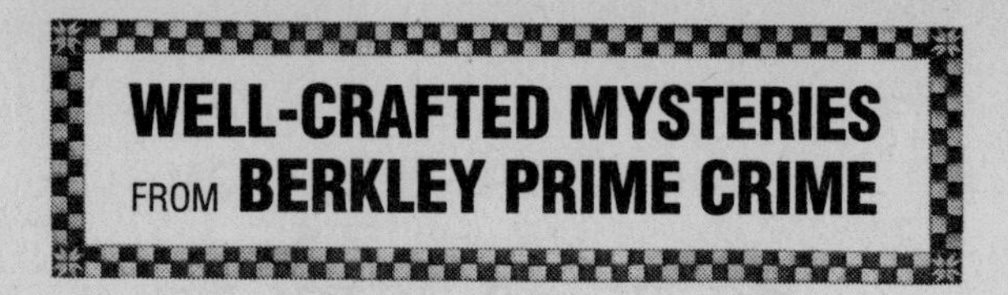

- **Earlene Fowler** Don't miss this Agatha Award–winning quilting series featuring Benni Harper.

- **Monica Ferris** This *USA Today* bestselling Needlecraft Mystery series includes free knitting patterns.

- **Laura Childs** Her Scrapbooking Mystery series offers tips to satisfy the most die-hard crafters.

- **Maggie Sefton** This popular Knitting Mystery series comes with knitting patterns and recipes.

SOLVING

M5G0508